THE AUNT EDWINA SERIES - BOOK 1

Aunt Edwina's
Fabulous Wishes

A family history novel

Lynne Christensen

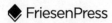 FriesenPress

One Printers Way
Altona, MB R0G 0B0
Canada

www.friesenpress.com

DISCLAIMER
This is a work of fiction. It is written in the form of a fun, charming, and fictitious
genealogical adventure. Names, characters, places, organizations, businesses, and
incidents are either products of the author's imagination or are used fictitiously. Any
resemblance to actual events, locales, businesses, organizations, or persons, living or dead,
is entirely coincidental.

For help with your own genealogy and family history research, please seek guidance from
a trained expert at a genealogy organization and/or family history organization. Guidance
and many helpful websites, articles, and blog postings are available either for free or via
payment from a variety of sources. Note that the research strategies and advice in this
work of fiction may not suit every person or family's goals.

ISBN
978-1-03-913444-7 (Hardcover)
978-1-03-913443-0 (Paperback)
978-1-03-913445-4 (eBook)

1. *FIC016000 FICTION, HUMOROUS*
2. *FIC051000 FICTION, CULTURAL HERITAGE*
3. *FIC045000 FICTION, FAMILY LIFE*

Distributed to the trade by The Ingram Book Company

Dedication

———

To Dr. Penelope and Dr. Gustav Christensen —
two wonderful, educated, and dedicated parents

AND

To Brenda and Val — two ladies who bring such joy

"A lightweight, warm, and often charming adventure."
— *Kirkus Reviews*

List of Characters (People)

—

Alfred Meadows: Lady Susan Marcelon's chauffeur. Discreet and polished, he is privately bemused by the antics of his boss and her friends.

Algernon 'Algy' Holgarth: Heir and proprietor of Holgarth Hall in Plumsden, Kent. Has penchant for tweed suits and formal estate living of yesteryear. Manages plant nursery and petting zoo at Holgarth Hall. Lance Holgarth's elder brother.

Amelia Georges: Director of the Pixleton Family History Society research site in Devon.

Angus Garfield McTaggart: Lobster fisherman in Scotland with a few choice words for reporters.

Bernard 'Bertie' Preswick, Fourteenth Duke of Conroy: Julie Fincher's aristocratic art patron. Incredibly wealthy owner of Scotford Castle estate near Oakhurst, Kent and a country house in Brambleford, near Medchester, Kent. Reliable friend of all family history adventurers who need help getting out of incredibly outrageous scrapes.

Brian Flintmerle: Old codger who volunteers at St. Olave's Church in Ludring, Kent. Insists his forty years of residency doesn't qualify him as a local.

Carlene Munsonthwaite: Flirty and devious public relations consultant who pokes her nose into others' business without guilt or scruples.

Chris Undermead: Julie Fincher's fiancé. Penniless stockbroker who foolishly sells when he ought to hold.

Clint Yamamoto: Owner/operator of The King's Arm pub in Plumsden, Kent. Has dispensed perfect ale and dry wit on site for over twenty-eight years.

Constable Bud Snowdrop: Ludring, Kent police constable trying to make his mark but forever blotting his copybook.

Diana Marlee Resman: Friendly, funky senior who owns an antiques shop in Kipbourne, Dorset.

Donald Jerome Fincher: Julie Fincher's father. Furniture shop manager in Carlingheath, Kent.

Ewan Kilburn: Owner/operator of Kilburn's Outstanding Antiques in Plumsden, Kent. Kind, handsome Scotsman who serves as treasurer of the Plumsden Family History Society. Uncle to one piano-playing nephew and one highland-dancing niece.

Fanny Gardiner: Churchwarden at St. Olave's Church in Ludring, Kent. Solid, sensible woman whose keyring causes extreme janitor envy.

Finn Severs: Duke of Conroy's ex-security-service chauffeur trained in evasive driving techniques, bodyguard protection, and rescuing his employer's friends.

Frederick 'Fred' Aloysius St. John Todling: Pixleton, Devon-based, newly qualified intellectual property solicitor who moonlights as a bookshop minder. Verbose with legalese and opinions. Owns potbellied pig named Barnaby.

Gertrude 'Gertie' Porringer aka 'The Apricot Powerhouse': Boisterous female priest and slightly older cousin to Julie Fincher. Always available for a detailed pedigree chart review and exuberant karaoke.

Harriet Tibbets: Antiques appraiser and auctioneer based in Medchester, Kent. Well-connected and quick as a whip.

Jacques Lesabrioux: Stoic bellman at Fizzleywick Hotel in Carlingheath, Kent. Able to handle anything, including guests dressed as tomatoes.

Jalaal Kahanis: Ewan's friend with Springer Spaniel painting commission. Lives in East Tysonford, Kent.

Jerry Elegant: Owns and runs Jerry Elegant's Pawnshop in Carlingheath, Kent. Has firm handshake and intricate knowledge of how to resell secondhand luxury goods flogged by high-net-worth people suffering from overextended lines of credit.

Julie Fincher: Twenty-something bohemian-style painter who marries for family duty but soon realizes she's taken the wrong path. Daughter of Donald Fincher. Favorite of Lady Edwina Greymore. Lives in converted barn on Scotford Castle estate near Oakhurst, Kent.

Lady Edwina Greymore: Family matriarch and aristocratic owner of Greymore Hall estate near Oakhurst, Kent. Has second home in Clothberry, Devon. Well-preserved, ninety-two-year-old community philanthropist connected to all the right people. Helped raise Julie Fincher after Julie's mother died.

Lady Susan Marcelon: Effervescent, tall grandmother and widowed owner of Marcelon Manor near Ludring, Kent. Likes bright-colored, flowing caftans, purple nail polish, and tacky stained glass. Member of Lady Edwina Greymore's exclusive, upper-crust Sherry Club.

Lancelot 'Lance' Holgarth: Younger brother to Algy Holgarth. Failed spicy chili-banana samosa kiosk owner who lives at Algy's beck and call for hound walking, vegetable rescuing, luggage heaving and general gopher duties. Lives at Holgarth Hall in Plumsden, Kent.

Lisette Gilbert-Durand: Museum director of Brown's Customs and Trades Building in Pixleton, Devon. Member of Lady Edwina Greymore's exclusive, upper-crust Sherry Club.

Lorelei Stoneton: Proprietor of Treemoreland Farm Antiques located in Waverly-on-Sea, East Sussex. Curious, organized seller of furniture and bric-a-brac from past centuries.

Major Barry Whitcombe: Retired military man who uses his pork chop sideburns, vast people network, and army expertise to reunite families with their history. Hobby is buying vintage uniforms then rehoming them at regimental museums. Based in Medchester, Kent.

sident of Plumsden Family History

n vast Petmond Grange estate of

r of Lady Edwina Greymore's exclu-

Club.

er/operator of Eppelton Military
Specializes in getting history into

g, Kent postmistress with waist-

nt for social history of the local area.

msden, Kent main-branch post-

cial hair adornment the world has

ed man in his seventies. Keeper of

s located in Ludring, Kent. Keen

s.

Smythe, MP: Grandchildren of

ar Two hero. Both spend most of

don.

and Lancelot Holgarth's long-

ith loose farm animals racing

Hinghurst Grange, Medchester, Kent, where a ring was hidden.

William Murlow: Man who struggled with a hitching post.

Maude Livingstone: President of Plumsden Family History Society. Rattles around in vast Petmond Grange estate of Plumsden, Kent. Member of Lady Edwina Greymore's exclusive, upper-crust Sherry Club.

Michael Eppelton: Owner/operator of Eppelton Military Memorabilia in London. Specializes in getting history into the right (or left) hands.

Primrose Smears: Ludring, Kent postmistress with waist-length hair and a penchant for social history of the local area.

Roger The Mustache: Plumsden, Kent main-branch postmaster with the biggest facial hair adornment the world has ever seen.

Stan Trentworth: Wizened man in his seventies. Keeper of mysterious secrets in sheds located in Ludring, Kent. Keen fixer of mechanical things.

Vera Smythe and **Dudley Smythe, MP:** Grandchildren of Horace Griffins, World War Two hero. Both spend most of their time working in London.

Zenith Parsons: Algernon and Lancelot Holgarth's long-suffering butler. Puts up with loose farm animals racing through the painting gallery and strange tourists arriving for their bed-and-breakfast stay.

List of Characters (Furry Friends)

———

Barnaby: Potbellied pig often on the lam. Owned by Fred Todling.

Daisy: Farmer Jones's donkey who makes an unusual friend.

Gilligan: Blond-caramel-coated Afghan hound who herds lettuce and rabbits. Owned by Algy Holgarth.

Norris: Blue-grey coated Afghan hound puppy. Registered name 'Northern Thunder of the Gables'. Owned by Algy Holgarth.

Various llamas, rabbits, goats and other petting zoo residents: All owned by Algy Holgarth and lovingly tended by Lance Holgarth.

List of Characters (Ancestors, Infamous and Portraits)

—

Admiral Sir Leonard Byron Gyntonne: Famed seventeenth-century naval man adored by Queen Anne. Died after being shipwrecked off coast of Ireland. His famed ruby ring was hidden for centuries at Hinghurst Grange, Medchester, Kent.

Basil Yardley: Royal Air Force gunner shot down during World War Two. Gertie's mother, a bus driver, used to drive him every day so he could visit his dear wife at her care home.

Horace Griffins: Famous British Special Operations Executive agent in World War Two. Saver of fifty-one lives and recognized for his bravery.

Lady Mary Burlisle: Unfortunate fifteenth-century aristocrat who was forced to marry a knight in dented armor.

Lord Bruce Greymore: Lady Edwina Greymore's deceased husband, né Bruce Fincher.

William Hinghurst: Deceased Medchester estate owner whose will dictates an estate sale with all proceeds going to charity, specifically the greyhound rescue society. Lived at

Hinghurst Grange, Medchester, Kent, where a famous ruby ring was hidden.

William Murlow: Man who struggled with a milkman and a hitching post.

County of Kent – Aunt Edwina's Version

River Thames

London

Medchester

Ludring

Brambleford

Carlingheath

Oakhurst

Scotford Castle

Plumsden

East Tysonford

The Weald

COUNTY OF EAST SUSSEX
(Adjacent County to South)

United Kingdom — Aunt Edwina's Version

Chapter 1

**Fizzleywick Hotel, Carlingheath,
Kent, England. Morning.**

No bridal magazine ever described a sweaty, paint-splattered, twenty-something arriving at her wedding venue like this. Entering the luxurious, seven gold-whatevers hotel dressed like a seedy vagabond firmly strayed outside the borders of polite society. This hotel's rates were in place to keep people like me away from the plush carpeting and fancy, etched glass walls.

It couldn't be helped. My last art class of the semester ran late and my phone battery died. I'd only slept three hours the night prior thanks to a wayward crow cawing outside my window just after four o'clock in the morning. He then invited three friends to join him. Having no idea of the time, I got into my battered SUV and took off for the upscale spa town. Carlingheath was a place for the rich and famous. Its fabled waters served as a royal retreat for centuries. And now, it was where yours truly, Julie Fincher, was going to marry her recently acquired live-in: Chris Undermead.

I never really understood what attracted Chris to me. He was tall, good-looking, and a stockbroker who checked all the boxes. His betrothed was a bohemian art teacher with stained fingers and hair tied back with odd bits of baling twine. We'd been together for three years and I truly believed I loved him. That was, until I discovered why he really proposed. I went ahead with the betrothal out of family duty. My widowed father was ill, worried his daughter had an uncertain future. When Chris and I got engaged, Dad was over-the-moon thrilled. He was excited at the prospect of grandchildren, and that sealed my fate. I would marry to give my dear father hope. My large gift would give him much-needed peace and a rested mind.

Chris knew I was my wealthy, elderly, titled aunt's favorite niece and joked about it often. He tried to make light of it, and I tried to laugh along with him, but deep down inside I knew he was serious about wanting money over me. Talk about deflating my balloon containing hopes of a happy matrimonial existence. All that remained was the need to deceive my family, akin to grin and bear it. Life shouldn't allow for these major affronts to human decency. It wasn't the kind of wedding or life I'd envisioned, yet I had to forge ahead with confidence and purpose. Selling this painful fantasy was my only choice to make my dear father happy.

I drew up to the hotel's fancy porte cochère. It formed a huge dome, one that had tons of fancy plasterwork underneath, pot lights dotted at even spaces. I greeted it with a sense of awe and respect, plus a grand feeling of not belonging. I got out and immediately heard a voice.

"Welcome to the Fizzleywick Hotel. Shall I have your bags sent up to your room?" I turned to see a stocky bellman. He was bald and had a pencil-thin mustache, a pert little man who seemed quite curious at my presence.

I remembered my paint-splattered attire and dirty fingernails. The bellman—nametag Jacques—looked at my battered suitcase as if it contained some radioactive material.

I smiled back, faking like I was one of the eccentric rich. "Yes, please."

"Very good, miss," he replied, somewhat pained. I was an anomaly in his day, and I sensed his eyes lingering on my fringed purse with the fleeting idea of a tip. "And your vee-hic-ewwwel, miss?" He said it coolly, dragging out the last syllable.

"I'm sorry?" I felt like apologizing for everything I'd brought, wore, and said.

"Your parking preference, miss?" he asked. He looked sure that his fancy side-striped trousers, brass-buttoned jacket, and smart white gloves were all wasted on me.

"Oh, right. Valet, please." I handed over the keys, knowing not to spoil the rich illusion by asking how much it would cost. Likely a single night would consume my entire month's teaching salary.

Bellman Jacques looked at the limp stuffed toy goat on my keychain that had pride of place beside my key fob.

"My aunt, she keeps miniature goats," I rapidly explained. I'd now descended into blathering idiot status. *Who on the planet explains a goat on a keyring to a bellman?*

"Ah, yes," he said. He now officially thought I was bonkers.

"Perhaps you know of my aunt? Lady Edwina Greymore?" Truth be told, Aunt Edwina was really my grandmother; however, she insisted on being called 'aunt' just to make sure she didn't feel old. Even at ninety-two. Even though she'd already aged herself down five whole years on her marriage certificate to look a couple of years younger than her husband when they were wed near the end of World War Two. There was no going back from that number on the marriage certificate. So, 'Aunt Edwina' it was amongst us of the younger generation.

A wasp buzzed in and took a liking to the paint aroma floating around me. Jacques swatted the wasp away. "My goodness, you are Lady Edwina Greymore's niece? To be married this weekend?" Mr. Hospitality's eyes widened about a mile and half. He stood up straighter.

"The very same." I issued him a syrupy smile.

The pearly gates opened wide. He issued me an ear-to-ear-grin and snapped his fingers at a young colleague. "Bell cart!" he called out with alacrity. My battered suitcase, a hand-me-down from a distant cousin, was now ticketed and afforded all the respect given to a famous gem or a solid gold statue.

I handed Jacques a five-pound note. Inside I was gulping down the mental calculations of what else I could buy with the crisp bill: two very fancy coffees, a shoe heel repair, a new sable-hair paintbrush ...

Jacques calmly took the note and made it disappear into his pocket in the most elegant fashion. After all, this was the Fizzleywick Hotel.

"Our very best wishes to you, miss," he said. "It's not every day that Lady Edwina's niece gets married."

"Thank you."

It wasn't every day that I name-dropped either, but in this place I needed something, anything, to give me a hope of fitting in.

The lobby was my second red flag down this extremely steep slalom course. The registration desk was my ultimate destination, however I had a sea of unfathomably fashionable guests to wade through first. Somehow a fancy corporate party involving high heels, satin, tuxedos, and deep-red lipstick had spilled out into the lobby. The clinks of glasses were everywhere, and the culprit was the champagne fountain towards the back of the room.

A bit early for that, but who was I to interfere with others' amusements?

I had no idea what was being celebrated, or by whom. I slunk my way around the perimeter of the throng, trying to fade into the background so as not to disturb the height of elegance.

FLASH!

A camera went off right beside me, and I cringed, thinking that I had ruined someone's elegant picture. I looked like some desperate hobo who'd invaded the party, eager to snatch a few freebies off the buffet. I continued to skulk around the room, certain I was captured in a few other unfortunate photos along the way. I felt terrible ruining some fancy, corporate event in my painting clothes and unkempt hair. I was dying to get upstairs, have a shower, then change. The registration desk was starting to look like a desert oasis that I was crawling towards on my stomach. My only hope now was to avoid running into anyone I knew.

Too late. Bernard 'Bertie' Preswick, the present Duke of Conroy and my generous art patron, spotted me and made a beeline. I gave him a hapless smile and waited for the tuxedoed aristocrat to reach my side. He gave me a curious look.

"Julie, how nice to see you," he crooned. He was a handsome, refined man, and why he wanted to possibly be captured in a photo with such a disheveled creature was far beyond me.

"My apologies, I'm straight out of the art studio and look a fright," I started to explain.

"Never mind, never mind. How is my latest watercolor coming?" he asked. "I'm going to give it pride of place in my study."

One thing I'd learned over the years: once an art patron got enthused about a muse, there was no backing down. He wanted everything, anything, in rapid time. The only true reason I was modestly successful with my painting was that Aunt Edwina put her good friend the Duke onto my art at a local exhibition. Bertie really liked it, and then we struck up an unlikely platonic friendship. I ended up living on his Scotford Castle estate in an outbuilding, a converted barn, which had a ton of space for my art. And Chris. Never forget Chris.

Bertie bought a lot of my work for his estate and for his friends; I took care of his barn as my fiancé pounded away on his laptop, oblivious to the wondrous countryside and most everything else. The only thing Bertie asked was that I create three large watercolors for him every year for the next five years. It was an artist's dream come true, and I didn't want to be ungrateful.

What I did want was a shower and some privacy, on an immediate basis.

The aristocracy can be a bit blind at times. Bertie whisked two champagne flutes off a nearby waiter's tray and handed one to me. "So, what are you working on?"

"Well, your watercolor, I just finished teaching, and I'm getting married tomorrow."

His face fell. "Here? Tomorrow?"

The aristocracy could be amazingly forgetful at times.

Great. Either he'd totally missed it or we'd neglected to invite him. Neither one was good, but I hoped for the first one. It was so unlike Aunt Edwina to make such a glaring faux pas amongst her set.

The biggest faux pas I could ever make was publicly calling Aunt Edwina 'Grandmother'.

Bertie's face broke into a smile. "Gotcha!" He gave a delighted chortle. "You don't think I'm that dense, do you?"

"No, but–"

"Nonsense. I would never forget your special day." He leaned in, somewhat conspiratorially. "This is our annual fundraiser for the local cat shelter society. I'm their proud patron." He pointed to a banner that showed five cats' paws, all different colors, stacked on top of each other like a baseball team's motivational gesture. He looked awfully pleased with himself. I highly suspected Bertie was responsible for the recyclable, super lifelike feline face coasters scattered on each high-top table. Bertie was like that. He went all in and had the financial backing to do so.

Rich, powerful people, some of whom would likely be at my wedding tomorrow.

Bottomless wallets.

Felines in need ... a very worthy cause to support.

So why did I feel so out of place and nervous?

Chapter 2

After profuse apologies and a couple of necessary distractions—"Oh look, isn't that so and so? I'm positive she wore the same dress to the Wilson wedding last week"—I reached the registration desk. It had cool, mixed-pebble color granite countertops, brass lamps, and the latest in contactless payment machines. I stood on a red carpet that led right up to the members-only desk where Aunt Edwina had told me to check in. I'd never stayed here before, just had tea with her on site as we planned the wedding over the last few months. Of course, the hotel made all its best rooms available. She wanted this event done right, and Lady Edwina Greymore would take nothing from my father's wallet. Dad was a modest man and never liked all the pomp and circumstance associated with the Greymore name. In fact, he did everything he could to disassociate himself from it, never wanting to be in the spotlight.

Chris, my fiancé, hadn't wanted anything to do with it either. He just told me to tell him the time and the place and that he'd wait for me at the top of the aisle. He didn't care what color theme it was. He'd wanted a bachelor party. I'd banned strippers. We'd compromised on a private party at a high-end London pub instead, all glitz, sports, and glamor. I heard about it later.

I felt suitably uncomfortable as the woman at the registration desk fawned all over me. Jacques in the Fizzleywick's bellmen department had obviously telepathically told her who I was. All staff were to snap to attention. I hated it: it *so* wasn't me.

The clerk's face fell as she checked something on her computer. "Oh dear," she said. The downward droop on her mouth was unmistakable. I was surprised her eyeshadow didn't start slipping off her eyelids.

"Is something wrong?" I asked. My fingers were now gripping the side of the cool granite countertop. Perhaps they were going to throw me out for embarrassing her hotel in front of all these fancy guests.

"Miss Fincher, I'm afraid there's been a water-pipe break affecting the bridal suite. We were told it would be repaired in time, but it appears that the work order's been revised so the suite won't be ready until late next week."

She was waiting for bridezilla to appear, but I wasn't going to give her that satisfaction.

"That is rather unfortunate," was all I said.

I was impressed with her recovery. The desk clerk leaned over to me and offered a fantastic compromise. "My manager is providing the catering for tonight's rehearsal dinner on a complimentary basis to make up for the inconvenience, Miss Fincher. I hope that will be to your satisfaction?"

"That will be fine," I said. "I always thought my Aunt Edwina was spending too much on this anyways. I mean, it's a wedding, not an international political summit."

The desk clerk giggled, pleased I was taking this so well. "We've put you in the presidential suite instead, and it is quite fabulous, I promise."

"Very well."

"It is rather a catastrophe of the most enormous proportions," the desk clerk said.

You don't know the half of it.

"Don't worry about it. Chris and I have been together for a while, so it's not like we need the bridal suite for, well you know ..." I gave her a wink.

I guessed the desk clerk wasn't used to a relative of a titled lady aristocrat speaking so frankly. The color in her cheeks rose as she handed me the keys.

"Thank you, and the bellman has my bag?" I started.

"Just behind you. At your service, Miss Fincher," she said.

I nodded my thanks and scarpered. Jacques rolled the luggage cart behind me as we walked into the elevator. Inside were gleaming brass buttons and rails, plus an inlaid crystal ceiling décor. All quite fancy. All super expensive.

We met a plumber in the elevator. More apologies were exchanged as his heavy wrench bumped into the bell cart. He wore a tool belt that clanked plus baggy, sodden overalls. I knew it was bad news, seeing that the tradesman himself was half-soaked. When he got off on the next floor, he exchanged places with a man dressed up like a red tomato. My eyes must've hit the ceiling. I couldn't help but notice our new floor-travel buddy's red fishnet tights, tall black-leather lace-up boots, and puffy vegetable jumpsuit that stopped at the top of his thighs, plus matching gloves.

It occurred to me that his discomfort at the moment would be mirrored by mine tomorrow. Stuffed into a tight, poufy costume to make everyone ooh and aah. My costume was off-white. His was red. Practically costume cousins.

There were two seconds of uncomfortable silence before Tomato Man felt compelled to talk. "Um, I'm here for the Comedy Festival. You know, tomorrow? At Molmuns Manor?"

"Riiiight," I said. "I have a friend who's going as a cauliflower."

Joke. Of course it was a joke. None of my friends had vegetable-dress tendencies in mind. At least that I knew of.

Jacques hid a grin and stifled a cough. I did believe the man was warming to my slight eccentricity.

Tomato Man looked relieved and got off two floors up.

Jacques nodded. "We don't need all types, but we do have all types," he offered in a prim voice.

"Quite."

I knew what Jacques was thinking inside that little bald head of his: Lady Edwina's favorite niece, the one who was bringing a lot of money to the brand-new hotel, had not been recognized upon arrival, didn't get the bridal suite that was booked months ago, and was now being entertained by a caricature of a man wearing a vegetable costume.

"Miss Fincher, I must apologize for your introduction to the Fizzleywick Hotel. It is certainly below the standard expected of this hotel establishment. We will do everything in our power to make this up to you, I promise," he said.

Did I detect a French accent in his voice?

"Where are you from, Jacques?" I asked him. It occurred to me that perhaps he had a secret in his past, something tantalizing that could be coaxed out of his lips with the right form of encouragement.

We reached our floor. He held the open-door button on the panel to let me exit first and then followed me with the humongous brass cart. The cart looked quite silly carrying just my single, battered suitcase, but Jacques was game to try and improve my luxury-hotel experience.

"I am originally from Paris, miss," he replied.

"I thought so. I spent two years there at art school."

"How delightful. Do you paint with oil, acrylic, or water-color?" He was intent on keeping up a running conversation as he rolled the brass cart down the plush carpet in the hallway.

"Acrylics and watercolor. I dislike dealing with the solvents and flammability associated with oils. I teach classes at the local college too."

"I shall have to remember that. I dabble in art once in a while myself," Jacques said. "And here we are, miss." With great efficiency, he touched his electronic skeleton key card to the lock pad, which emitted a green light, and he pushed open the door. Ahead of me was the opulent, four-thousand-square-foot presidential suite. It looked as if an upscale department store had sold the hotel five rooms full of furniture and the staff had laid it out in the most attractive groupings. Of course there was expensive artwork on the wall, and a modern shag rug down in front of the sixty-inch television. A mahogany dining table sat twelve, plus there was a wet bar and a full kitchen. Two bedrooms, two bathrooms. Vases of fresh cream, pink, and lavender roses everywhere. A side table even held a small plate of fancily wrapped gourmet chocolates with what I assumed was a welcome note from the manager.

"Will this be adequate, miss?" Jacques asked. "Your wedding dress, reception clothes, and all your accessories are safely stowed in the closet."

Safe. Something I wished I felt from my fiancé. To me, Chris was like a milkshake ready to avalanche down my back, making me shriek with disdain at its surprise iciness. There was nothing warm or comforting talking about our love, and that was a real shame.

I turned to look at Jacques and raised my eyebrows. "I think eighteen people would be quite happy in here. It's fine, thank you." Secretly, I was still dying for a shower and a change of clothes. It was only 11:00 a.m., but I felt I'd lived a lifetime since getting out of bed this morning.

Right now, I was sincerely wishing that Chris and I had eloped. Aunt Edwina would be beside herself when she found out about the water-pipe leak, about me not being recognized, heck, even about Tomato Man. She wanted a genteel, upscale wedding for me and was going all out. I just hoped she thought the expense was worth it.

Chapter 3

———

Aunt Edwina stood five-foot-six-inches tall and influenced the world through firm, steady eyes. Her grey hair was always done up in an elegant style. Her self-appointed daily uniform consisted of a business suit with either a pastel or calm-toned jacket and matching skirt. She wore stylish yet chunky heels and always had a triple strand of pearls around her neck. Her skin was well-moisturized, and she exuded the aura of an experienced woman who cared deeply for her family, friends and community.

I'd given up years ago trying to conceal the tiny scar on my cheek—a car accident remnant. It was now part of me. I did, however, wear a crisp, summery pantsuit in order to gain Aunt Edwina's approval.

I could tell she was disappointed the moment I walked into the pre-conference meeting. Not at my appearance, but at the circumstance. In the hotel industry it didn't matter if you were having an annual general meeting for a non-profit society, a large wedding, business sales training, or an eightieth birthday party. It was always called the 'pre-conference meeting'. It was a chance for the client and the hotel event leaders to sit down in a quiet room and go over the schedule of events, including all banquet event orders. Practically, it was a chance for hotel staff to figure out how difficult the client was and what accommodations could be made to avoid any failures, clashes, or disruptions.

My reaction to the water-pipe leak was anything but annoyed. I'd been gracious. Aunt Edwina would be gracious. As Lady Edwina Greymore, it just wasn't within her DNA to make a fuss or tarnish the family name. However, she had a subtle way of making people know that she was not amused. And disappointing her with her niece's wedding plans was an unwise thing to do if they wished her patronage in the future. If influential Lady Edwina Greymore mentioned to her friends that she wasn't pleased with the Fizzleywick Hotel, then it was highly likely the grand opening would soon be followed by a grand closing. The lady of the local manor always needed to be satisfied.

"I really don't think it's too much to expect that the bridal suite be ready for my niece's wedding." Aunt Edwina looked at the entire cast of senior managers who sat around the table for the discussion. She took a slow sip of her probably perfectly brewed tea, one lump of sugar plus a thin slice of lemon.

The hotel general manager dove in first. "Of course, Lady Edwina, we understand how utterly frustrating this must be. We are horrified to be in this position yet did not anticipate our contractor needing a week to fix what they initially said would only be three days." He was a thin man who earnestly leaned forward in his chair, hoping to soothe his VIP client.

He looked at their catering manager and gave her a slight nod. She took his cue. "We are providing complimentary catering for this evening's rehearsal dinner, including hors d'oeuvres and beverages."

Aunt Edwina looked around the table and clasped her hands in her lap. She had the unmistakable appearance of an efficient, upscale woman who was used to getting what she wanted, yet in a very nice way. She represented Oakhurst, the village closest to her home, located about nineteen miles away from Carlingheath. She started slowly. "Well, it is most disappointing; however, we shall have to make do. Are there any other mishaps we should anticipate?"

She surveyed each of their faces with an eagle eye, glad to see blank expressions and shrugs.

The general manager started in again. "We thank you for your understanding, Lady Edwina, and wish you, your niece, as well as your family and friends a very lovely event. Rest assured that we will do our utmost to prevent all other challenges."

"Do you mean problems?" Aunt Edwina asked.

"Well, yes," was his hurried reply. "But 'challenges' sounds much gentler to a client."

Aunt Edwina stiffened in her chair. "I am ninety-two-years-old, sir. I have survived over nine decades and do not need gentle. I need facts and truth. Understood?"

"Certainly, Lady Edwina. I shall make a note."

And there it was. The utterly pristine difference between a traditional British aristocratic lady and a modern business-man. Current language trends had no impact on Aunt Edwina, nor should they. It was all namby-pamby rigamarole meant to elicit confusion and even worse, docile acceptance of the status quo. Aunt Edwina was made of far stronger stuff.

The meeting then diverted into extreme detail about who was sitting where, the music to be played—a classical string quartet—how to handle party crashers, what guests to keep away from each other due to longstanding family feuds, the flowers and, of course, the catering. It was to be a three-course meal: smoked salmon salad, prime rib, a chicken or vegetarian entrée, followed by an elaborate lemon multi-tier cake with amazing decorations. Most incredible of all the decorations was the cascade of roses elegantly winding their way down the cake, floating on a pond of gold leaf at the base. I was impressed, because they really pulled out all the stops for us, trying to make us happy.

I felt a gentle touch at my elbow. I knew that expensive fabric from playing dress-up in her closet when I was little. "Aunt Edwina, I'm sure this will all be just lovely," I said.

"I'm trying to make this the most perfect day for you, dear," she said.

We looked into each other's eyes and saw the love and friendship we had shared for over two decades. Half of me truly wanted to run away with Chris when he first proposed, however I knew Aunt Edwina would never forgive me if I'd taken this opportunity away from her. She sincerely wanted to help my father, who was sorely lacking a wife and only had the one child. My mother died when I was three, and Aunt Edwina had graciously made up for that void for as long as I could remember. She took in other spare relatives at Christmas; my cousin Gertie, for example, was one such soul.

Aunt Edwina was very kind. Kinder to me than any school friend I'd ever had. Kinder than my favorite cat I had as a pet while growing up—the tabby scratched me—and that was how I made the distinction. On a scale of one to ten, Aunt Edwina was an eleven, and bravely so with me, as I constantly plagued her family with non-traditional vocations. I was the one who brought splatter painting, crochet, and beekeeping into our households' purvey.

I leaned over and gave her a hug. "Thank you for making this such a special time for me."

"Not at all, my dear. Not at all. Let me spoil you." Aunt Edwina turned to look at the hotel staff. "Am I correct in stating that Julie and I will wear the special hotel pins signaling that if we need something done immediately, we have the power to order it?"

The general manager hummed and hawed. "Well, Lady Edwina, yes, that is typical for the client conference leads, however I wouldn't dream of asking you to wear such a thing because you're so well-known and we have such respect ..."

She brushed away his comment with a wave of her hand. "Piffle. Treat me like any other client. I just want to make sure I understand the protocol."

"Very well, Lady Edwina." He pulled a small, clear-plastic envelope from his breast pocket and opened the seal. He shook out two golden pins with back closures that secured them onto a garment. Each bore the hotel logo on the front. "These pins grant all-access to the hotel kingdom. Anyone wearing one can order anything they want at any time. No questions asked."

One pin disappeared into my aunt's hand and the other one into mine.

She issued a mischievous grin to the staff. "And the flowers?"

The wedding specialist on staff took that one. She looked at me with a shy glance in her eyes. "Miss Fincher, we never did get your reply on the specific arrangement of roses that you wanted, so we ordered some of all three for the ceremony and reception hall. All that's left is for you to decide on the exact flowers for the bridal bouquet."

Waste not, want not. And I'd been busy teaching my painting classes. Hadn't read all the emails stacked up over the last few days. Oops.

"Well the theme is cream, lavender, and pink, so I'm sure it will be fine," I said.

Aunt Edwina sat up straight. "Julie, you *must* take a greater interest in the floral decor. Your bouquet will be the foundation of all of the family photographs taken. They will be photographs you will cherish for the rest of your life and show your grandchildren. The flowers must be perfect."

"Of course, but ..." I knew enough to keep my opinion out of this. Besides, she was a lady, and I was, well, a modestly successful painter, a hanger-on-er if I'd ever known one.

"Does anyone have anything else for the group before the dinner tonight?" the general manager asked.

No one said a word. Aunt Edwina finally looked satisfied.

They took it as their cue to pack up and get on with the rest of their assignments.

Aunt Edwina stayed with me, alone in the cavernous ballroom. Far off, about two miles away, a couple of waiters were collapsing circular tables and stacking chairs.

Aunt Edwina leaned over across the white tablecloth. "Don't discount the importance of flowers, my dear. I didn't have the luxury of fancy ones for my wedding. I always regretted it, and it's a blight on my family history photo collection."

"Well, there's time for me to go to the flower shop right now," I said.

Aunt Edwina's eyes lit up. "What a wonderful idea. I think you should take this opportunity to march right down to that shop and make your final choices for the bridal bouquet."

"You're welcome to come along, if you wish. Brandywine Walk makes for a lovely outing," I said, referring to the colonnaded shops in the exclusive area of Carlingheath. With her beside me, I had a much better chance of fitting in with this fancy town.

She shook her head. "With all this excitement, I think I'll have a little lie-down before lunch. I already had the medical clinic board committee meeting earlier this morning, and I'm starting to find it more tiring than usual."

"All right. I can take care of it by myself, no biggie."

"No biggie?" Aunt Edwina asked, a quizzical look on her face.

"Not a big deal. Not a problem," I explained, a grin on my face. "Sorry, I slipped into artist lingo."

Aunt Edwina gave me a sweet smile. "Not befitting a young lady," she warned in that beguiling manner of hers. "Perhaps it is I. Perhaps I'm just out of touch with everything. Last week I saw a television show that simply horrified me. Something about the family history of an earl who'd made up his entire genealogy just to slink his way into the family fortune. Honestly!"

I nodded in agreement. "It's a scary world out there. I think I should have been born in the safe, picket-fenced 1950s."

Aunt Edwina leaned over and patted the back of my hand. "Dear girl. The 1950s weren't all fairies and ponies." She got a serious look on her face. "Rationing went on for years and the entire population was still recovering from the war. Never doubt how difficult it was."

Chapter 4

———

Brandywine Walk was exactly as I'd imagined. Cool, elegant, and framing a multitude of exclusive boutiques and offerings that were unique to this part of the world. Tourists came from all over the globe to see Carlingheath. They'd heard about the famous spa waters and wanted to partake in their healing properties. An English king had indeed brought his barren wife here early in their marriage in hopes of healing. Later on, a woman actually held a job as a dipper of the springs, bringing up a cup of water for any person worthy of receiving one. Nowadays, the local tourist board replicated this offering during the warmer months for the thousands of visitors who descended upon the city each year.

Today, I was one of them. The multitude of columns, supporting first-story railings, signs, and a large clock, all contributed to the utmost charm of the place. It was a long, winding walking street where trees and throngs of people coexisted. Flowers were plentiful, and bright hanging baskets spilled over with a rainbow of colors and greenery as the street slowly curved up ahead. The second through fourth stories appeared to be living quarters above Brandywine Walk. Various cafés had set out chairs and tables, and today's sunshine made it all that more pleasant.

'Kirsten and Katrina's Floral Wonderland' was at the end of the road, a large enough shop to need two retail spaces combined into one. It had a dizzying display of colorful flowers outside. I knew to go inside to look for my roses because they were still a little ahead of the season here in town and had to be imported from a warmer climate.

Aunt Edwina had approved the cream, lavender, and pink color theme. She asked me to pick, but because it was not a huge deal to me, I chose her favorite colors in deference. And of course they looked lovely in the photo of the sample bouquet that I'd been emailed.

Kirsten looked up when I walked inside, the doorbell yielding a loud musical chime. "Julie, how nice to see you!" She was one of those gardening types, happier with plants than people, and instead of paint had constant soil stains under her fingernails.

Her shop was a feast for the senses: gorgeous flowers of every shape and size. The scent was overpowering, a heady concoction of incredible sweetness and freshness. It was like simultaneously walking in a meadow and a formal rose garden.

"Hi, Kirsten. I'm here with a rather chagrined look on my face. I think I missed an email from you."

She nodded. "Never mind. I just need you to sign off on these bouquet flowers for tomorrow. We have all the stock, and I wanted to make sure you are okay with what we chose on your behalf."

Of course the bride's bouquet and matching boutonniere for the groom were perfect. The sample pew flower arrangements were lovely, as were the ones for decorating the area up front with the priest. The roses she'd brought in were very healthy, turgid at the base of the petals, and emitted a glorious scent.

"Do you have anyone with allergies coming to your wedding?" she asked. "The scent can be a bit overwhelming if you have a flower issue."

I leaned in deep and took a huge whiff. "We asked on the invitations to let us know if anyone had allergies we needed to accommodate. All we got back was one person who has a problem with bananas and another one with strawberries. Nothing else."

"That's a relief. That was the only worry I had for you. To double check, you would like us to deliver to Scotford Castle by 8:00 a.m. tomorrow morning?"

"That's the plan. My aunt has staff there who will set everything up. I'm really quite spoiled."

"Your Aunt Edwina has done a lot for this area. You should be proud to be related to her."

"I am. She's been like a mother to me ever since my own died." I looked around the shop. There were various floral arrangements as décor, many of them behind big, glass-fronted coolers. Dried-flower arrangements as well as loose stems were on display throughout the shop on various shelving units and in black, water-filled buckets. There were also the accompaniments that went with flower arrangements, such as teddy bears, chocolates, cards, balloons, other gifts, and ribbon. It was an established shop, one that took orders from across the globe due to its stellar reputation. I signed off on the work order with more profuse apologies for my lack of attention to the paperwork. I was then on my merry way.

As I headed back to the hotel, I heard a woman's throaty voice pouring out of a nearby café. A crowd of curious onlookers had gathered, numbering about twenty-five or so. I stopped to take a look, and inside I saw a woman with bright-red hair in a modest, floor-length, loud floral cotton dress, belting out a hit pop song. She was slightly off key, and the high notes were reaches the chanteuse really shouldn't have tried.

Then I remembered. In my peripheral vision I'd seen her at the hotel. She was with a few other people and held two champagne flutes in her hand. There was something about that face. And the bright-red hair. As in, fire-engine or tomato bright red. I didn't remember that at all.

And then it hit me. It was my vivacious cousin, Gertie Porringer. She was nicknamed 'The Apricot Powerhouse' fifteen years ago after a particularly shocking, bad home hair-dye job. Gertie was the cousin who'd looked out for me on campus at boarding school in America when she was sixteen and I was just ten years old. She'd been absolutely wonderful, showing me all the cool hangouts and things to see. She also warned me off drugs and alcohol, telling me all they would do was mess up my education and my head. Turns out she was right, as we'd both seen what substance abuse did to other students.

Gertie wasn't vivacious because she was a leggy model that all the men followed. No, she was a female priest who was unafraid to speak her mind. I hadn't seen her for the past two years as our lives had gone in massively different directions. We'd been close friends growing up.

But karaoke? This was new. And scary.

Gertie was on the last few notes of the song, drawing it out in a slow, nasally whine. Then it was over, thank goodness. The crowd dispersed, after a smattering of polite applause. Gertie had provided a good ten minutes of free entertainment for their day, and I guessed they all thought she deserved some appreciation.

I made my way to the front of the crowd. The café's staff had opened its full-length windows, collapsing them back into a scissor pattern so the air could flow in freely from outside. I waved at Gertie, and she recognized me instantly.

"Jules!" she cried out, making a beeline for me after she put the microphone back in its stand.

I was the recipient of a firm, unyielding hug from my cousin. It was great to see her because she always made me smile. I pulled back and looked into her sparkly hazel eyes. "You changed your hair color again!"

"Stress and deceit, my dear. Stress and deceit." She said it with a gleam in her eyes, and I didn't know whether to take it as truth or not. Priests weren't supposed to have personal stress and deceit. It wasn't supposed to be in their nature.

Right?

We settled at a nearby table.

"Fire-engine-red hair, Gertie? Blue eyeshadow?"

She nodded, sounding parched. "I've got a few greys coming in, so I gave myself a makeover. Consider me the modern look of religion." She looked me up and down, checking out the engagement ring. "So I see Jules has found her one and only. Whatever happened to 'I'm never going to let a man control my life'?" she teased good-naturedly.

I shrugged. "I compromised. He's a good cook."

She gave me that look, the one I'd known since I was three years old. "You're getting married for food? Okay, at least you're being honest."

She missed my forced poker-face grin, opened a packet of cashews, and took a swig of her iced tea. "Belting out that tune, wow, it sure dries out the pipes."

I smiled. "This a new venture of yours? The singing priest?"

"Not really. It's kind of a hobby, an allure."

"Karaoke bars?"

"Well, not technically always bars. Cafés sometimes have stages and the machines. I even found one at a college lounge. I used to be the auditor for various church sermons around the County of Kent for a few years. It was during my travels around the Garden of England when I discovered my true calling." She grinned.

"It's great to see you, Gertie. I've missed our chats," I said.

"As have I. Remember all those winter holidays, us sitting together under Aunt Edwina's Christmas tree?"

"The ones so tall they always scraped the ceiling plus the paint from her angel ornament's head?"

"The very same. Boy, we had some good natters, looking at her family photo albums."

I smiled. "So how did we lose touch? I got busy painting and with Chris."

"And I drove around every back road, hedgerow, and lane in Southern England, auditing sermons. Some good, some pretty bad."

The world of today was so busy—too crazy—and it affected family ties. It was so bad that first cousins like us drifted apart; quite a feat considering we both lived in the same county. Life had turned young people into dominoes tumbling downhill, to heck with whatever went flying.

"It's sad how family loses touch. Because it's certainly not intentional," I said. "It's so important for future generations that we keep the stories and bonds between us alive."

Gertie took another swig of iced tea. "Oh, come on, admit it. I'm the obscure, jolly cousin everyone assumes lives alone in a timber-framed cottage with a thriving herb garden and eleven cats. I'm also completely forgotten until needed. Except by you. You never missed a birthday or Christmas card. Thank you!"

"I wouldn't dream of sending you an impersonal email. We always promised to do snail mail so we can scrapbook the cards later. I still have all the scrapbooks we did. It's a great way to look back and enjoy all the things we did as children."

"And I've broken that promise too." Gertie sighed. "Where did the time go?"

"You're only thirty-one. And you made up for it by being here to officiate at my wedding ceremony. I really appreciate that, Gertie." I gave her a furtive stare. "If you have eleven cats, you need to talk to Bertie. He's got just the cause for you."

Now it was her turn to shrug. "Do you remember all those Christmases at Greymore Hall doing Aunt Edwina's puzzles? She would always create a riddle for us to figure out before we could open any presents."

"That's because our presents were always hidden at the end of the riddle!" I said. Aunt Edwina's drawn-out present-seeking adventures were the stuff of family legend.

Gertie laughed. "We had to do a hide and seek to find the gifts before we were allowed to even consider rattling them or opening them in front of the family."

My phone rang. "Hi, Dad? Guess who I'm sitting here with? It's Gertie!" There was a squawking on the end of the phone and Gertie saw my face fall. I tapped the red 'end call' button, then gave her a focused look. "It's Aunt Edwina. She's been taken very poorly. We need to leave. Now."

Chapter 5

———

I didn't understand how 'taken very poorly' translated into 'dead'. But in this case, unfortunately, it had. Poor Aunt Edwina was laid out in her beautiful, lavender silk nightgown and robe on top of her pristine sheets and comforter. She looked beautiful, as if she was just resting, like she promised she was going to do before the evening's activities.

I burst into tears as soon as I touched her elegant hand. It was stone cold.

My father pushed a note into my hands. I read:

> *Continue on with the wedding as planned.*
> *And Julie, please open my gift last.*
> *Love to you all, Aunt Edwina.*

I shook my head. "Did she know that she was unwell?" I looked up at the sea of faces surrounding me, including my father, Gertie, the hotel doctor, and two paramedics.

My father, a tidy, middle-class man who worked as a high-end furniture shop manager in Carlingheath, started gently. "You see, Julie, my mother didn't want you to know she was fighting stomach cancer. She thought you wouldn't go ahead with the ceremony, when it was her greatest wish to see you have a lavish wedding day. She wanted you to go ahead with what is planned for tonight and tomorrow. Her instructions are for her to be cremated, and then for you and Gertie to arrange a suitable funeral in two months' time, no sooner."

"Two months? Why two months?" I asked.

He shrugged. "If the burden is too much–"

"No, it's fine. It's just, well ..." On one hand, it seemed completely unfathomable. On the other hand, it was a dying lady's wish that I had an obligation to fulfill. I looked to Gertie for some guidance.

"What would you do?" I asked my cousin.

She had a very sorrowful look on her face, and her eyes welled with tears. "Heavenly Father wants all his children to be happy. The one he's taken back into his arms had a last wish, and it's well within your power to fulfill it."

"But it seems so disrespectful, holding a celebration when someone so dear has just passed away," I said.

"Nonsense," Gertie replied. "She and I were on the phone for hours talking about today when we first started planning the event. She was absolutely thrilled to get her family together and to see you settled in this world."

"How can I smile on my wedding day when she's died the day before?" My shoulders felt like they were carrying a weighty sack full of stones. I knew Aunt Edwina would expect us all to carry on, stiff upper lip and all that, but it would be so hard.

Gertie gave me a hug. "Because she wanted you to, Jules. You were always her favorite, ever since you nursed her that one summer after ankle surgery. Everybody knew that. Don't disappoint her, because she's still watching."

I looked back at the dear lady who was laid out on the bed, completely still. Her eyes were closed, and it looked like she had simply passed away in her sleep. I hoped that was the way it was for her, because this good lady didn't deserve anything else but a peaceful departure from this world. I dared myself to reach out and touch her cold hand once again. I leaned in close. "I will do it for you, Aunt Edwina. I promise."

***

Scotford Castle, near Oakhurst, Kent. Next morning.

The portcullis was open. The lights were on. The marvelous carved wood paneling was on display. The fifteenth-century childhood home of Lady Mary Burlisle was a lovely tourist destination in the beautiful County of Kent. Chris and I were to be married outside on the grounds, in front of three arches wound with garlands of roses. These arches overlooked Scotford Lake, a small body of water with a fountain feature built by a previous owner centuries ago. Swans glided over its glassy surface, ruffling their tail feathers when they settled down for a gentle paddle. It was a quiet location, away from the hustle and bustle of the rest of the tourist trade, and seemed perfect. We once considered the interior of the castle as a possible venue, but there wasn't anything large enough to accommodate the number of people Aunt Edwina wanted to invite. Our wedding group increased by twelve people every time she invited one additional guest. That was just the way it was with aristocrats; if you invited the duchess of one county, then you had to invite the three in surrounding counties. If you invited a viscount, then all the others plus a few barons would have to be thrown onto the invite list as well. Basically, if you moved in these circles on a restricted budget, it was a sincere hope that some invitees would come back with a decline RSVP.

However, if Lady Edwina Greymore was sending you the invitation, it was the social kiss of death to decline.

Scotford Castle. I always thought that getting married at this particular venue was quite the stroke of genius. The title of 'doomed bride' suited Lady Mary Burlisle and I equally well.

Lady Mary was wed to a knight in dented armor who would soon desert her.

I was to marry a man who saw dollar signs when he looked at me.

Same type of horrid deal.

Lady Mary was a social climber whose father demanded a good match, not love, for his daughter.

Later today, I would marry out of duty to protect and give hope to my dear father. Chris and I got along well enough; it was just that, above all else, I'd hoped to spend my life with someone who wanted me for me rather than a potential inheritance down the road. My nuptials were akin to hitting 'pause' on the next phase of my life. Thank goodness Gertie was able to officiate. She did such a lovely job standing at the head of the congregation as Chris and I exchanged vows. Aunt Edwina was right about the cream, lavender, and pink flowers; a small bouquet hung off the end of each row of chairs, all looking absolutely stunning.

Placing my lace-covered arm in the crook of my father's elbow made me cry. Dad did the right thing and stood up in front of the entire group of attendees before the ceremony started. He told them it was Aunt Edwina's dying wish for the ceremony and celebration to continue. Everybody understood.

Chris took my hand in his and squeezed hard, possessive and confident. I bit the inside of my cheek and soldiered on. By the time we'd both said our 'I do's', I was firmly convinced that 'I did not'.

Back at the Fizzleywick Hotel for the reception, I got all glisteny-eyed listening to my father extoll my virtues. I nearly cried, partly because of his pronounced love for his daughter, and then once again because of the horrific deception I was creating. I was close to my father, closer than most daughters. He was a cardiac stroke survivor, and after recent successful triple-bypass surgery, I'd nursed him back to good health. He'd tried to give me profuse thanks, but they weren't necessary. My father helped give me life and cared for me when his spouse unexpectedly died so young. He owed me nothing. Dad said his greatest wish was to see me married and settled. Sure, he was supportive of my art career, largely because I taught classes as well as sold canvasses. But the instant I'd told him I was engaged, I literally saw a couple of worry lines completely vanish from his face. He was old school, and there was nothing wrong with that; all my father wanted was the best for his only child, and that meant the safety and security of a life partner.

Dad didn't know I wed because of my non-customary obligation. I looked over at my husband doing fist bumps with his friends from university. Chris was slightly boring, moderately controlling, and overly patronizing towards my art. On the outside, he was a gregarious, charming breadwinner who would take care of me for the rest of my life. He even had Aunt Edwina fooled, at least as far as I could tell. The dead giveaway was when I'd overheard him on the phone one night. He'd told a friend he wanted out of the rat race and boasted he'd done everything it took to marry an heiress to old money, including pretending to like her, her family tree, her friends, and her art.

It really hurt. It really stung. But I had no other prospects. And at the time, my father's health was still so fragile I didn't want to upset him by backing out of the engagement. So I gritted my teeth.

A noise to my right snapped me out of my self-absorbed thought.

"Julie! Wifey!" Chris yelled from the entrance. "We're taking pictures beside the water ... I'm going to push my best man into the lake. You coming?" His eyes were drunk-wide with excitement at his little boy prank.

How utterly silly and trite. Did he think he was a young hooligan in short trousers?

Aunt Edwina would be horrified.

"No, thank you. I'll stay here with our guests," I said. Polite and steady. Butter wouldn't melt.

"Sure thing!" And with that, my husband of twenty-nine minutes left me. At least it wasn't at the altar, but close enough. His earlier shots of whiskey courage no doubt led to this unabashed boisterousness. I knew not to interfere when Chris and his financial markets buddies got wound up.

I turned to see my father, pleased as punch to see me in my wedding gown. We embraced. "Julie, my precious little girl, all grown up now on your wedding day." He wore a grin as wide as the River Thames and had wonderful color in his face. He kissed me on both cheeks.

My father's words tugged at my heart, and I knew I'd done the right, albeit challenging, thing. It was imperative that I made him happy and unstressed; that would ensure Dad would be with us here on earth for all that much longer.

I had to admit, Chris made all the single women present look extremely jealous as we walked back down the aisle as a married couple. But Chris made me feel ill ever since I discovered his longing for an easy gravy train. His thirst for money haunted me. Not like a ghost, because belt-and-braces people like me were too practical to believe in the supernatural. No, Chris was just a murky pool of deep, unyielding water, but I refused to sink beneath it.

The tipsy relatives and friends had all soon forgotten why they were there and, later on, even their own names. Gertie made sure she got to each of them before they over-imbibed, especially Cousin Devlin from Ireland. She rounded up each relative to ensure all new hatches, matches, and dispatches were added to the latest computer-generated family tree she'd brought. Family history was her passion, something she'd inherited from Aunt Edwina, and some of the intrigue had also rubbed off on me. We'd spent hours together over spring break and summer holidays combing through online census records and parish registers. Then we'd put on our wellies and visit remote graveyards, hunting for more ancestors to add to the family tree.

The family tree was now over twenty feet long and tacked to the wall for all to see. Gertie had printed out a fresh copy at the local office services shop, sweet talking the clerk into letting her use the continuous roll of paper that was linked to some new-fangled architectural software program. Luckily, the hotel had a cork strip for this exact printed display purpose running around the wall at eye level to ensure its fancy wallpaper was protected. Gertie was a fanatic about entering details online in her genealogy program and then uploading the revised family tree for the world to enjoy. She had our ancestors' photos on there too and absolutely delighted in receiving messages from people all over the world who were thrilled that they'd joined up their family tree with ours. Many of them raved about the photos she shared online. Her only lament was that the program wouldn't let her post living persons' photos, just those who had passed on. I supposed it was for privacy and security reasons.

I read over the edits that were all there in Gertie's neat penmanship. Oops. She hadn't caught Cousin Devlin in time. I saw his crude marking of 'Fudgie the Dachshund' near his name. It was his drunken way of adding levity to a rather serious business, altering a well-developed family tree. I always thought it odd, drawing a twig that was expected to support each new marriage. Truth be told, I was certain the branch Chris and I created was rotten from the start.

Then it was over. My fantastic, extravagant, and over-the-top expensive wedding was finished. And I felt empty because the woman who'd helped organize it all right down to the very last canapé hadn't been there to enjoy any of this special day.

Chapter 6

Gertie's Suite, Fizzleywick Hotel. 11:30 p.m.

As if it was a perfect omen, my new husband passed out the
second we got back to our presidential suite. He was face
down on the sofa, his forehead pressing right on to his watch.
I moved his arm to the side so he wouldn't have a huge, ugly
impression on his skin when he woke up. I took off his shoes
and just left Chris there, his sweaty, tuxedo-clad body lolling
about, certainly not giving me any inkling of a comforting
husband or superhero. Come to think of it, lately he'd never
made me feel that way. It was rather depressing, thinking how
my fun, art-filled life had degenerated into an ill-fated version
of some perky housewife's magazine. I married at 11:00 a.m.
this morning. By 11:00 p.m., I wanted out of the marriage.
Aunt Edwina got her fantasy wedding event, but there was no
luck in my upside-down horseshoes. How romantic ... not. I
needed Gertie.

It was like we'd rewound the clock back to our teenage years together. Gertie and I sat beside each other on her suite's sofa, pouring over the wedding photos she'd uploaded to her laptop. We giggled, we commented and rejuvenated a deep, close friendship that we'd somehow lost over the last two years.

She looked at her watch. "It's just gone 11:30 p.m. Don't you have somewhere to be? Someone to be with?"

"No, ma'am. Chris won't wake up until sometime after nine tomorrow. The guy can't function without eight full hours of sleep, minimum."

"And he's a stockbroker?" She gave me a confused stare.

I stared back.

We both burst out laughing.

"Yes, one could call it a rather interesting career move for him," I said. "Hong Kong and London don't wait for sleepyheads."

"Is there something you wanted to tell me?" Gertie asked. She had a knack of reading me, sussing out anything I was trying to hide.

I stared at the floor. It was covered in plush carpet resplendent with tiny replications of the hotel's logo. It was fancy and quaint all at once. At the present moment, I felt like that carpet, stretched taut and without any give left. There on display for everyone to see, yet not an inch for me to move out of place. I was subservient to the establishment, to family duty. The kicker was being walked all over by Chris. I was his carpet, he the eager pair of muddy boots. People shouldn't be allowed to possess a doormat spouse.

She put a gentle hand on my shoulder. "You can tell me. Your secrets are safe with me."

I looked up at her, my eyes starting to feel tears. I had to tell somebody. A priest was a safe person, right? I took a deep breath and told her, "My husband doesn't love me for me. He's after the money he thinks I'm going to inherit in the future."

"What money?" Gertie asked. "I thought Aunt Edwina was leaving it all to Bertie's cat shelter."

My mouth fell open.

"Kidding. Just kidding. Although I'm sure Bertie's already roped her in for some sizeable donations. Why else would they have Greymore Hall tea towels on display in their booth at the local village fair last month?"

She was trying to cheer me up and it was an honorable attempt. I sniffled. "I never understood why Chris had so much fervor for me. Not until I overhead him on the phone with a work colleague talking about his pending life of leisure."

We thought on it for a minute. Our eyes roamed the room. Gertie was also given a suite because we needed somewhere safe to store the mountain of wedding gifts after the reception.

"Perhaps Chris thinks this is just the start?" Gertie said, spreading her arms wide.

I looked around the room at all the gaily wrapped gifts. "Did he really bind himself to me for the rest of his life for a few blenders and toast racks? Because I've never once breathed a word to him about any inheritance."

She shook her head. "He's a risk taker in business. He thinks that Aunt Edwina would get you much more than a few small kitchen appliances."

I shrugged. "I never asked. I was happy to have her guidance and her companionship since I grew up without a mother."

"It was enough for Chris to know she's rich and adores you." Gertie tilted her head to the side. "How's your husband's business been doing over the last couple of years?"

"Not good. He decided to sell all his tech stocks right before the market jumped up. He also missed a few currency trades he should have made."

"Didn't tech stocks go through the roof?" Gertie asked.

I nodded. "And so did his temper."

"So, rather than working himself out of his hole, he decides to marry and move on to easy street. Let me guess, he's started to talk about taking up golf."

I sat up straight. "How on earth did you know that?"

"Because the retired couples that I've married all talk about having a new golf partner. He's thinking easy street to retirement, Jules. That's my guess."

"Perhaps the best thing for me to do is open all these gifts and then give him the tally. I'm sure it'll be much less than he's counting on."

She shook her head. "I think you need to open these now and keep quiet about whatever Aunt Edwina has planned for you. Chris is up to no good."

"You and I both know that's a fact." I sighed. Then I looked at Gertie. "Do you remember all those Christmases we had to wait until the adults were down from their bedrooms and the dishes cleared away from breakfast before we could open any presents?"

"Agony for a seven-year-old," she said.

I issued her a somewhat conniving grin. "Let's not do that tonight," I said, handing her the first present.

"Seriously?" she replied.

"Seriously."

She grinned. "All right. I can handle it."

Two hours later we were surrounded by a mountain of torn giftwrap separated out from fancy bows and ribbons. A neatly printed, long column list showed items received plus gift givers' names. The amount of money people had spent on their gifts for the supposedly happy couple was staggering. The number of engraved items we received was even more disturbing. I'd much rather have received un-engraved glasses than the boxes of glassware items delicately etched with an elegant, intertwined *J* and *C*. I didn't want to sound ungrateful; I was simply amazed at how generous people were. It was just such a lie that I was living, and engraving things for perpetuity just didn't feel right. There was no going back from an engraved set of glassware. It wasn't like a gentle scrubbing with a sudsy cloth would remove it. No, *J* and *C* were permanent, tilting sideways every time one took a drink.

Gertie picked up the list again. "So that's £150,000 in cash, three blenders, two lazy Susans, fifty additional pieces for your fine China set, a couple of ornamental vases, a £10,000 travel voucher plus a one-year lease on a new luxury convertible." She looked at me with focused eyes. "And you say Chris had no idea about any of this?"

"Not a one. All he said was to give him the list after we were done opening."

"Well, there is still one item left."

We both stared at Aunt Edwina's gift. It was likely a beautiful piece of artwork, judging from the rectangular shape of the package, which was about two by three feet in size. There was an envelope neatly affixed to the top of the package, and everything was wrapped in the most beautiful lavender and cream paper. A handmade bow, covered in small bits of glittery pink confetti, finished off the ribbon. She was always one with the greatest flair for wrapping. It was an Aunt Edwina special and deserved to be last because of its splendor, not just because she told me to.

Gertie nudged her head over in the gift's direction. "She'd want you to open it. Go ahead."

And it was like we were back at Aunt Edwina's house at Christmastime, sneaking down early in the morning hours before any adult was awake, rattling the presents to see if we could guess what was inside.

I approached Aunt Edwina's gift with some trepidation, holding out a hand while looking ever so bittersweetly at my rings. The engagement ring was worth well over £10,000, something Chris bragged about to all of his friends. They didn't know that I saw the bank loan paperwork he signed to buy it. When I spoke to Chris, he told me not to worry, that everything was taken care of. All he needed was another turn in the stock market, and we'd be right back on top again. Unfortunately, the turn never came for him, and his business had spiraled downward over the last eight months and count-ing. I was glad that we didn't own property together because Chris would likely have tried to mortgage that too.

My cousin brought me back to reality. "Her gift won't bite, you know," Gertie said.

"I know. I'm just thinking of her wrapping it. It's one of the last things she did before she passed away." I felt the salty tears slip down my cheeks. My skin felt heavy. The entire past forty-eight hours were such a whirlwind of emotions. Now that I was in a safe place with my favorite cousin, everything just started pouring out. Pretty soon we were both blubbering away, tears streaming down our swollen red faces as we cried at the loss of Aunt Edwina.

"She was so good, so kind," Gertie started. "Remember the family trees we did?"

"We already remembered those," I said in between heaving sobs. "Mine were in crayon."

"Mine too, but I used yellow crayon, so you couldn't really see them," Gertie cried, her chest expanding in and out for breath.

I looked at her and shook my head. "Gertie, how could you not know that yellow isn't a good match for white paper? You can't read it."

We stared at each other. Then we broke out laughing. It felt good to release the pain and anxiety. Pain over losing Aunt Edwina, and anxiety, at least for me, of being married to someone I didn't want. Chris didn't count right now. This was about us making the best of a rotten situation.

"Right. So then the only thing left to do is open the present." I reached for Aunt Edwina's gift and started to undo the bow and ribbon. I wondered what kind of artwork she'd given us, what type of painting she wanted to adorn my new marital home. As the wrappings fell away from the frame, Gertie and I looked upon a beautiful watercolor painting signed by an artist named 'E.E.'

"'E.E.' Do you know him?" Gertie asked.

"I do not. It could be a her, you know."

"Of course, cousin, of course," she said, putting a friendly hand on my shoulder. She peered closer. "It's an image of a pond with some foliage all around it."

I looked the painting up and down, front and back. "There's no description about where it's located. That's odd. I wonder if her note explains it a bit more."

We looked. Aunt Edwina's beautiful cursive writing was on her elegant, pale-lavender stationery. I unfolded the notepaper with the gold-embossed Greymore Hall drawing at the top. It was sophisticated and only said the name of the house plus the closest village: Oakhurst. Aristocrats didn't need any more than that on stationery because everybody knew where the big manor house was located. Aunt Edwina's had 350 acres to boot.

Aunt Edwina wrote:

Dearest Julie:

Please accept this gift on your wedding day from me. I hope this special event was everything you hoped for and more. I asked you to open this gift last because it has special meaning to me, and also it's about to send you on an interesting journey.

I ask that you read this letter with an open heart and that you forgive an old lady for her entertainments. As you know, I was a code analyst for England during the Cold War. I've always been fascinated by puzzles, riddles, clues, and mysteries. I offer you a wonderful treasure, yet you will have to work for it, seeking it using your wits.

Here's how this game works:

This letter comes with a watercolor painting, a key, and a riddle. Figure out the riddle accompanying each watercolor, and they will both guide you to where you need to go. At the end of this journey is a wonderful treasure for you to enjoy for the rest of your life.

Here is your first riddle:

> *Brandy, tobacco, lace, and velvet were brought,*
>
> *By stealth of darkest night as local conscience was fought.*

A hundred gang men called them-
selves after this purple fruit,

Wreaking havoc on dear villages 'til
resistance called out, we'll shoot!

Julie, be aware that all locations are public places.
Just ask the likeliest-looking person on site when
you arrive, and they will help you. All the places
are in Southern England, reflecting my homes near
Oakhurst, Kent and Clothberry, Devon. Remember,
assumptions are dangerous. The clues lead you to a
nearby place, but you'll need to use your wits to get to
the exact location. It could be the town you're in OR a
nearby village.

This watercolor is one in a series of four. I leave this
with you because you've been like a daughter to me.

With love and good wishes for much success and
beauty in life.
Aunt Edwina

PS: Now you understand why I wanted you to wait
two months for my funeral.

Inside the envelope was a brass key.

Gertie gave me a bit of a shocked glance. "Well, that's certainly not something one expects as a wedding gift. I was thinking artwork for a wall, then maybe a gift certificate to a furniture store. Maybe even an art supply store. But this? This is exciting."

"I wonder why she's sending us on a treasure hunt," I mused. I thought back to the wonderful woman our family and the world had now lost. She would be dearly missed. Yet somehow, she was determined to stay a part of our lives. That's how it was with families and their history; everything was entwined, and rightly so.

Chapter 7

Chris and Julie's Suite. 9:00 a.m. Next Morning.

I watched Chris as he slept, knowing he must've woken up halfway through the night to use the toilet and then made his way over to the bed. It irritated me that he snored. I never slept well with that foghorn blaring beside me. Over the years, life had proved to me that a decent night's sleep made a significant difference to one's day. I tended to stub my toe or miss my alarm if I was only granted snatches here and there of sound sleep.

I held my hand up to the light and saw the diamond glint. I looked over at him, unshaven and disheveled, and knew that what I had done wasn't worth it. Not in a thousand years.

I prodded him. "Well, Mr. Romance, are you ready to get up? You need a shower. Big-time."

"Carlene, Carlene," came out of his mouth. It was like a tumbling brook, a babbling, incoherent set of two words that I could just make out.

It was shocking. Especially a day after our wedding.

I decided to play a little bit more drunken truth game with my new husband. I ruffled his hair. "Yes, darling, it's Carlene. I can't wait to see you again."

"Mmmphh," was all he gave me back. I got up, heading for the shower, but saw a text message come in on his phone. I picked it up and read *Golf Course. Our place. 11:00 a.m.*

Interesting. My husband's friends didn't play golf, at least not well. They were more into friendly football and rugby games. *Our place?* Chris wasn't on golf courses enough to warrant a special place. *Bizarro.*

Perhaps it was just an uncle being friendly, or even my father welcoming his new son-in-law to the family. But one little tidbit of information told me that wasn't the case. The reason I knew? The text was from Carlene.

***

10:45 a.m.

Gertie and I staked Chris out on the golf course, hiding behind a tall set of pine trees. The day was lovely, with sun breaking through the clouds and yielding a wonderfully calm day for anyone who wanted to chase a little white ball around eighteen different over-herbicided micro-meadows.

"How did you get away from Chris this time?" Gertie asked.

"Pretty easy. I showered and left him in bed with room service," I said. "He's taking full advantage of Aunt Edwina's generous hospitality."

"Well done, cousin," she said. "And looks like you were right. Here comes Carlene."

I saw Chris look around to make sure no one else was near them. Carlene was a mid-height brunette with a sporty figure and a whitened, toothy smile. Long false eyelashes and a hint of blush on her cheeks completed her flirty look under a high ponytail. She was the kind who didn't play sports well but loved dressing up to look the part. I bet she wore an exotic orchid perfume.

They stepped behind a fence, expecting that no one could see them. Chris had his arm around her, and he bent down and kissed her in that boyfriend-girlfriend type of way.

I'd turned off the flash on my phone's camera so they wouldn't know I captured their special moment.

Gertie tugged at my sleeve. "I need to tell you something, Jules," she said.

For some odd reason I was literally frozen in place. I'd married out of family duty, yes, and thought I knew what I was getting into. But now? The bets were off. Seeing Chris with Carlene so few hours after we exchanged our vows really tore at my heart. It bothered me immensely that he had all the guests fooled, including my dear father.

Eventual payback—and it was coming someday—would be sweet, swift, and effective.

I looked at Gertie. "I need out of here, now."

She raised her eyebrows and nodded. "I'm with you." She laced her arm through mine and we marched out, heading to a secret place of our own.

***

Gertie's Suite, Fizzleywick Hotel.

I met my cousin back in her suite half an hour after we got into the hotel from the golf course. I'd already made a quick trip to my suite and grabbed the note Chris left me. I held it up in my hand and then passed it over to Gertie. She looked at me with a skeptical glance.

"So, this is his excuse? An apology rolled into a note?" she asked.

"Something like that. Pretty lame, hey?"

She slid the hotel stationery out of its envelope and read:

> *Julie:*
> *I'm at the golf course with buddies.*
> *See you for dinner.*
> *Love from Chris.*

"Not exactly the kind of missing-you-something-awful note that comes from someone you married yesterday, right?" I said.

Gertie put a careful hand on my forearm. "There's something I really need to tell you."

I had to hang onto a wingback armchair to steady myself. "Don't tell me that you've seen my husband with other women as well? That would be the icing on my day."

"No, nothing as dastardly as that," Gertie said with a woeful grin. "Unfortunately, it's something rather important I've been concealing from you. I can't keep it quiet any longer." She looked quite chagrined and embarrassed with herself.

I put a gentle hand over top of hers. "Gertie, you've just witnessed my brand-new husband kissing another woman. I don't think you have as much to be embarrassed about as I do."

"Well, I don't know about that. This one's pretty bad." She pulled her hand away from mine, then clasped her palms together and stared at the ceiling, as if to gain some type of heavenly inspiration. The look on her tortured face told me such help wasn't forthcoming this time.

I went and sat down on the sofa in front of the dual-wall fireplace. It was a gorgeous suite that Aunt Edwina had arranged for Gertie, and it was so nice to have a hideaway from my philandering husband. I couldn't help but let my mind race through other signs I had missed leading up to the wedding. All those nights I'd worked alone late in the art studio, when Chris claimed he was out playing rugby or at the pub with his mates.

Carlene.

I'm an even bigger chump than I first thought.

I shook myself out of the reverie and focused back on Gertie. She still looked semi-horrified at what she was about to tell me. "Come on, Gertie, it can't be all that bad, especially after seeing my day."

"Actually, considering your current circumstance, it might make you ecstatic." She looked at me, hesitant.

"Well, come on, out with it then," I said.

"Er, remember how I said I married you?" she asked.

"Yes. Just yesterday, in fact. I was there, remember?"

She continued, slowly. "Well, there was a slight problem with my qualifications."

"Oh, don't worry about that. Aunt Edwina had all that checked out with Scotford Castle's conference manager months ago. They're nondenominational. You could have an intergalactic alien wedding ceremony complete with little green beings on site if that's what the bridal party wanted. Don't sweat it."

"Er, no, that's not quite it. When I say qualifications, I mean qualified within my own religion." She peered at me as if looking through a cloudy window.

"What do you mean 'qualifications within your own religion'?"

She took a deep breath. "Well, the long and short of it is, I've been defrocked."

Chapter 8

———

I felt my mouth drop down a few inches. "When did this happen? What about our ceremony? Are Chris and I even legal?"

"Number one, I found out when I checked my email after the ceremony. Defrocked at 1:00 p.m. Your ceremony at 2:00 p.m. Number two, the ceremony was invalid. Number three, you are not legally married."

I sat there staring at her. I could see Gertie was starting to panic that I would throw something at her. Instead, I reacted the complete opposite way that a bride would normally do the day after her wedding. I got up, went over to Gertie, and gave her a big hug. "This is all just too deliciously good to be true," I said.

"So you're not even the teensiest bit worried?" Gertie asked with a tentative smile. She rearranged her exceptionally loud floral dress over her knees.

"Far from it. Would you be upset to learn that you're not really married to such a bad example of a husband?" Inside I'd been doubting my decision ever since 'I do'. I now knew there were some things in life not worth selling: dignity, common sense, and creative freedom were at the top of my list. It was time that I chose in favor of them. Surely my father would understand, especially after I told him about Carlene.

Gertie grinned. "I was hoping you'd feel that way." Then she sighed. "Dear Aunt Edwina. I've let her down. She was so in love with the idea of me marrying my cousin, er, I meant not me marrying you, what I meant was you marrying and me conducting the marriage ceremony ..." She was all flustered now.

Fluster. That's how it always was with Gertie when she let loose with a secret that really upset her. It did give us pause for thought when she decided to become a priest, because that vocation required calm and presence in the middle of strife and chaos. We just assumed there was a class she could go to and learn it. I guess we were mistaken.

"Well, Aunt Edwina always used to say that hindsight was twenty-twenty, so knowing what we know now about my husband, or rather my non-husband, Aunt Edwina is likely up there in heaven thinking things turned out the exact way they should have," I said. It was true. Aunt Edwina had a gift with these types of things. "Furthermore, she thought that Chris and I were in love, so she could likely overlook his greed for money. But him galivanting off with another woman? That is absolutely unacceptable to any member of our family."

I settled into the sofa, relaxed now. A world of possibilities was opening up in my mind, now that I knew I was rid of the ball and chain named Chris. It was deliciously exciting, a second chance at making myself whole again without Chris chained to my side. "I can just see it now. Aunt Edwina's shaking her fist at him, her lavender scarf perfectly arranged as she issues him the dreaded furrowed brow."

"Aunt Edwina would make mincemeat of Chris," Gertie said. "If only she knew."

"She does!" we said in unison.

"That's quite a bombshell piece of news, Gertie," I said.

"I guess I was holding out for the most appropriate moment."

"You have no idea how good your timing is. You just saved me from a lifetime of pain," I said.

There was a question just begging to be asked. Our eyes met again. She rolled hers.

"I suppose you want to know why I was defrocked?" Gertie asked.

"That would be the cherry on top of my day," I replied. "You've been holding out on me."

She gave a big sigh and stretched her arms out across the back of the sofa. "It's all rather embarrassing, to tell you the truth. You ever hear of a little village called Mossmarleigh in the West Midlands?"

I shook my head.

"Well, it's like this. I was in town to surprise-audit a different territory's sermons. I got in the day prior because it was too far for me to drive on Sunday morning from my last audit location. So, I found a nice pub that also rented rooms. When I went down for dinner that evening, they had a karaoke night on."

"You didn't?"

"I did. And I won the contest." She gave a sheepish smile.

"What type of contest? And was it legal?" I asked.

"Let's go with 'not illegal', yet not something one would expect a priest to be doing on Saturday night."

"What type of contest was it?"

"Crooners night." She grimaced.

"You sang up on a stage, in front of live people." It was a statement, not a question, because it was really too unbelievable. "You. The woman whose voice was purposely drowned out during the last family reunion singalong?"

"I was good," she pleaded.

"Gertie, in all the years I have known you, no one has ever complimented you on your singing voice. In fact, remember that Easter dinner when–"

"I know."

"How much alcohol was involved?"

"That's the problem. They were serving punch. I just thought it was only ginger ale and floating strawberries. Boy, was I ever wrong. Next thing I knew, I was up on stage belting out a show tune. Next morning I woke up to discover my performance had gone viral, my audit was cancelled, and I was due in London to answer why I didn't notify my superiors in a timely fashion. I was to expect further correspondence regarding my priestly status, but didn't expect them to take so long to decide."

"But it only just happened the night before. When were you supposed to have time to notify them?" I asked.

"Apparently as soon as I was let out of the village's holding cell."

"No."

"He was a rather persnickety police constable. He was horrified that I'd taken over the local pub. He found me very offensive and said that the likes of me had no place stepping foot in the church. I took offence and we had a minor scuffle."

Now was my turn to roll my eyes. "Gertie, you were a champion wrestler back at high school in America. Tell me that you didn't take on the police constable."

"He started it!"

"You got drunk on spiked punch, sang karaoke, which was videoed and uploaded to the internet, then wrestled the police constable? All this before midnight and without telling your boss?"

"That's about the sum of it."

"In your priestly robes?"

She sighed. "The very same."

"How about some nice herbal tea?" I offered.

She got a bit huffy. "I just explained the most embarrassing night of my life, and you want to make me tea?"

"I have nothing else better in mind." I paused. "Gertie, once again you have broken the mold on proper comportment in society."

She looked rather dejected. "I feel like such a failure. I can't even marry my cousin properly. Er, I mean marry you to Chris–"

I held up my hands. "You've made your point. Quit being so down on yourself. I think this is a new beginning for both of us." I gave her a reassuring smile as I handed her the tea box. The hotel provided nine delightful tea bags from which she could choose.

She looked up, hopeful. "You're not disappointed in me?"

"You just gave me the best present I've had in two decades. The only question now is what we do with Chris."

"Payback?" she asked.

"Big time." I selected apple-cinnamon tea. She took mint. I boiled the kettle and then served. We were like ladies of leisure, laying back on the sofa, conniving together how to best drag Chris through the mud after we'd exposed him for the phony philanderer he truly was.

"I've decided to live my life to its fullest, rather than cower under the cloud of a past mistake," I said.

She toasted me with her tea cup. "Well done, cousin."

I spun the rings on my left fourth finger. "I guess I won't be needing these anymore. Is there a good pawn shop in town?"

"We should ask Jacques. He'd know," Gertie said.

I'd return the wedding gifts as soon as the news of the marriage's dissolution was made public. For now, I'd ask the hotel to store them for us in one of their offices and safety deposit boxes. The cash gifts were going to the bank for safekeeping. "About Aunt Edwina's treasure hunt, Gertie," I started.

"Use it to distract you from the breakup of your marriage that really never was," Gertie offered.

"You really think it's as simple as that? I mean, I'm all for jumping in the car and giving this a go but–"

"But what?" Gertie asked, deadpan.

"It's just so, so ..." I trailed off. "You know what? You're right. We should just seize this opportunity and go. To heck with Chris. The guests are all leaving later today, so we're free."

"What are you going to tell Chris?" Gertie asked.

"That he'd better not come after me unless he wants the photo I took of him at the golf club with Carlene to be emailed to all of our wedding guests along with our thank-you notes."

"Nice," Gertie said. She giggled.

I shrugged, then I frowned. "I want to lose that man's number. As soon as I possibly can. Right now I just need some time away from him so I can figure out what to do next."

"So let's do it," Gertie said.

"My vehicle won't make it that far. And I need to raise some cash first," I said.

"Don't worry about the vehicle. That I've taken care of already," she said.

"Company car?" I asked her with a grin.

Gertie shook her head, sorrowful. "Alas, I lost that beautiful pastel-blue sedan when I lost my frock. But I replaced it with a stunning eight-person vintage van."

The gauntlet was thrown at our feet. Aunt Edwina had given us an elegant way to escape. But we had to do it on our own and prove we were worthy of her treasure first.

"You provide the vehicle, and I'll provide funding for fuel and food," I said.

"Four different towns all around Southern England. We could be gone for a while," she said. "Your art classes just finished, right?"

"I've got two months off teaching duties. And we know that you have nothing pressing in your future at the moment, so we're both free to go. Now about that local pawnshop ..."

Chapter 9

——

Jerry Elegant's Pawnshop.

Pawning one's wedding ring set the day after the ceremony wasn't a normal thing to do. In fact, it would classify as a rather unorthodox way to say a rapid goodbye to the recent past. The fact that the priest officiating had no license to marry us made the payback even sweeter.

I didn't care if Jerry's real last name was 'Elegant' or not.

I didn't care that Chris had taken out a loan to pay for these rings. To me, they were tainted, false, and something to be rid of as fast as possible. Bad karma. I wanted to move forward with my life and lose this horrific baggage in the form of two bands of platinum and diamond along with their elegant, leather hinged box.

The shop was an upscale one, not a seedy place one would expect to be filled with guns, bad taxidermy, and scratched televisions. This shop, with more high-end jewelry and silver, kept in tune with its clientele who lived in and about Carlingheath.

One got buzzed in by pressing the doorbell and after making visual contact with the proprietor. Jerry was a middle-aged bald man. Very jolly and with a firm handshake. He invited us to browse. When I told him I had my rings on offer, he gave me the standard spiel about his percentage and how quickly they may sell.

"They may go tomorrow, they may go in a month, but just realize once you give them to me, they go on my sales roster. That's how I make my money, see?" he said.

"With these, the faster you get rid of them, the better. Lots of bad memories attached to these things. Although a new person–"

"I'm not one who believes bad luck travels from marriage to marriage. I'm sure a new lady would be honored to have these rings. And because the wedding band is so simple, it would be quite easy to find a matching platinum band for her betrothed."

I sighed relief. "You have no idea how happy I am to hear you say those things."

"Bad relationship?" Jerry asked.

"You guessed right," I replied. "Lucky I got out before it was too late."

"How many years in, if you don't mind me asking," Jerry said.

"Er, yesterday. Biggest mistake of my short life."

"Well, I never. Good for you. I like seeing people take action when they know they've made a mistake. You sure it's not too late for an annulment? It worked for Henry the Eighth."

I grinned. "I like your style, Jerry."

"Yeah, Chris was a mistake, all right," Gertie said, coming over. "Jerry, do you have any amber pendants?"

Jerry took her on with dignity and aplomb. "Certainly. Over here, please." He proceeded to show her five different pieces in another display cabinet. I sat and contemplated the sorry pile of two rings in front of me. Even when Chris proposed, it was in a halfhearted way, kind of like 'hey, do you want to get married, oh, and by the way, I'm going out to play rugby tonight.'

"How is one supposed to respond to that?"

Jerry and Gertie both looked up at me. I hadn't realized I'd spoken my thoughts aloud. I shrugged and pretended to focus on something else in the display case in front of me.

Soon enough, Gertie came back clutching a beautiful amber pendant and a ring with a matching stone in it. She handed me the ring. "You need to get something more positive on your finger. Put this on."

I tried, and it fit like a dream. No resizing necessary. This one wasn't the typical yellow amber, it was more of an orangey, coffee kind of color, almost coppery. It was unique and set in a beautiful sterling-silver ring base.

"How much do I have to haggle with you, Jerry?" Gertie said. She'd always handled the negotiating process with everything since we were children. No matter whether it was getting front-row seats, a two-for-one ice cream, or an extra hour to complete an essay, Gertie was the go-to person everybody wanted on their side. All I had to do was stand back and watch her poetry come alive.

"What do you say, Jerry?" She put her elbows on the cabinet and leaned over the prizes. "You already know Julie is going to give you an excellent deal on her platinum rings. How about giving us a bit of a break on the amber so we can all walk away feeling like we've won?"

Jerry held the platinum rings up to his jeweler's magnifying glass to take a closer look. Of course the craftsmanship was exquisite; it had better be for £10,000. "Tell you what, ladies. I'll give you £6,000 for the rings and throw in the amber."

He looked at Gertie, wondering if she'd take the bait.

No dice. She sighed. "Jerry, Jerry. And here I was thinking that we'd get out of here in a reasonable hour." She refocused a hard stare on him. "£9,000 plus the amber."

He whistled through his teeth. Then he shook his head. "That leaves me no profit when I resell these." He looked at Gertie again, then over at me. I looked back at Gertie: her face hadn't changed. Nerves of steel. They didn't call her 'The Apricot Powerhouse' for nothing at boarding school.

Jerry tried again. "£7,500 for the rings, and I'll throw in the amber. Best offer."

Gertie looked at him, then looked at me. "Jerry, £7,500 for the rings, and you throw in the amber plus that leather jacket hanging up on the wall."

Now everybody was hard-staring at everyone else. It was like a showdown at some dusty corral without any guns, tall hats, or horses.

The Apricot Powerhouse brought it to an industry standard as her calm, cool hand pressed its palm against Jerry's. "Done."

We left the shop, me wearing my new amber ring in all its delicate finery. Gertie had the heavy amber pendant around her neck, against yet another one of her curtain-like floral dresses. She wore the leather jacket on top; it was likely too hot in the sunshine, but she wanted to try it out.

I gave her a sideways glance. "Thanks for your help back there. I feel much freer."

She nodded. "Don't mention it. I think we got a good deal. By the way, whose name was on the bank loan paperwork for the rings?"

"Just Chris. At least he didn't make me co-sign for a gift he was giving me."

"Smart girl." Gertie strode ahead, down Brandywine Walk and back towards the Fizzleywick Hotel. I had to hustle to keep up with her because she always strode with purpose.

"Why the leather jacket?" I asked her.

She grinned. "I've always wanted one, just didn't think it was befitting of a fully fledged priest. Imagine me standing up in church at the pulpit looking like that. People would've thought that the place was invaded by a biker gang."

"But you live in floppy dresses covered with flowers. And those sensible, T-strap walking shoes that you're so fond of? They don't quite fit in with the motorcycle set."

"Calm and logic from my cousin wins again." She gave me a sneaky glance. "You know, I read a few months ago that one's supposed to mix and match styles. You know, designer top paired with high street bottom? I happen to think that this jacket is quite fetching with this dress. Kind of like a former-preacher-on-the-edge type of vibe."

I snickered. "Just stick to the karaoke and you'll be as far over the edge as you'll ever want to be. You don't need a leather jacket."

She put an arm around me and pulled me close. We laughed all the way back to her suite.

Chapter 10

———

Our getaway vehicle was a 1963, two-tone, mint-green-and-cream, eight-person van. It was the kind that predated all the other people-movers. The van was cool to those who attended 1960s music festivals and drove it new, yet it was also cool as vintage with younger generations. But I knew better than to call Gertie's pride and joy names. She called the vehicle 'Athena' after the Greek goddess of war. It really suited Gertie's personality and the way she attacked everything in life with gusto. Including the odd karaoke machine.

We escaped at 2:00 p.m., definitely much too soon to expect Chris back from his golf outing. Jacques held Athena's door for me as I hopped in the front, ready to settle into seats that were the color of spearmint gum. "Miss, I do hope that life works out well for you." He cast a furtive glance at my bare ring finger. "You do have them safely stowed?"

"Oh yes, they're safe. Very safe, indeed." I handed Jacques an envelope that contained a fifty-pound note. "For your trouble, and for taking such good care of our family in awkward circumstances."

He issued me a small half bow. Jacques had done us a great service and I was very thankful. Aunt Edwina had taught me to always make sure that hospitality staff were well compensated for their efforts. Their help and more importantly, their silence, was earned through pleasant conversation and a decent tip. It just astounded me how many people I'd seen over the years be incredibly rude to waiters, bellmen, and housekeepers. It made absolutely no sense to me. I didn't care if somebody was a CEO or a janitor, we were all people and everybody deserved basic respect and courtesy. That's what my father had taught me, what my Boston boarding school drilled into me, and also what Aunt Edwina had demonstrated.

"All settled then?" Gertie asked from behind the wheel. She had on these incredibly large, round tortoiseshell sunglasses. Add to that Gertie's bright-red hair, gold glitter eyeshadow, leather jacket, floral dress plus her sensible shoes, and it all made for a rather madcap appearance. I had to admit this was likely the most fun adventure I was about to go on this year, perhaps in my entire life. It hands down beat sitting at home playing housewife to my philandering husband.

Wait. He wasn't actually my husband after all. *Oh joy and ultimate rapture!*

I settled back into my mint-green seat. "Let's go home," I said to Gertie.

She smiled. "Let's get on the road to freedom."

***

Julie's Home, Scotford Castle, Near Oakhurst.

I liked the converted cow barn on Bertie's estate where I lived with Chris. All the mod cons were there, including an amazing bathroom with touchless faucets and a rainfall showerhead. My kitchen had a lovely island with a soapstone top plus an eating nook in a conservatory that welcomed the morning light. There was a sink-in sofa in the media room plus a bedroom that had a super comfortable king-sized bed. Right now the place was cluttered with Chris's man things, and my closet held too many of his suits. I put together what I thought I would need for a two-week road trip and then left the rest as it was, his suits slightly jammed together to ensure creasing. I took comfortable shoes, business casual and leisure wear, a couple of nice dresses plus my toiletries bag and a raincoat. Umbrella. Sunglasses. Cash and plastic. My art diary where I wrote down inspirations for new pieces.

Chris would find my note inside its pale pink envelope when he returned to the barn. I had already left him one at the Fizzleywick Hotel, and it was pretty simple:

Husband:
Had to go out for a few things.
Julie

He didn't deserve *love* in front of my name.

The trip back downstairs had the suitcase banging against the carpet on each step.

Gertie was checking out some of my watercolor artwork hanging on the walls. "These are really good."

"I'd love to know who 'E.E.' is on Aunt Edwina's watercolor," I said.

"Did she ever mention anybody by that name?" Gertie asked.

"No, and her husband's name was Bruce, so I'm wondering if he was a secret artist that the family just didn't know about."

"Perhaps that's where you got your talent from, your father's side of the family," she said.

"Perhaps. My mother also had an amazing sketchbook with pencil and ink drawings, plus she loved to write poetry. Sounds like it's on both sides of our family." I gave Gertie an expectant look. "We're packed. Let's get out of here."

"And go where?" Gertie asked.

"To where the riddle takes us–"

Gertie play-bashed her palm against the side of her temple. "And that would mean we had the answer to the riddle. We haven't even started yet."

"Good point." I hauled out Aunt Edwina's letter and read the riddle out loud:

> *Brandy, tobacco, lace, and velvet*
> *were brought,*
>
> *By stealth of darkest night as local*
> *conscience was fought.*
>
> *A hundred gang men called them-*
> *selves after this purple fruit,*
>
> *Wreaking havoc on dear villages 'til*
> *resistance called out, we'll shoot!*

Gertie nodded. "Brandy, tobacco, lace, and velvet. Those were all smuggled goods. So we're looking for a town quite involved with scamming customs and excise men. Did you know that customs and excise authorities actually used to move their officers around the country on a frequent basis just to ensure they never had enough time to set up frauds of their own?"

"My, you're just a fountain of knowledge," I said.

87

"As those smuggled goods came in on ships from France, we're looking for a place that has a large body of water nearby."

I laughed. "Gertie, we live on an island. There's nowhere in England far from a river or the sea."

She shook her head. "Somewhere with a sheltered cove, somewhere where they could unload things at night without risking being seen too easily. Now the next clue, a hundred gang men. That means it was quite a large smuggling operation. This wasn't just a local vicar and his wife accepting two prized cases of brandy courtesy of the local ne'er-do-wells. No, this was a large, organized operation."

I had it up in a flash on my phone. I'd done a search for 'smuggling in England' with promising results. "Here's the answer. It's Plumsden in Kent. About twenty-five minutes away from Oakhurst. The purple fruit is obvious. A plum. Kent's High Weald is famous for them. And there were up to a hundred men in their crew, depending upon the job. Pistols, brandy, tobacco, lace, and velvet. They even carried blunderbusses!"

By now Gertie was looking over my shoulder, nodding as I spoke. "I believe you found the destination, my dear. But I think it's pretty odd. Aunt Edwina liked intricate riddles and clues. Why would she make up something that was so easy for us to figure out?"

"Perhaps she's starting us off gently. Because I agree with you, this is way too primary school for her," I said. "Also, her letter mentioned that the clues will guide us, then we have to use our wits to find the exact location."

Gertie was at a loss.

"Is the Spearmint Wonder ready to depart?" I teased. I felt like I was about to leave earth, heading for a spectacular lunar landing.

"Does it rain in England? Of course Athena is ready for you. She's very much looking forward to our trip; she told me so herself," Gertie said.

"Please tell me that doesn't mean her engine is making weird sounds."

"Hold your tongue. I just had her serviced two weeks ago. She's in tip-top shape." Gertie patted the door with a caring hand.

"So I'm putting my life in the hands of the 1963 mint-green van?" I grinned at Gertie.

"And the man above. Never forget him." She took my hands in hers and gave me a reassuring smile. "I can't see any more bad things happening to you in the next little while. You've been through so much. Now you deserve some good in your life."

"I certainly hope so. I never really wanted the life I took on at my wedding."

"Consider it a practice run for when you really do meet that special someone."

"What was the best wedding you ever officiated?" I asked.

"The best one?" Gertie thought on it for a second. "Likely Pat and Rob's. Both in their fifties, both had really figured out what they wanted in life. All their friends and kids were there and it was a second marriage for both. One spouse had died in a car accident, the other was lost to kidney disease."

"And why was it the best?"

"Because it was about honesty. And love. That's the best mixture for a copiloted life together."

We settled down against Athena's front seats, all my luggage safely stowed in the back with Gertie's. I had to laugh at the three suitcases she was carrying on board. That many suitcases made for an awful lot of floral dresses and sensible T-strap shoes.

I was glad to see the barn fall away behind us as we headed out to the road leading to Plumsden. It was only afternoon, and I would quickly book our bed-and-breakfast en route. Somewhere. Anywhere. Far away from my false husband.

***

I fed Gertie some takeaway pizza we grabbed at the restaurant next to the petrol station on the way out of town. "Aunt Edwina forgive me," I said, looking up. "She hated these fast-food places taking over any quaint English village."

"Do you blame her?" Gertie said. "It's like they're bulldozing our heritage."

She took a swig of her lemonade. It was probably filled with too much sugar, but we needed high energy to get on the road and leave all of this nonsense of the past forty-eight hours behind us.

About ten miles out of town, Gertie pulled over to trundle down a side road. "I hope you don't mind, but I've got a small bit of business to do here."

We were in a churchyard. There were over fifteen cars in the parking lot. I gave her a sideways glance. "You're not thinking of doing a crash sermon, are you?" I asked.

"No, you need not worry. I've made a personal pact to drop a two-pound coin into every church donation box that I pass on my travels. Kind of like karaoke penance."

"You want to spend the rest of your life paying for your one night mistake?" I asked.

"It makes me feel better," she said. "Only ten thousand or so more to go."

"That's a lot. Luckily, I just sold my wedding rings." I hauled out the wad of cash from my purse and held it up in the air.

"Already taken care of," she replied. "Look inside the glovebox."

I opened it up and saw rolls and rolls of two-pound coins. "Gertie, let me guess, one of the suitcases is filled with these as well?"

"Yes, the heavy one. I thought if I did penance the church might consider taking me back. Because I really miss having a congregation. Although I don't think I could start preaching again in the same church. Not after what the youth choir did. They did their own imitation video of me in full crooner mode. It also went viral."

I leaned back in my seat and sighed. "Go and make your donation. I'll stay here and watch the suitcases."

"Back in a flash," she said. She closed the door carefully, respectful of Athena's elderly joints. I watched her stride up the pebbly path with purpose, her two-pound coin firmly clutched in her fingers. She was a good cousin, full of hijinks and glad tidings that I never expected. And she was exactly what I needed during my time of misfortune.

I supposed the older generations looked at my wedding as all for the greater good, preserving the family name and all that jazz. Chris did have a good family name; he was just dead broke. I wasn't willing to settle for his name alone. I wanted more. Heck, it wasn't like there was a world war on, creating a shortage of men in the area. Was it too much to ask for someone I could truly love and trust?

I was shaken out of my self-analysis with the sight of Gertie leaving the church in a hurry. She hiked up the hem of her floral dress and hustled over towards the van at a pretty good clip. There was no one after her, but her face looked rather panic stricken.

I leaned over to grab the door handle and let her in. She jumped in the right front seat, buckled up her seatbelt, and backed out of the parking stall, spraying pebbles as she went. I knew not to say a word until we were clear of whatever she was outrunning. It was our expected form of communication, developed when we were both young girls role-playing an adventure mystery we'd just seen on the television. I put both hands on the dashboard to brace myself as she took the first corner with alarming alacrity.

"Sorry," she muttered. "Had to leave pronto."

"Alright, Miss Songbird, care to share what happened back there in the church?" I asked.

"We shall not discuss it." She shook her head. "Surely some notorious celebrity has done something more noteworthy since then to kick me off the cyber map."

"That bad, hey?"

She gave in. "Fine. All I did was put two pounds in the donation box. As soon as they heard the coin drop, two choir boys in there practicing recognized me and started pointing fingers. I beat a hasty retreat before I was asked to leave." She checked her appearance in the rearview mirror. "I used gold glitter eyeshadow. I should have used the lurid blue. That's why they recognized me."

"I was going to ask you about that. You've really changed your look since I last saw you."

"I have to change it some more. I don't want to be recognized."

"One day you'll have to play the video for me," I said.

"It's on the internet. Sixteen million views and counting. Bon appetit."

"I haven't looked, out of respect for our close familial relationship," I said.

"At least there's one person in this world I can trust," Gertie said.

"I don't get pleasure out of somebody else's pain," I said.

"Then you are one of the few in a cast of thousands." As soon as we were on a safe stretch of road, she turned to look at me. "Thank you."

"Look on the positive side. At least you got your donation done."

"Yes. Three down, nine thousand, nine hundred and ninety-seven-plus to go."

Gertie started fiddling with the radio. She settled on a country station playing a twangy classic song where a woman lamented another stealing her man. Not exactly the kind of music I thought a priest would've chosen, but at least it passed the time. Pretty soon, both of us were belting out the sappy chorus, grins on our faces.

The song ended. Gertie changed the station to a symphony. "So why do you think that woman wanted to take her man?"

"Maybe because she lured him in with falsehoods?" I said.

"Okay, that's the woman scorned response. What are some other reasons?"

"Because she liked him? Because he asked her? Because he was comfortable?"

"You make him sound like a bedroom set," Gertie said.

"I do not! But in my case, I'd be better off if it were true."

"Was Chris a pine dresser?" Gertie teased.

"More like a footstool. Better yet, a toadstool." I grinned, starting to feel like my old self again.

"And that's what a lot of this life is about, isn't it? Multiple answers to the same question. As I grow older, I learn that's more and more the case," she said.

Gertie drew up on the shoulder and rolled down her window. "See that over there?" She pointed at a busy shopping center. "My mum once worked at the bus depot that used to be there. Spent years driving in and out of that place. Now it's a supermarket."

"She was a bus driver? Good for her."

Female bus drivers always had my attention and respect. The job, filled with wads of used chewing gum in the most unlikely of places, wasn't for Nervous Nellies. It wasn't easy driving snoring winos, shrieking schoolchildren as well as seniors who needed the front seats but somehow always had to ask for them. Bus drivers held their own little fiefdoms inside the hulking metal boxes they lumbered down roads on a prescribed schedule. I could never be a bus driver: too many moving parts and projectiles. I liked a bit more order in my life.

Gertie leaned forward over the steering wheel. "She used to tell me, 'Gertrude, I drove Mr. Basil Yardley to see his wife today.' She lived in a care home, you see."

"That's sweet."

"She drove him every day like clockwork. Out on the 9:13 a.m. and home on the 2:49 p.m."

"He went every day?"

Gertie nodded. "My mum told me that he was one of the RAF gunners shot down during the war. His face was totally disfigured, but it made no matter to his wife. She nursed him back to good health, stood by him, and deflected the awkward stares from people walking by."

"What happened to her?"

"She got dementia. And so Mr. Yardley, his facial injuries then well-repaired with plastic surgery, told my mum it was the least he could do to repay her kindness."

"That's quite a testament to their love."

"It's always stayed with me. It's one of the reasons I became a priest, actually."

Silence pervaded. Then Gertie harrumphed. "Their story was written up by a local historian, thank goodness. Saved for posterity."

"And your mum's memories?"

Gertie shook her head. "She left me a few diaries. I'm slowly plowing through them. One day, I'd like to write a book about my mother to preserve her legacy."

Chapter 11

We drove through Plumsden high street and then further south. Heading out into the country, we came upon a huge field of wildflowers fronting the road. It was part of a grand estate, and the brass name plaque on the stone pillars out front read 'Holgarth Hall, Plumsden'.

"Appropriate name for this place," I said, taking out my phone to check we were in the right location.

The tall gates were open, so we drove straight through. It was a truly lovely property, the front drive lined with laurel hedges trimmed to perfection. The drive was paved with dark asphalt, and one could sense that even if the hint of a crack showed, it would be repaired posthaste.

As we neared the manor house, the tall hedges gave way to twelve mature topiaries, all done in floral designs. How they managed to get simple green hedges to grow in the shapes of daisies, sunflowers, and orchids was beyond me. It truly was an amazing sight. Each topiary was ringed by a low box hedge, with hostas and delicate pink saxifrages surrounding the showpiece in the center. On the other side of the drive was a paddock with brown rail fencing that enclosed a beautiful herd of llamas.

"This is a modern estate, Gertie. I would've expected a showcase stallion racehorse in the paddock. Instead we have doe-eyed wool-bearers." I peered over at the five brown-and-white llamas, grazing as if our intrusion meant nothing to them. They chewed sideways and were clearly enjoying the lush grass.

Gertie slowed Athena down to a crawl. This estate was clearly someone's pride and joy, and we certainly did not want to get into trouble by driving too fast and damaging something.

"And you found this place on your phone? A bed-and-break-fast?" she asked. "Score one for Jules!"

"Power of the internet. I think we're supposed to sign in at the main house and the bed-and-breakfast accommodation is around the back."

She drew up in between an expensive black sedan and a cherry-red two-seater convertible. "I don't think Athena can blend in with this lot," she said.

"We don't need all types, we just have all types," I replied as we both exited the vehicle.

Just off to the side we could see a massive greenhouse filled with an explosion of color. This was the nursery touted online as one of the best in England. The earl who ran this place was chairman of the Plumsden Horticultural Society, and rightly so. He appeared to have ten green thumbs and counting. Perhaps he aimed for a showcasing on a popular televised garden show.

"What a lovely place," Gertie explained. "I wonder if it has its own church?"

"Ladies, greetings to you both!" A rotund man dressed in impeccable tweed suddenly appeared in front of us, seemingly coming out of nowhere. A tiny mustache grazed his upper lip, and it matched the shock of dark-brown hair that kept falling over his left eyebrow. His posh accent said fancy school, very upper crust. If he wasn't the earl himself, I would eat my fringed purse.

I extended my right hand. "We're Julie and Gertie. We made a booking for your bed-and-breakfast?"

"Algernon Holgarth. But everyone calls me Algy." He shook our hands. Next he rubbed his hands together with glee. "You are visitors number eight and nine since we opened last week. This manor house costs a packet to run, so we converted every-thing we possibly could into a commercial enterprise." He smiled. "It prevents us from having to sell off the Rembrandts."

"Mmmm, we have the very same problem in our house," Gertie teased.

I jabbed her in the ribs.

"Algy–"

"Yes, just like the pond scum," we heard a teasing voice add from our right. We turned to see the younger version of Algy spring up the path. There would be more purse eating by yours truly if these two weren't brothers.

"Lance Holgarth at your service, ladies," the younger man said. He looked about ten years younger than his older brother.

"His full name is Lancelot, an odd name to bestow upon my little brother," Algy said. "Knights are supposed to be reliable."

"Algy, please don't start. I've already finished building your rabbit hutch and am now starting on your sunflower garden."

The older brother frowned, as if he was dismayed that his brother had not yet built a spaceship to the moon in a single day.

It was odd because Lance really looked capable of so much more.

Algy wasn't done yet. "If I told you once, I told you a thousand times, a million times, our guests must come first." He slapped his palm on the top of a stone half-wall with each word spoken, adding emphasis to his diatribe.

Gertie sensed the friction. "Well, we've only just arrived, and our bags are still in Athena, I mean, our vehicle, so we'll be just fine starting off now."

Her small slip appeared to catch both brothers off guard.

Algy was the braver of the two. "You've named your vehicle Athena?"

"Yes, it gives her the courage to dash up and down all these narrow country lanes. Plus, we're on a mission to find meaning in a mysterious vintage watercolor painting left to my cousin, so who better to do it than the fearless goddess of war!"

Lance grinned ear to ear. Clearly he knew that he was on territory that his brother, the practical one, was finding a bit odd. "A mysterious ancient painting? That's right up Algy's alley. He sits inside all day surrounded by dead ancestors hanging in gilt frames." He gave a huge smile to his brother.

Gertie and I both sensed that had we not been there in front of the pair, there would've been a full-on verbal row at this very moment.

Algy ignored his brother's comment. He whipped out tiny reading glasses and held up his mobile phone. "I see you are here for three nights. If you'd like to bring the painting up to the main house later on today, I'd be glad to take a look at it for you."

"Indeed. That would be very kind. We're wondering if it's by a local artist. You see, my Aunt Edwina left it to me. Perhaps she would've supported a local painter ..."

It was like a thunderclap had gone off in Algy's head. He stood up straighter and gained an inch in height. "Good grief! You're *not* Edwina Greymore's niece?"

I nodded.

"Blast! I was away in France so I couldn't make the wedding, and then heard Edwina had passed so sent flowers to the house, but why the devil aren't you on your honeymoon?" His words tumbled out in a torrent of perfect elocution.

It was a valid question. And I supposed I should be prepared to answer that frequently. So I did, using the words that came to mind. "The honeymoon was cancelled, and we're on a quest for Aunt Edwina instead. You know how she was: when Aunt Edwina got a bee in her bonnet, it had to be done immediately."

Algy nodded. "That was Edwina. Was there no service?"

"In two months. At Aunt Edwina's request," I confirmed.

Algy took a deep breath. "She was a marvelous lady. Old-school, yet the glamorous lady of the house who held the community together. She will be sorely missed." We sensed that with Aunt Edwina's passing, Algy felt that a part of his familiar world had been stripped away too. As he stood there in his bespoke tweed sporting jacket and trousers, he looked a bit like a relic from the past.

There was a slightly uncomfortable silence, and now Lance was starting to act rather nervous, continually looking over towards the vegetable garden. In fact, he looked quite pained.

"We should get unpacked. Could you show us to our room, please?" Gertie asked.

"Lance?" Algy instructed. His brother shook out of his reverie and jumped to attention. "And your luggage, ladies? Is it in the boot?"

It was clear that Lance was the dancing gopher and his brother was the one tossing out circus directions.

We headed over to Athena, where Lance ably got our luggage put onto a brass-railed trolley cart, shiny and new, just like the one Jacques had at the Fizzleywick Hotel. It was quite clear that Algy had gone all out to ensure Holgarth Hall's guests' comfort. They'd even gone so far as to pave the narrow path around the manor house directly out to the converted stables a few hundred yards away.

"It's a lovely estate," I said to Lance as he put his back into it to get us up the small rise before the converted horse stables. It wasn't a steep incline, but Gertie's suitcase full of coins made all the difference, for the worse. Lance looked like he was scaling Mount Everest.

"Been in the family since the sixteenth-century. My brother is very proud of the fact that we supported the crown during the Civil War. The first earl was rewarded appropriately with Holgarth Hall."

"Are you in partnership with your brother?" Gertie asked.

"Partnership?" Lance snorted. "Try servitude. As the elder one, he inherited everything. I was supposed to go to London and make my fortune, but unfortunately my spicy chili-banana samosa kiosk franchise went the wrong way, so I'm stuck here being his gopher."

"Oh dear," Gertie said.

"Well, you live in paradise, so it can't be all that bad," I said.

"Oh, it's fine until Algy goes off on one of his rants. Blaming me for anything that goes wrong. His latest venture is a petting zoo for the children to enjoy while their parents shop in the nursery. Have you ever tried to keep seven boisterous five-year-olds out of mischief around a herd of inquisitive goats, llamas, and rabbits?"

We both shook our heads.

"Believe me, it's not for the faint of heart." He rolled us up to our room and unlocked the door. It swung open to reveal a pleasant two twin-bed arrangement, with fully modernized bath, tea station, and wardrobe. I daresay the wardrobe was an antique, all gleaming and shining from its weekly polishing ritual. The bathroom was all glass and brushed nickel, and the towel warmer was wonderful. The tea station had a multitude of cups and mugs, a tea caddy, sugar, spoons, and even fresh packets of biscuits. Everything was branded *Holgarth Hall*, Algy's smiling face on every sticker, visitor guide brochure, and embroidered throw. It was a bit creepy, especially on the shiny biscuit packets that made Algy look like he'd just rolled his forehead in a thin layer of olive oil.

"You see what I mean?" Lance said with despair. "It's paradise but my brother is everywhere!"

One couldn't help but feel sorry for the little brother, the one who'd been cast out into the world without the comfort, security, and riches of the family estate. I suppose one would say that it was kind of the eldest boy to take care of the younger after a failure in London, but the hierarchy was still maintained and painfully obvious. It was indeed quite the comical farce.

Lance continued his running patter about how things in the room worked. "Please run the fan after you've had a shower, otherwise in this climate we tend to get mold issues. If you want your towels changed, please leave them in the bathtub; hang them if you wish to reuse them another day. If you are out of tea-making supplies, then just ring up to the main house and I'll bring them to you. I do keep a small container of milk in the fridge here for you, but if you need more just let me know. There are extra pillows and blankets in the dresser beside the wardrobe. Breakfast tomorrow is what time, ladies?"

I looked at Gertie. "Around seven-thirty?"

She nodded.

"Does that work for you, Lance?" I asked.

He took another pained look outside towards the vegetable garden. It was quite an expansive one filled with lettuce and cabbage. I could see carrots and beet tops poking over the raised rows of earth, and I also thought I saw squash and potatoes.

"Lance? Around seven-thirty tomorrow morning for break-fast?" I asked. "Is that suitable?"

He heard me this time. Refocused. "That's fine, just fine. Feel free to walk the grounds. If you visit the main house, come to the front door and see Parsons, else you risk catching Algy dictating one of his excessively boring Battle of Waterloo books into his computer."

"Oh, is Algy a writer?" Gertie asked.

Lance grimaced. "A very bad one. He thinks a big publisher is going to take him on, pay him a huge advance, and then make him ultra-famous. I keep telling him to stick to the nursery and the llamas."

It was just too funny. We all broke out laughing. It was quite clear that Lance was an alright guy, just in a terrible position. It was hard for someone so young and eager to be so downtrodden. Heck, I'd heard that sentiment before, talking to myself at the wedding ceremony.

"Well, I shall take my cart and leave you to it," he said.

"Great, thank you for your help," I said. I waited until Lance left, and then looked over at Gertie. "He looks nervous, don't you think?"

"I think I know why. Didn't he say there was a new petting zoo on site?" We looked out the front window, and she gestured towards the vegetable garden. We were just in time to see Lance dive headfirst into the dirt, a white-and-black spotted rabbit leaping out in front of him, just out of his grasp. But Lance wasn't giving in. He got up, brushed himself off, and scrambled after the rabbit again. This time he used stealth.

He stood up from the vegetable patch the next time, the escaped rabbit firmly gripped under his arm, moist soil clinging to him, covering the front of his neck right down to his upper thighs.

"I'll wager that Algy has no idea what his brother gets up to when he's not watching," Gertie said.

"Probably just as well. I'd wager that Lance is the one saddled with making Algy's harebrained schemes work while his brother sits in his study writing his books."

"Still, his new bed-and-breakfast, what a simply brilliant idea," she replied.

I picked up the kettle, preparing to make tea. "So many of these fancy, big estates are cash starved. They need to commercialize to keep afloat. I read about one that just spent over half a million on roof repairs alone."

Gertie whistled through her teeth. "Half a million? Thank goodness Aunt Edwina always had plenty of money. Can you imagine her opening a petting zoo at Greymore Hall?"

"No. It wouldn't fit with her social committees and high teas."

We watched Lance take the rabbit back over to the petting zoo and firmly lock it inside. He examined the sturdy lock and shook his head.

"I wonder if somebody left it open by accident?" I said.

"My money's on Algy," Gertie said.

The quiet was pierced by a huge flash of long, flapping blond-caramel hair that whipped past the window.

"What the heck was that?' Gertie asked.

"This is better than going to the movies," I said. "It looked like a hairy deer."

We left our room and went outside to see what else was going on in the animal kingdom. The hairy deer was hotly pursued by a man in flapping tweed—Algy—who looked alarmingly uncoordinated as he dashed after it.

"Gilligan! Gilligan! Come here at once!" he yelped.

Algy suddenly realized he had an audience. He circled back at a slow jog, a defeated smile on his face. "My late wife's Afghan hound, Gilligan. Beautiful dog, but aloof and independent to a fault."

Gertie looked over at the dog's trajectory. "Er, perhaps check out what he's up to ..." she started.

Algy and I both looked over towards the vegetable patch and petting zoo. Gilligan the Afghan had leapt the fence and was now herding the goats. This wasn't good. The goats looked terrified and bleated their discomfort.

Algy's face went beetroot red as he picked up the chase again. "Gilligan! Gilligan! You stop that right this instant!"

"I'm surprised that dog could jump over a fence that high. It must be at least four feet tall," Gertie said.

The younger brother got his payback, and we sensed it wasn't the first time. He pretended to be weeding the vegetable garden, nonchalant, as his brother hopped around like a leprechaun trying to recapture the escaped hound. We watched Algy cry at his brother for help, and Lance dutifully rose and left the beets in order to call the dog over to the fence. For some reason, he had an uncanny knack with the Afghan. As soon as Lance called the dog's name, the racing frenzy stopped and Gilligan came over for a head scratch. This distracted the dog long enough for Algy to clip the lead to his collar and march him smartly out of the pen.

There was no money exchanged, and Lance wasn't granted any type of promotion. However, a little smile emerged on his face as he watched his sweaty, red-faced brother walk away with the now-tired dog. Somehow we both knew that they were even, at least for today.

Chapter 12

Later that day we found ourselves under an ornate brass lantern. It cast a warm glow down onto the sturdy beige stone arches that framed where we stood. We were in the covered hallway leading to the main door. When we'd arrived, we never made it past the front steps because that's where we were greeted by our hosts. This time, however, we had Aunt Edwina's watercolor securely in hand, both of us eager to see if Algy could help us identify the painter.

I rang the front bell, and we were greeted by Zenith Parsons, the estate's tall, lanky butler who announced himself as 'Parsons'. He had smooth English skin with rosy cheeks. The butler looked able to instantly discern if one was amusing or offensive, so Gertie and I rolled out our best boarding school behavior.

We saw Gilligan in the massive library first. The Afghan hound was on a lead and tied to an eighteenth-century desk leg. The desk was sturdy, heavy oak, and there was no way the dog would escape this time. The dog laid his head over his front paws and looked quite sorrowful at being jailed. Afghans were regal, noble animals. To me, they always looked like they needed to wear a crown. This one was obviously very well cared for due to his immensely long and mat-free blond-caramel-colored coat.

"Earl Holgarth will join you momentarily," Parsons announced and then left.

The library was a wonderful place, half a football field long. The entire room was ringed with carved cherry bookshelves that held gilded tomes of every height and width imaginable. Two brown leather, dimpled-button sofas had pride of place in the middle of the room facing each other. Wingback chairs in a complementary Holgarth crest upholstery ringed the larger pieces of furniture. Ancestral portraits hung high above the shelves, and many smaller pieces of furniture including side tables, tropical plant pots, and lamps of various sizes were placed at tasteful intervals about the room. The ornate plaster ceiling contained six matching chandeliers, all with tiny stems that glinted under miniature individual lampshades to send warm light below onto visitors. The hardwood floor was covered in an elegant oriental rug in shades of blue and grey. It was a well-loved home, one with unflagging nobility and attitude that kept it going through the centuries. It was as if the current owner couldn't help but heed the ancestors high up in their gilded frames looking down on him, as if he was constantly on display, being gauged for their approval.

"Perhaps it's not so easy being the eldest son," I whispered to Gertie.

"Not in the least. Can you imagine being responsible for all of this, keeping it all going for the next generation?" Gertie said.

"There you are, ladies!" Algy's booming, positive voice descended upon us as he came into the room. We'd gotten to the point of believing he was rather forgetful, because he was wearing not one but two pairs of small reading glasses on his head. "And is that the painting in question?"

I nodded. "I take it Gilligan knows he's not been a good boy, hey?"

Algy nodded. "Afghans have an immense amount of energy. My late wife was quite the enthusiast, but I just don't have the time to spend with him like she did. We also have a twelve-week-old puppy in the kennel, just weaned, and I'm hoping he will be a good companion for Gilligan. Lance is in charge of the puppy's well-being and training."

"I assume you'll let the dogs be together once the puppy's housetrained?" Gertie asked.

"Of course," Algy said. "I just have to be very careful with the carpets in here. Some of them are centuries-old, utterly irreplaceable. Priceless. Absolutely priceless."

"Is the puppy the same color as Gilligan?" I asked. I'd always had a soft spot for dogs. Especially beautiful ones.

"He's what they call a blue Afghan. Almost like a darker bit of Danish blue cheese." Algy shrugged. "I'm not into all the details, but can appreciate a good pedigree. Gilligan over there is from a top bloodline and took Best in Show at several local and regional events when my wife was alive."

We refocused on the watercolor.

"Let's put it down here on the desk," our host offered, sweeping off this morning's newspapers into a recycling bin. I gently put down the watercolor so he could examine it. Algy started patting himself down. "Now if I could just find my glasses, I'd like a closer look ..."

"Ahem," Gertie said, tapping the top of her head.

He reached to his temples. "Good grief! Not one, but two pairs! I think I should lose my head if it wasn't screwed on correctly!" he said. "Rather embarrassing, wouldn't you say? I'm not exactly in my dotage yet." He took off both glasses, put on one pair and then peered closely at the painting. "Interesting, very interesting. I've seen this before."

I leaned forward, intrigued. "You mean you know who 'E.E.' is?"

Algy shook his head. "No, but I can tell you the location of the scene. It's the old pond in Plumsden, just down the road from here. You probably drove right by it and didn't notice because there are some very mature trees around it now. I've got a landscape very similar to this one. Follow me and I'll show you," he said.

We all trooped out of the library. Gilligan gave us a sorry glare as we walked past him and didn't bring him along. We entered into a long art hallway, and this was where we saw that Algy kept an extensive collection of landscape watercolor paintings. He whipped the glasses off his head and gestured with them at each painting as he talked. "And this, this is art. The elixir of life, something to strive for in all that us humble humans do. This is why we commercialized Holgarth's. To save beautiful antiquities such as these."

We peered closer. The watercolors were all by one artist, a 'G.Z. Norton,' in the 1860s. And what a collection it was. There were fifteen of them in total, and apparently that caused our host a bit of angst.

"I have fifteen of them, but the sixteenth has gone missing. There was a rumor that a predecessor Earl of Holgarth sold it, but it's never shown up in any auction catalogue. I fear that it's lost in some private collector's hands, destined never to see the light of day again."

"Do you know what the subject was for the sixteenth painting?" I asked.

"I only ever found a reference to it in an old family guestbook for this house. It said something about 'boy and girl sitting on a stone bridge'. I never saw or knew anything else about it. And it hurts me to know that it's out there somewhere, languishing all by its lonesome."

There was a tick tack of tiny paws on the cool tile floor. Lance came into sight with the twelve-week-old Afghan puppy on its lead. It wasn't really clear who was walking whom. When they reached us, the puppy was all tongue and paws, leaping up onto us to say hello. This one was a stark contrast to Gilligan, the young one being completely shorthaired and with stubby legs. The curl of the tail had started but it was only just the beginning. As Algy had explained earlier, the puppy showed the blue-grey coloring quite regularly through its coat.

"What a darling little dog," Gertie said, bending down to pat it. She got a face full of kisses from the puppy. "What's his name?"

"Northern Thunder of the Gables." Lance tried to hold in his laughter.

We didn't.

Algy looked mystified at what we all found so hilarious.

Lance continued in a serious tone. "His house name is Norris. This is the only place we allow him, er, the only place my brother allows him, for now," Lance explained. "He's still got his tiddling schedule to figure out."

"I'm afraid I can't help you much more than that with your painting," Algy said. "It's a very familiar scene of this locale, but

I do not recognize the painter's 'E.E.' initials. What you should do is go down to the local Family History Society right here in Plumsden. Ask for Maude Livingstone, and mind, it's only open on Wednesdays."

"Shall do, and thank you for trying to help," I said.

"Not at all, not at all," Algy said.

"I'll be taking Norris out for his daily training now, Algy," Lance said.

"Good. And don't forget to water the vegetable garden afterwards." Algy gave his brother a serious glance as if to say, 'I dare you to defy me and my generosity allowing you to mooch off me, living on my estate.'

"Of course, dear brother," Lance replied. It was obvious he was trying to butter up Algy for something, we just weren't quite sure what it was yet. With the two brothers so contrasting each other, we simply wanted to hang around to see what type of family catastrophe would occur next.

Lance disappeared down the hallway heading to the tiled cloakroom at the end of the hall, which in turn led outside. Algy looked at us and issued a half smile. "He's up to something again, don't you think?"

We played dumb. This brotherly rivalry wasn't something to get involved in ... because we were guests. Guests were to merely observe and stay out of the way at a bed-and-breakfast. Owners didn't want strangers continually underfoot. It was a curious paradox: opening up one's home yet being concerned that the daily routine would get upset. I decided to stick to painting.

"Do you know my brother actually tried to get me to invest in an on-site distillery? He sold it to me as a moneymaker, but I knew he'd be drinking all the profits every week," Algy said.

Something came to mind as we walked back to the library. I looked over to the side of the massive room and saw a huge liquor cabinet covered in paned glass that was resplendent with a tiny diamond pattern. Behind the glass one could see a collection of about twenty different opened whiskey bottles.

"So you turned Lance down, then?" I asked.

"Family-friendly is the way to go," he said. "So when I came up with the brilliant idea of the petting zoo, that's what I put him in charge of managing. That will be his legacy to this estate."

It seemed quite pathetic, with all of the ancestors in the room, that the younger brother was relegated to keeper of the estate's menagerie. It wasn't exactly a station to aspire to in life, but I sensed that Lance would've been happy with his lot were it not for Algy's constant badgering.

"Plumsden Jubilee Gardens are quite close to here, aren't they? Does your nursery supply them?" Gertie asked.

Algy looked proud enough to burst. "Yes, we do. It's only ten minutes away. It's one of the pre-eminent gardens in Kent, and we donate many plants as a corporate benevolence. These grand estates have to band together and survive, you know. We're on the tourist map with them, and we need both properties looking as perfect as possible." He emphasized his P's as he spoke.

"The garden rooms were revolutionary for their time. And the rose collection is simply stunning," I said. "Aunt Edwina used to take Gertie and I to those wonderful gardens as children."

"It is simply heaven on earth," Algy said.

Chapter 13

——

The next morning we had a full English breakfast in a delightful sunny dining room up at the main house. Two other tables were occupied by vacationing couples, one from France and the other from Germany. We made our polite nods to each other as we walked into the room and then quietly settled in to a hearty breakfast. Everything was there, and all was wonderfully farm fresh. Eggs, bacon, sausage, fried tomatoes, mushrooms, an assortment of rolls and breads, umpteen types of homemade jams, yogurt, cold cereal, and assorted coffee, tea, and hot chocolate. We were well set for a good morning's work. We went back to our room and packed a day bag each. We'd only been at it for ten minutes when we heard a frantic rap on the door.

Gertie looked around the curtains and saw Lance standing there, looking rather panicked. She opened the door with a bright smile. "Good morning to you. It's a fine day. We're going out to the town center and ..." She halted mid-sentence. "What the devil is the matter?"

Lance looked like he'd swallowed a too-large piece of Stilton cheese. "It's the rabbits. All five of them. They've escaped!" He spoke with a strangled voice, as if it was some massive conspiracy to dumbfound him.

"Rabbits? Have you tried lettuce? Carrots?" I asked, coming around the corner of the door frame. "I used to have one as a child. Vegetables always worked to bribe Harvey."

Lance's shoulders sagged. "It's not just the rabbits; there's only the nasty one left on the lam. It's my brother's vegetable garden, his prized vegetable garden. And I was doing so well with Norris and my bed-and-breakfast guest attendant duties–"

Gertie picked up her floral dress and hiked it out into the yard. "Right then," she said, giving him a mock salute. "Where is the soldier who's gone AWOL?"

Lance bit his lip, looking a bit unsure. "I really don't think that's your problem, although it is most kind of you to offer. This one's the ringleader, you know, getting all the others up to no good." Lance held out his phone and showed us a picture of a brown-and-white Dutch rabbit.

Gertie and I both shook our heads. No, we had not seen a brown-and-white Dutch rabbit cross our threshold in the last twelve hours.

"He's cute enough, but obviously it's a clandestine furry disguise," I said.

"Algy is going to absolutely kill me," Lance moaned.

Gertie put a gentle hand on his shoulder. "Come, come now. It can't be all that bad."

Lance asked us to follow him, and we were soon upon the large vegetable garden. "It's worse, I'm afraid. My brother's won the horticultural fair's best lettuce prize two years in a row. But last year he lost out. This was supposed to be his comeback year. Oh, what a terrible mess!"

There were two rows of what once were prized lettuces. Now they'd been nibbled down to mere cores, little white stems standing up in the sunshine, mocking whoever grew them, saying, 'thank you for growing us, but now we've departed.'

"So you're left with stubs?" Gertie said.

Lance nodded, sorrowful. "Just like the painter. What am I going to do? Wait! There he is!" A brown-and-white bullet darted in between the rows and Lance was after him like a shot. He cornered him up against the beets and faked left when the rabbit went right. It was all over. Lance held him up, triumphant, cradled in the crook of his arm. The man had a smear of steer manure on his left cheek and nose.

We followed Lance back to the petting zoo and saw that all the animals were now securely inside, under lock and key.

"What will you tell your brother?" I asked. "A rather massive attack of the slugs?"

Lance shrugged. "As long as it can't be traced back to me–"

"Good morning, all. Enjoying the lovely Kent sunshine?" we heard behind us in a familiar voice. Algy was upon us, out for his morning walk with Gilligan securely on a heavy leather lead. It was the perfect scene, a regal-looking dog with perfectly groomed hair, attached to his master, a gentleman in tweed. No doubt they would enjoy tea at elevenses and perhaps a fire later on in the day if the evening grew chilly and damp.

Lance frantically wiped his face on his shirt sleeve then turned to greet his brother.

"It's a lovely day," Gertie said. "We were just admiring your petting zoo. What a brilliant idea for the visitors' children."

Algy puffed up with pride. One might think he would burst his tweed jacket. "All in the name of smart commerce."

"We're driving around Plumsden and surrounds today, doing a bit of touring," I said. "I'm so glad it's not raining."

"You're in the High Weald now, the Garden of England. There's nothing finer than a sunny day in this part of the world." Algy was in wonderful spirits. His estate was running like an established business, the Afghan hound was under his control, and his brother was looking after their guests plus the petting zoo, just as he was instructed.

"Well, we'd better be off then," Gertie said. Furtive glances shot between Lance and us two ladies. Luckily, Algy missed all that, busy crooning to Gilligan about being such a good dog.

Lance beat a hasty retreat, but not before he heard the inward gasp of the estate owner, one that was building fury by the millisecond. We turned and saw Algy's face was a pale shade of plum and rapidly growing darker. "Is nothing sacred? My prized lettuces! Lancelot, what have you done?"

Lance was nowhere to be found.

Gertie and I left Algy alone, seething. We hightailed it out of there and a few moments later found Lance hiding around the side of Athena, cowering: "Let it pass, let it pass. Hopefully Gilligan will escape again, and then he'll forget about the wretched lettuces."

Gertie tried to be helpful. "You know, it's really not fair for the chairman of the Plumsden Horticultural Society to win a prize that his own society is sponsoring."

"Exactly! That's what I keep telling him, but he won't listen," Lance said.

"I will not listen to what?" Algy said, striding up to us, glowering, hands on his hips as he stood before us. Gilligan was in tow, nonplussed.

"The puppy, Norris. I'm trying to teach him to stay," Lance said, saving himself with beautiful nonchalance.

"Oh, right." Algy took the opportunity to survey his brother's face, deeply and with a very pensive, probing look. He could find nothing there. No hint of lettuce thievery or mangling. "Wipe that vacant stare off your face and get out the slug bait.

We have a massive intrusion of the slimy pests in our vegetable garden."

Lance saluted him and clicked his heels together, military style. "Right away, brother. Right away."

We somehow held in our laughter until Algy had walked away. The elder brother muttered up a storm to himself as he kept his elegant hound in check.

Chapter 14

We were about five minutes away in Athena when she started to make some odd noises. It was like little squealing starts and stops, spaced apart every couple of seconds.

"Is this the ghost of 1963 coming back to haunt us?" I asked Gertie.

"I just had Athena serviced. She's in tiptop shape." Gertie looked slightly offended.

"Maybe we should pull into a garage and have her checked out?"

Gertie held up a finger and now she heard the noise too. "Well, I don't know what it could be. Radiators hiss. Tires flap. And oil burns. This is more like a ..."

The sound turned into a howl. Definitely canine and not vehicular.

"Norris!" We both said it at the same time.

"I'll pull over to the side of the road up ahead," Gertie said. "We just passed the sign for the lay by."

I turned around and strained my neck, trying to see what on earth was going on behind the third-row seats. All I saw was spearmint-green vinyl upholstery.

The howling got louder. It was a bit farcical because the howling wasn't that of a well-developed adult dog. Rather, it was a puppy trying to show his disdain for being disturbed from his cozy little hideout, none of his familiar people nearby.

We stopped under a shady tree, and Gertie clambered over to the back row of seats. "I'm not going to open Athena's doors, because if he shoots out like a gazelle then we've lost him," she said.

"Good idea. We've witnessed how fast these hounds can run."

I watched her move onto the back bench and then start speaking in soothing tones to Norris. She picked him up and brought the puppy up front. "Aren't you a naughty little boy? You're a vagabond." She looked at me. "Can you please phone the house and ask what we're to do?"

I pulled out my mobile phone and dialed Holgarth Hall. "Hello, Parsons, it's Julie Fincher, your guest? Is Lance about?"

I got a very polite reply. "Master Lancelot is outside tending to his zoo," Parsons said with a rather smiling tone in his voice.

"And you do know that the zoo is courtesy of Algernon and not Lancelot, correct, Parsons?" I asked.

"Indeed, miss." This was household staff loyalty at its finest. "How may I help?"

"Could you please get Lance to come to the phone? It is rather urgent."

"I shall do my utmost, miss. Please hold one moment."

I was put on hold and subjected to a pre-recorded spiel of everything Holgarth Hall offered for sale. I put the phone on speaker because I had no idea what type of crisis Parsons would be pulling Lance away from this time. While we waited, we heard about Holgarth's homemade jam, vegetable stand, plant nursery, and petting zoo.

I was right to put it on speaker. My arm would have gone numb with the phone up to my ear as long as we had to wait.

I heard a scuffle and then Lance came on the phone. "Julie? Is everything all right?"

"Gertie and I are fine, thanks. Have you seen Norris lately?"

"I took him out for training this morning and then put him back in his kennel." It was a rather tentative voice Lance was using at present, unsure of why this guest was asking this particular question.

It was precisely at this moment that Norris decided to take up another round of decisive howling.

"Right. I'll come and fetch him. How far did you get?" Lance asked.

I explained where we were on the A road, and Lance told us to sit tight. Twenty minutes later he pulled up in the cherry-red convertible, sunglasses on, full of the joys of life. He'd brought a crate for Norris in the back seat that was strapped in with a seatbelt. Pretty soon the escapee puppy was safely ensconced inside.

"You look rather pleased with yourself, Lance," Gertie said.

"Of course I am. I'm experiencing continuous fits of laughter just watching my brother trying to figure out what happened to his lettuces. I put out all the slug bait as commanded, but for some reason it just doesn't seem to be attracting any. It's curious, like the little devils have all chosen to take early hibernation."

We all had a good laugh.

***

Beyond the tidy cottages with their picture-perfect, brilliantly colored flower gardens and throaty songbirds, the high street in Plumsden offered many things similar to other towns. Rows of quaint little shops and boutiques, and one would walk under their eaves, dodging long trailers from overhead hanging flower baskets. A plein air painting group was working on the tidy village green today, adding to the ambience. It was an affluent area with many toney shops to choose from. We went directly to the main-branch post office with our questions. Once inside, we made a beeline for the burly postmaster doing time at a wicket. Luckily it wasn't too busy inside. As we proceeded to his counter, we noticed he bore a huge red mustache that spread from one side of his face to the other. He gave us a smile and welcomed us once we had reached the head of the queue.

"How can 1 help?" he asked. His shiny nametag read 'Roger'.

1 stepped forward and held up my brass key. "Good afternoon. 1 was given this key by my aunt, who sent me to Plumsden to open a box. Do you have one here that it would fit?"

The postmaster took the large brass key from me, turned it over in his hands, and nodded. "You'll need to come around the counter for this one. We've been expecting you."

Roger's meaty hands held open the security door at the side of the counter. His colleague stepped in to help the only other person in line, an elderly lady with a stack of greeting cards to mail.

Gertie and 1 followed Roger the Mustache behind the main public area and into a small room containing a wall of brass-fronted safety deposit boxes. "Leftover from when this place used to be a bank," he said. "We knew your Aunt Edwina quite well in this town. Lovely lady, did a lot for this community ... sadly missed. We keep these boxes as a favor to certain clients who bought lifetime leases. We use the empty ones for our stamps and commemorative coins. All the others were let go, all except for hers. And now you're here, the end of an era."

"We don't know what we're going to find inside," I started.

"That's your business, miss. Please take your time," he said. "And do let me know if you still need the box or not."

"Thank you," I said. "You've been most helpful."

He left us, closing the door behind him. Gertie watched as I put the key into the only remaining locked box. The small door swung open with a slight creak and inside was a single sturdy envelope.

"The moment of truth," Gertie whispered in my ear.

I removed the envelope, carefully tore open the seal, and pulled out a letter on Greymore Hall stationery. It was written in Aunt Edwina's beautiful cursive script. Her letter simply read:

> *Dear Julie:*
> *You'll need one more key to find the next painting*
> *and riddle. Remember, ask the most likely*
> *knowledgeable person.*
> *Love from Aunt Edwina*

The envelope felt heavy, so I looked inside again and saw a different key, this one far older and with more weight to it. It was also brass and definitely not post office issue.

"I wonder what she means by 'the most likely knowledgeable person'," Gertie mused. "Does she mean a librarian? A research scholar, perhaps?"

"I'm not sure. She never discussed it with me at all."

"I'll bet she's sitting up there on her puffy cloud, wearing her halo, smiling down on us as she watches us trying to figure out her clues. That is *so* Aunt Edwina."

"I agree. So do we keep the box?" I asked.

Gertie shook her head. "It seems to only be a personal safe. It's not associated with a mailing address."

"So let's save Greymore Hall some money and cancel it," I said. "I'll let her attorney know. We should probably tell Roger that's what we're planning on doing. I don't like leaving people hanging."

We showed Roger our new key, and he seemed a bit baffled by it. "That key is from something historical, definitely not post office issue. If it were me, I would try an old outbuilding at Greymore Hall and see if I could fit it there somehow."

Otherwise, the big man looked stumped.

"So it's not worth us trying any other nearby post office branches?" Gertie asked, as she checked the map feature on her phone.

"I would say not," Roger replied. "We're the only one in the area that has these ancient boxes for the key like you just used.

And as for the new key you just found in the envelope, none of us have anything that would fit that."

"Thank you so much for your time. I'll ask the estate attorney to get in touch about closing the box with official paperwork," I said.

With Athena well-parked, we explored more streets of this charming town. We came upon the Plumsden Family History Society right beside a Red Cross thrift shop that was selling handknit sweaters by the ladies' hospital auxiliary. On the other side of the Family History Society was a small law office. We went up to the Family History Society's front door, and Gertie tried the handle, but it was locked.

The sign on the door told us why.

She looked back at me with a pained grin. "Remember what Algy said? Only open on Wednesdays. Today's Tuesday, so we're out of luck."

"Excuse me, ladies?" a man's voice behind us started.

We turned to see an attractive, sandy-haired man, nearly six feet tall, offer us a confident smile. His blue-grey eyes crinkled up in the corners in a very pleasant way. He was a very personable man in his early thirties, I guessed.

He continued. "I'm Ewan Kilburn. I own the antiques shop a couple of doors down and also volunteer as Plumsden Family History Society's Treasurer. Do you need some assistance?"

"Do you have a crowbar handy?" Gertie asked with a grin.

He smiled back. "You must have a desperate need to find some ancestors."

We laughed.

I looked at Ewan again and decided he'd made a very good first impression. With me, first impressions were everything, and I put a lot of stock in them. For example, Chris was a two, that conniving, smarmy, welching ogre. Lance was an eight, in a friends-only sort of way, and he'd have the extra two points if he grew a backbone. Ewan was a ten because he impressed on every note: kind, capable, good looking, volunteered with seniors. There was nothing not to like.

Ewan continued. "Ah, the Wednesday thing. It frustrates a lot of people. Unfortunately, we just don't have the funding or volunteer base to open it more often, unless it's by appointment."

"That's a shame," I said.

"I do have some of the book collection and a computer with genealogy research site access back at my shop if that's of any use. What exactly are you seeking?"

"We're researching this old key plus a painter with the initials of 'E.E.'" I held up the key we retrieved from the post office box and showed him a picture of the watercolor on my phone. Wisely, I'd left the original back at Holgarth Hall just in case something nefarious happened to Athena while we were out on our tour today.

Ewan gestured for us to follow him. "Please follow me, ladies. Fancy a cuppa?"

Chapter 15

Ewan's antiques shop, aptly named 'Kilburn's Outstanding Antiques', was a charming little shop cram-packed with furniture from multiple centuries, all polished to a high gloss. He had solid silver tea services, Art Deco mirrors, ancestral portraits, chamber pots, a moose head, hat pins, and a multitude of books and other paper items further in the back. It was a real treasure trove where one could get lost in history for an entire afternoon. I emailed him the image of the watercolor.

We sat at the back in his lunchroom and bookkeeping alcove. The ceiling was sloped, so we all had to sit in a line against the wall opposite his desk, but it was cozy enough. Ewan was an obvious lover of antiques and apparently meticulous with his record keeping. One could tell by looking at how orderly all the letter slots were on the roll-top desk he'd commandeered for his business operations. He used a computerized inventory system, and this was nice to see because it was a modern business necessity. It was odd, modernizing the antiques trade.

Kind of like reassembling a vintage dress using a slightly different pattern.

Ewan brought up the image of the watercolor on his big monitor. "So, your watercolor painter. 1 do not know of anyone with those specific initials working in this area. However, I'm not an art expert but do have a colleague who is a painter, and 1 can take you to see him tomorrow morning, if you like. As for the key, it looks like it would fit a seventeenth-century cabinet, likely a sideboard where one keeps the fine china."

Gertie and 1 looked at each other like we'd struck gold. "You can tell all of that from a key?" 1 asked, slightly shocked.

Ewan nodded. "One tends to pick up a lot of knowledge along the way in this business. I've seen my fair amount of keys over the years, and that one is definitely a good candidate for a seventeenth-century sideboard."

"So the next question is where would we find it in Plumsden? Aunt Edwina said that all of these were public places, so it's not like we have to go round the private homes and cottages looking like complete crazed persons trying to fit a key into an elusive object," 1 said.

"You're welcome to try the ones in the shop, but that's a longshot because my inventory moves fairly quickly. 1 only bring in the larger pieces when a buyer asks me to find something in particular, or 1 know that another dealer will always take that type of piece off my hands." He gestured out towards the middle of the shop. "As you can see, space is always at a premium, and I just don't have the room to store dozens of large pieces."

"Quite," I said.

"I'd also recommend you come back to the Plumsden Family History Society tomorrow and ask the volunteers there to take a closer look. If the painting is by a local artist, one of the volunteers may recognize it. One of them is actually a wealthy lady—quite house poor, mind you—Maude Livingstone."

"That's who Algy recommended to us," I said, quite glad to make the connection.

"Ah, so you're staying at Holgarth Hall, then? How are the newly converted stables?"

"Very comfortable," Gertie said. "We're thoroughly enjoying our stay. Especially watching Lance and his 'zoo', as Parsons likes to call it."

"I went to the same grammar school as Lance, almost went into business with him after a career day visit. But I count my blessings I'd retreated to the antiques world long before he experienced his spicy chili-banana samosa misfortune," Ewan said.

"At least Lance has a place to live," I said.

Ewan scoffed. "Oh, Algy would never leave his brother out in the cold. And the banter between those two, well, it's always been unworldly."

"Should I tell him about Gilligan's antics?" Gertie asked me.

Ewan looked puzzled, and I thought he should be put out of his agony. I went ahead and nodded at Gertie.

Gertie regaled us with the story of the Afghan hound bounding through the yard, having escaped his master. We then somehow got onto the rabbits and the lettuce montage, and by then we'd all finished three cups of tea and were roaring with laughter.

Ewan looked at his watch. "Well, I do have to close up and run. I'm shuttling my nephew off to his piano lesson right after his tea. My sister's taking her daughter in the complete opposite direction for a highland dancing lesson, so that's when Uncle Ewan needs to step in."

Wow. Any further goodness emanating from this man would require someone to grant him keys to the city.

"Thank you so much for your time, it's been a scream," I said.

"My pleasure, ladies," he replied, shaking each of our hands. "I'll be back in tomorrow at 9:00 a.m. and then we can go down to the Family History Society together and ask your questions."

***

I checked my phone once we were back inside Athena's safe confines. I groaned.

"What is it?" Gertie asked.

"Chris. He just texted me an hour ago: 'When are you coming home?'"

"Tell him never ... wait, tell him when ostriches no longer bury their heads in the sand and drink chocolate milkshakes." She looked rather pleased with her witty statement.

"I think I need something a little less antagonistic," I said.

"Why? It's not like you were the one sneaking around with Carlene."

"No, but I did theoretically marry him."

"You left him a note, so he knows you're fine. Why not just blow him off?"

"He has all my stuff. I don't want him to slash all my canvases in a fit of rage."

"Can you get Bertie to evict him?"

"Bertie just attended our wedding! I doubt he's going to help me throw my husband out the week after the ceremony."

"You should try him. Aristocrats lead stranger lives than you and I. He may have seen this kind of stuff before," Gertie advised.

"I think that is a bizarre idea."

Gertie shook her head. "Artists are supposed to be a little off the wall. Why don't you just play that up, use it to your advantage?"

"Because I don't like using people like that." I set my mouth in a firm line and stared straight ahead. I didn't know what to do. "Gertie, with Chris, I just don't want to push him that hard. I don't trust his reaction. Besides, he still thinks we're married."

"I think he knows you're on a treasure hunt. We should be careful about that. Especially since he's trying to finance Carlene."

"Finance her, what do you mean?" I asked.

Gertie looked pained. "A friend of mine works in IT, actually a facial-recognition software development company. I sent him a picture of Carlene and asked him to look her up. You know what he found?"

"I have no idea."

"She's in public relations, damage control. A for-hire consultant who fixes companies' public issues. Even serves as a spokesperson when needed. BUT, Carlene's not that well-known and the consulting world's a tough one, especially since her banker ex-husband's done all he can to persuade people against contracting with her."

"Interesting," I replied, not really meaning it. "Ewan's nice, hey?"

"And I didn't see a wedding ring either," Gertie said. "Perhaps–"

"Perhaps you should focus on getting us home safely. We can stop at the supermarket and pick up some odds and ends for dinner. I'm really not too hungry after eating that huge cinnamon bun Ewan fed us."

"What did you text Chris?" she asked.

"I kept it short: 'Have more art projects than expected. Home in a couple of weeks.' He's probably doing cartwheels right now because that means he can spend more time with Carlene."

"At your place?" Gertie shook her head.

"Ugh. I'm going to call Bertie and see if he can get the nearby fields fertilized this week. That scent will put anyone off staying there."

"Clever girl," Gertie said with a wink.

"There wasn't much else I could say, really," I replied. "I'm keeping it cordial yet distant."

We had a girl's night in the bed-and-breakfast room, eating our dinner and watching a couple of old movies from the 1940s. We both loved black-and-white films, so we were in our element when we discovered a movie marathon playing on the telly.

"It was such a simpler time back then," Gertie observed as she dove into her salmon and cress sandwich. "Not so much frenetic running around, worrying about who said what about whom on the internet, posting social media things eight hundred and ninety-four times a day. I mean, who has time for all that?"

"Social media influencers," I said, swigging back some spring water to wash down my roast beef and cheese sandwich. "They live and die by the number of followers they have."

I looked at her, she looked at me, and it was all good. It had been quite the day, and we were both ready for a good night's sleep. As I nearly drifted off, Ewan's face scrolled through my mind: such a kind and helpful man. I was very much looking forward to seeing him tomorrow.

Chapter 16

———

Next Morning.

We asked Lance to have breakfast ready earlier today, and he came through with alacrity. We started breakfast by 6:30 a.m., arriving well ahead of the other two sets of guests. One could always tell what type of travel a fellow guest was doing. If they were eating alone consistently, just gulping down a quick breakfast before the office world opened, then you knew they were there on business. It was nice during a business trip to try and get away from the hustle and bustle of a city core, and that's why the bed-and-breakfast routine was popular with lone travelers. With families, one didn't normally see them at breakfast till about 8:30 a.m., either with small kids in tow, or reluctant teenagers who wanted to sleep till noon.

Gertie and I were the oddballs: two single women traveling the countryside, sorting out a family history mystery. It was a fun time, certainly, only clouded by the person I'd have to deal with once I got back home. It was like a clock's pendulum slowly ticking me forward to that agonizing moment of truth. For now, to help get over the shock, escaping into Aunt Edwina's mystery tour was the best possible medicine for me. I intended to make the most of this precious time, rekindling my friendship with my cousin Gertie and ensuring that Aunt Edwina's wishes were properly carried out.

***

We were at Ewan's antiques shop at 9:00 a.m. He'd obviously been there for quite a while before us, stuck into some bookkeeping software on his computer screen.

"Good morning, Ewan!" Gertie called out in her most cheerful voice.

He got up from his desk and promptly whacked his head on the sloped ceiling. He groaned and rubbed his head. "Good morning, ladies."

I went over to him. "Are you all right?"

"Yes," he said with a sigh, grimacing. "It's only about the three-hundredth time I've done that this year."

"You're not bleeding?" I asked.

"No, us hard-headed Scots need to suffer a lot more violence in order for the red stuff to flow. But that ceiling? It's like my own personal Battle of Culloden."

We laughed.

"I pulled out a box of local postcards that you might find interesting," he said. "Many of the Edwardian and Victorian photographers would take pictures of streetscapes, local celebrities, farm equipment, and vehicular disasters. Of course, there are always the comedic ones, as well as the chubby babies. If you flip through the box, you might find something related to the area that can help you with your painting identification. You never know."

"He's right, Julie," Gertie said. "A couple of years ago, a friend of mine visited an antiques shop and found a postcard sent by his great grandfather. He was local to the area, but there is no reason why that postcard should've ended up in any collection other than the family album."

Ewan looked interested. "That's exactly the kind of stuff I'm talking about. Speak with the staff at the Plumsden Family History Society. They'd be interested to hear your friend's success story too."

So we all gathered up our things, Ewan promising me that I would have ample time to look through his box of postcards later on. It was important to get over to the Family History Society and have as much time there during opening hours as we could. Ewan had a couple of books he was bringing over to them, I had my watercolor painting, and Gertie had the day bag. Luckily, today we had no puppy in tow; we'd made a firm check of that before we left Holgarth's. There were also no rabbits, goats, or llamas in the boot. It was apparently quite important for us to check these things while we stayed with Algy and Lance.

The tiny bell over the door to the Plumsden Family History Society jingled politely as we walked inside. We must've looked quite the sight, Ewan and his two rescued travelers, one clutching a leather backpack and the other holding a watercolor of the local pond.

Ewan knew everybody on site and called out the names, one by one. Maude Livingstone, a thin woman with tailored clothes, perfect short, curly grey hair, and a shiny name tag, came over and shook my hand first. "Algy telephoned to say you might be dropping in. How lovely to see you, and please accept my sincerest condolences for the loss of Edwina. She was a fine, fine lady."

"Thank you so much," I said. "Were you great friends?"

Maude nodded. "We met every third Saturday of the month. Did a lot of good community things." She gave a welcoming smile to my cousin. "You must be Gertie. Edwina said you were thick as thieves with Julie when you were growing up."

Gertie looked shocked that she was recognized—well, recognized for something other than her viral video. And that was a really good thing.

Ewan chimed in. "I told both ladies that this is the place to come and get more local information on their mysterious painter's name, as well as what perhaps would be a good item to accept an old seventeenth-century brass key."

Maude's eyes opened wider. "An old brass key? Well, we do have some reference books in our library, and you're certainly welcome to use the computers to search locksmith craft guilds. Is there anything associated with the key at all?"

"We found more initials, I'm afraid. 'H.P.'," I said. "It could mean that the cabinet is located at Westminster, Houses of Parliament, you know."

Gertie shook her head. "The letter Aunt Edwina left said that everything was located in Southern England. Does London count as Southern England?"

Ewan and Maude shook their heads. He answered for both of them. "London is a country unto its own. At least, that's how we feel out here in our little English villages. I doubt Lady Edwina would send you up to the big city. She knows how security conscious they are in Parliament these days."

Maude took charge. "Do come back with me. I'll show you the books and the computer to get things started."

We were in good hands. Gertie and I followed Maude back as Ewan settled at a desk off to the side where a volunteer unlocked the cashbox for the society's treasurer to review and balance petty cash. An hour after we'd started, Gertie was well into a book about Restoration England locksmiths, and I was deep into a family history website with a very interesting article about the nineteenth-century watercolor painting scene.

Ewan popped his head round the corner. "I've finished tallying the month's receipts. I'll be at the shop for the rest of the day. Come see me when you're finished and let me know what you found. I'm curious."

We waved him off with big smiles and thank you's.

He was a good man. So helpful. In today's world, help usually only came after flashing about cash or a bit of skin. This was rather a pleasant departure from the norm.

Maude came over towards where Gertie and I were sitting. "Any luck?" she asked.

I went first. "Well, it's all interesting stuff, but there's nothing specific about the artist named 'E.E.' I get the feeling that this is going to be like jousting at windmills for quite some time."

"I have better news to report," Gertie said. "Ewan was right about the key. It is indeed seventeenth-century and should fit a lock from that era. Any type of sideboard, cabinet, perhaps even a secret bookshelf."

"Oooh, a secret bookshelf," Maude said. "We have one of those in the top floor of our home. When we put the key in the lock, we found out it was once used as a sealed room, a place where they boarded up a relative who was in the way." She shook her head.

"You mean, they just put somebody in there and forgot about them?" I asked, stunned.

Maude nodded. "It wasn't uncommon for aristocratic families to get rid of illegitimate siblings or mentally ill relatives, for example, in that matter. Imagine someone showing you up to your room, telling you that they'll bring you a warm cup of cocoa for the evening after setting up your fire, closing the door, and then locking you in. Permanently." She shuddered.

Gertie had to ask. "What did you find inside your secret room?"

"It was all rather exciting," Maude said. "There was a sapphire ballgown, a woman's diary, plus a skeleton lying in the bed."

We must've looked quite shocked.

Maude frowned. "We discovered it during renovations to the top floor. My family had listened to me get all excited about the history of our home. Then I found out that my now-late husband had already been in there. It was a Halloween joke, and the plastic skeleton was from his medical-school days. The ballgown he bought from a local thrift shop, and he had my daughter—only eleven at the time—concoct the victim's diary because she's quite the calligraphy artist."

"I hope you had both of them locked up in that room for a few days as punishment," Gertie said. "That's horrible."

"Not as horrible as having to sit with your housekeeper for a few hours at the hospital because she's fainted and clonked her head on the mantlepiece."

"Oh dear. Was she alright?" I asked.

"Oh yes, we all survived. She just had a little bump, not even a slight concussion. My family felt terrible. But keeping historical facts accurate, well, it's just something I've got a healthy respect for. That's why I always insist that the people I help are focused on finding three different sources proving their genealogical facts."

"How so?" I asked.

"It's not enough to have the birth certificate," Maude explained. "What if the parents lied because they weren't really married? Or the records clerk didn't know how to spell their last name correctly, and the parents didn't read and write enough to correct him? The marriage certificate—was it really for your family's John and Anne? Were there any other couples named John and Anne in nearby parishes who could also be your ancestors? How about that census record he looked at? Just because somebody wasn't listed didn't mean that they'd already passed away. They could've been traveling out of town, or in prison, and just weren't noted. That's why I always say triple-prove your genealogical sources."

"Food for thought," Gertie said. "But all I found for this key are some book references telling me it's seventeenth-century, along with the letter from Aunt Edwina. I can't check it any other way."

Maude held out her hand and took the key once more. "I think the initials 'H.P.' are what to focus on now. Did you find any cabinetmakers with those initials yet? If not, that's what I'd keep looking for. It's important to remember that even if you don't know the genealogy of the person, or any ancestors' names, you can trace them back using apprenticeships or crafts. Sometimes you'll be surprised at what you find. We had a patron in here last week who found her great-grandfather's name and birthplace simply by tracing the name of the photographer's studio on his picture."

"How did she do that?" Gertie asked.

Maude smiled knowledgeably. "By finding the photographer's studio, she knew what city to look for. She was lucky, the studio left wonderful records that got donated to the county archives. They were even digitized. So within two hours of sitting down at one of our computers, she was able to take her family ancestry back three generations."

"I sense that may be a lucky find?" I asked.

"Yes, that's one of my hero stories I like to tell," Maude admitted. "For most of us, finding a recalcitrant ancestor who doesn't want to be found involves multiple months or years of hard slogging through un-indexed parish registers, many false starts and dead ends. Oh, plus copious cups of tea."

Gertie nodded her thanks and got back to work.

Maude turned to me, placing a book by my side. "I did find this for you on our shelves. It's a book of Kentish crafts, including things like saddle makers, wood joiners, silk printers, and sign painters. It's a bit of a stretch; however, flip through it and see if you can find your mysterious 'E.E.' artist."

"That's wonderful, thank you," I said. "Perhaps the frame has a maker's mark, or the name of the miller who worked the pond. Either could provide a lead to the area."

And so we sat for another couple of hours leafing through references in books and searching online, finding that one clue would lead to another, and that there were endless rabbit holes to dive down. The key being, of course, to stay away from any headstrong, two-toned rabbits like the one Lance wrangled with back at Holgarth Hall.

***

Back at Ewan's shop, he was just saying goodbye to his last customer of the day. He locked the front door, turning the 'open' sign over to 'closed'. He looked at Gertie and I, who were slightly bleary-eyed from all that heavy concentration we'd just performed. "I'm all yours, ladies," he said. "Now about those postcards ..."

I headed to his side in an instant, eager. Perhaps too eager.

"I'm beginning to feel like the proverbial third wheel," Gertie whispered to me.

"So run along then, go try the key in all his cabinets," I said, shooing her away to another part of the shop.

Ewan came back, the box of postcards in his hand. "As I was saying earlier, the Edwardians and the Victorians had a fantastic eye for the intricacies of their respective time periods. Hundreds of thousands of these cards actually still exist, but I only have one box right now; I just sold a couple more to a customer last week. However, I'm at a large antiques fair starting tomorrow through the weekend and hope to acquire more stock."

I took the box from him. "This is really nice of you, thank you."

"You're welcome to sit at my desk to review them."

"That would be lovely, thank you." I settled in at his desk.

"Just remember, er, the sloped ceiling. She's got a wicked left hook," he said. He was really trying hard, and I sensed it.

"Got it. Thanks."

Ewan went into the back to rustle up some tea, and Gertie got busy trying our cabinet key into everything inside his shop.

Of course, Ewan had every single one of his postcards inside a clear, protective, acid-free sleeve. This prevented the card getting dinged at the edges and also kept out mold, mildew, and dust. Each one was priced individually, ranging from one to fifty pounds.

I felt someone hovering over my shoulder. Looking up, I saw Ewan staring at the card I had in my hand at the moment. It was a lovely portrait of a young woman wearing an elegant Victorian dress and matching hat. The sepia tone of the photo had been hand-colored in spots, showing the lovely rose-pink color of her parasol and her figure-hugging fitted jacket. There was an enormous amount of lace on her elbow-length sleeves as well as at the hem of her floor-length skirt. Her hair was piled on top of her head in a multitude of curls, and I was sure a couple of jeweled hatpins were buried in there somewhere.

"You found my most expensive card," he said.

"Why is it £50? The others are not even a quarter that much."

"Because this one is actually a real studio photograph. The others are reproductions and mass printed," he explained.

"It says 1894. Is that early?" I asked.

"It is. The writer was allowed a short message. On the reverse, one could only write the address—strict postal regulations, you see. In the early 1900s, the postal system ceded to popular demand and loosened restrictions."

"Hence the flood of holiday postcards from around the country and abroad?"

He nodded then went back to his mini-kitchen to answer the kettle's whistle. It had broken our conversation in a harsh manner, like all kettles did. It was as if their shrill call signaled an imminent catastrophe in the kitchen. Right now I hated that kettle.

Gertie came over and plunked herself down next to me. "The key fits nothing in here. I tried it in loads of furniture. Rather disappointing."

"Again, that would've been a little too easy coming from Aunt Edwina, don't you think?"

"Perhaps. But I have to ask Ewan. What the heck is this?" Gertie held up a tea cup and saucer set, which had a gold rim as well as an intricate design of roses entwined all over the base and around the sides of the cup. What was mystifying, though, was the bat-shaped piece of porcelain that was affixed from one side of the cup's interior to the other in sort of a half-moon shape, with a small hole letting liquid through between the bat shape and the rim.

I held the cup in my hands and was baffled too. "A manufacturer's defect with its die cut machine?"

"Incorrect, I afraid," Ewan said emerging from behind the tiny kitchen area with a tray laden with tea and biscuits. "What you are looking at, ladies, is a mustache guard."

"What?" we both exclaimed in unison.

Ewan found our stereo reactions quite amusing. "A mustache guard, of course, to prevent a sopping set of whiskers."

Gertie got a glint in her eye. "For the post office!"

I nodded. "He'd be my first customer."

Ewan looked confused. "Have I missed the joke? Am I the joke?" He made a self-conscious move to feel his clean-shaven chin and jawline.

I had to stop myself from laughing. "No, you're not the joke. We just met your postmaster, and he's got a red mustache that goes from one cheek right to the other. He definitely needs this product."

"Oh, the *main* post office. I was thinking of a smaller outlet. Of course that's Roger, and I can see exactly why you're smiling. You know, he's even had offers to shave it off for charity?"

"He'd make a killing," Gertie said.

"He did once, about five years ago. That's how we fundraised money to put new sod on our historic village green." Ewan got mugs of tea and biscuits into our hands. "You know, the antiques fair I'm going to be at this week on the south coast in Waverly-on-Sea is a great place to ask the dealers if they know anything about your mysterious 'E.E.' painter. People from all over Kent and Sussex will be there, about an hour's drive south from Plumsden. You're both welcome to come along if you wish."

"That would be lovely," I said. "Gertie, are you in?"

"Are there any churches nearby?" she asked.

"But tomorrow's Thursday," Ewan said. "Why do you need a church?"

I sighed. "It's a long story. How about we tell you in the car tomorrow?"

Chapter 17

Next morning. O'Dark Thirty.

I couldn't tell Ewan about Gertie's defrocking incident in the car. The reason being that we weren't in a car. Ewan had cleverly repurposed a hybrid-fuel horse box for his antiques business and painted his business name in bold, two-foot-tall letters on the side. We sat three abreast in the cab, with a bench seat behind us where we stowed our bags and Ewan's cooler. If one knelt backwards on the bench seat, one could see through a little window and look at the cargo in the large cube area behind us.

Ewan had cleared out half his shop, courtesy of a local football youth club. In exchange for a pizza party and a donation to tournament travel costs, Ewan had twelve boys between the ages of fourteen and sixteen show up at his shop the night before we left. They carefully loaded up everything from furniture to an eighteenth-century microscope. The end result was that we had a big cargo, and Ewan definitely had an interesting stall to show prospective customers.

We were on our way to Waverly-on-Sea, East Sussex. The event was held inside an arena, so rain would not be an issue. Even nicer, the facility was large enough for exhibitors to drive in their electric vehicles to unload next to the stalls. By the time we'd driven much nearer, it was a real comedy show inside the horse box. Ewan nearly had tears streaming down his face when Gertie recounted what got her defrocked.

"I never expected to meet a priest who got into trouble for singing. What on earth possessed you?" he asked.

She shrugged. "I blame the punch."

One learned a lot from how a man reacted to someone else's misfortune. Chris would have smirked the moment he heard Gertie was in trouble. Ewan waited to see my grin before he added his to the mix. That was the difference between a two and a ten.

He focused on the road ahead. "Ah, here we go."

Ten miles out, we'd started to see signs for the antiques fair. They were the same kind one would see promoting an open house or a brash business liquidation. They were weatherproof signs stuck into the ground with thin metal spikes on either end: ANTIQUES FAIR: Ten Miles. Then Five Miles. Then Two Miles. Then TURN HERE OR MISS THE ANTIQUES FAIR!

We pulled in. It was all extremely well-organized. We were met in the parking lot by an attendant wearing a high-visibility vest. It was the fancy kind with pockets and a zippered front. He had a flashlight, radio, and a badge that showed security guards he was cleared for access to the run of the site. He directed our electric vehicle towards the arena, noting we were in stall number twenty-three. The site map showed there were over 250 exhibitors. This was a huge event.

Gertie frowned. "How big is this stall? A single stall isn't going to be big enough for all of the stuff in the back."

Ewan looked surprised. "Is she always this blunt?"

"Devilishly so," I replied. "It's actually why I appreciate my cousin to a fault."

"We're fine, Gertie. Honest," he said. "Here we are." We were now inside a large arena where the exhibitor booths were called 'stalls.'

We lumbered up to a twenty-foot by twenty-foot space marked by event pipe and drape. The number twenty-three was printed on the temporary cardboard banner beside 'Kilburn's Outstanding Antiques'.

Of course, the first thing Ewan did was replace the cheap stall sign with a professional wood-carved one of his own that he'd brought along for that specific purpose.

The place was packed with other antiques dealers setting up their wares. This was obviously one of the premier events of the year, because all the stalls were bustling with activity, including our own. They were starting to line up rolls of industrial carpeting to cover the concrete floor, and thankfully put padding underneath to make sure our backs didn't get sore after so much standing. Padded shoe inserts were a must, and luckily Gertie had turned me onto them years ago when she first started preaching. I wore them in my art classes because I had to stand on my feet for hours at a time, roaming large studios watching my students apply paint to canvas.

Ewan parked right outside the stall and turned the engine off. All the roll-up doors on each side of the arena were wide open to ensure the fans prevented any outside fumes lingering inside the complex. We all got out of the cab and headed to the back of the truck. As if by magic, two burly men appeared, ready to help Ewan. I was given a box filled with hats, hairpins, and books, then instructed to keep it out of the way while they unloaded the big stuff. It looked like I was in charge of the 'last-minute throw-in' box, but that was fine, I wasn't complaining. I really didn't know what I was doing anyways!

Gertie had a similar 'last-minute throw-in' box, and we stepped back to watch the men put a heavy Welsh dresser, a nineteenth-century side cabinet, and a couple of Queen Anne chairs around the perimeter of the stall. These were the key pieces that would set up Ewan's 'room', so to speak. On the dresser and the side cabinet he placed an assortment of hand-embroidered runners to protect the surfaces. The Welsh dresser then received an array of china and silver, while the side cabinet held some candelabras and a glass display case of portrait miniatures. He strung two soft velvet ropes over the chairs to dissuade tired fairgoers from using his expensive antique chairs as a rest stop. It was like his own miniature museum exhibition, but with all the different time periods mashed into one tiny space.

Ewan came over to us. "Ladies, just be aware that there are some light-fingered visitors here, so keep your eyes peeled. In the stall and out on the floor. Nothing is for free, and if somebody looks sketchy, then they probably are."

Gertie looked excited. "Do we get a secret code word?"

Ewan looked a bit confused. "For what?"

"To flag the others about a nefarious person on site, of course," she replied.

"Sure, how about 'karaoke'?" he said with a grin.

She scowled. "That's low, really low."

We set about unloading the rest of the truck, which was now down to the lighter things we could manage without our two mountain men. I took out a box of poufy ladies' hats plus more china and was busy setting them up in an attractive display on the Welsh dresser. Ewan had a couple of pieces of rare sculpted glass, obviously his pride and joy; they got center stage and swanky price tags as well. He'd ordered a flat-screen television for the stall, and the show officials had run electricity to it as part of his stall package. Ewan brought a tablet preloaded with a few of his promotional videos as well as an instructional video on how to restore old furniture. He started playing the auto loop to make sure everything was fine with the electronics. The final touches were some royal-purple chair drapes bearing his shop's logo that he hung over the two barstools he'd rented from the show office. It was a smart move, because barstools allowed one to rest the feet while still making near eye-level contact with potential customers.

We stepped back and admired our handiwork.

"Well, ladies, this looks fantastic. Thank you so much for your help. This should be a really good show for us," he said.

"It looks marvelous, Ewan," Gertie said. "Definitely needed a woman's touch, though. I had my doubts once I saw your brawn arrive to help unload the big stuff."

"I agree one hundred percent." He gave us a kind smile. "Now, I have some important clients coming for a preview in half an hour. You're free to wander the hall if you'd like, so long as you wear your exhibitor badges." He handed us each a badge printed with our name, kept inside a plastic holder attached to a lanyard emblazoned with the sponsor's name 'Kilburn's Outstanding Antiques'.

"Hey, this is your shop," I noted. "Way to go on the market-ing, Ewan!"

He looked quite chuffed that I'd noticed. "It's all about name-brand recognition and supporting the community that supports you."

"Best of luck, then," I wished him.

"Come back for lunch, if you can tear yourselves away," he teased.

We nodded 'yes' to his arrangements. Gertie linked her arm with mine and we were off. The antiques fair didn't open for another three hours to the public, but looking at the other exhibitors who were struggling with setup, they would need every single minute left. This was the land of both kind biddies and con artists. One exhibitor had a wonky sign that we helped to straighten. One had a broken chair leg and was dealing with a child who'd spilt a fizzy grape drink all over the carpet. And the list went on. We tried to stay out of the way as much as we could, looking at what was being set out for sale without being invasive or annoying.

I had to admit, one dealer's booth drew me in immediately; three boxes of postcards sat on a lovely lace runner on a desk near the front of the stall. I headed over and said a quick hello to the owner sitting at the back of her stall knitting, totally prepared for the public to arrive. She had grey hair and bright-orange cat-eye glasses, a funky senior look.

We made our acquaintances and the owner, Diana Marlee Resman, turned out to be a lovely lady from Kipbourne in

Dorset. She did her antiquing on the side, in between babysit-
ting two very active grandchildren. I started to flick through
her box of postcards as Gertie perused the rest of the stall with
Diana's permission.

"Do you collect postcards, dear?" Diana asked me.

"Not so much for collecting, but for family history research.
You see, my aunt recently passed away and left me a watercolor
painting with a mysterious artist attached to it. We're trying to
figure out if it's related to anyone in the family or even in the
local area, the Oakhurst and Plumsden areas in Kent."

"Do you have the painting on your phone?"

I nodded and brought it up so I could show it to Diana.
"It's this mysterious pair of initial 'E's. Nobody can identify
the artist."

"Have you tried the local Family History Society?" she asked.

"That was one of our first stops. Unfortunately, no luck
there either. So we're here with Ewan Kilburn to do the rounds
and see if anyone else can help us."

"Oh, Ewan's very kind. Knows his stuff, too. I'm sorry
I can't be of more assistance. But do ask around, we are a
friendly bunch. In the meantime, feel free to browse through
my postcards."

"Thanks, shall do." Diana also had her postcards neatly
placed inside individual archival-friendly sleeves. I was going
through a bunch of holiday beach landscapes and a set of train

locomotives when I caught my breath. In between a couple of postcards was a series of five photographs, all on the original thick card stock that early photographers used. There was a set of three photos of a man in military uniform plus a young lady holding a flower and then another of a young rosy-cheeked child of about two years old. I thought it was so sad to see these family photos abandoned.

They should be labeled and in an archive.

"Excuse me," I called out to Diana. "Did you know you had photos in this box as well as the postcards?"

"Oh yes, dear, they landed up in there somehow, probably from another auction lot I bought."

A surge of responsible-rescuer emotions coursed through me, kind of like saving a forlorn kitten at a shelter. "Can I buy them?" I asked.

"Of course you can. How about £6 for all five photos?"

I had no idea about prices, but was absolutely determined to rescue these family photos from oblivion. These were the faces of the people who were war heroes. Homefront workers. A much-cherished child. Those who kept the country going in her darkest days. They deserved more than being forgotten, and at least now they had a cheering section of one.

It struck me that this was quite a serendipitous moment, a time where the proverbial light turns on and some faraway gong echoes through one's head. I didn't know these people from Adam, yet they called to me. I realized this was what family history was all about: reconnecting with lost loved ones and gaining a much stronger appreciation for the past. I understood what caused people to dash off to various record offices and graveyards in the hopes of finding another lost ancestor. Their goal was to bring them back into the fold, so to speak. It didn't matter if they were a lord or a highwayman, a princess or a milkmaid. No, what mattered was that there was a sturdy family tree, a thickly rooted oak that never failed to expand its canopy of branches to add another ancestor. It was all about belonging, and now I was determined to give the unknown people in the photos my best efforts at placing them on the lofty branches of their own family tree.

Chapter 18

I put my new purchases into my satchel that I'd slung cross body and decided to walk the rest of the show floor. "Thanks very much," I said to Diana as we left her patch.

She'd nearly gone back to her knitting and gave me an encouraging smile before we left. "Good luck finding out more details about the watercolor!"

I waved goodbye and took Gertie with me. We tried dealers at about thirty other stalls, ranging from those who were selling paintings to those who looked to be likely prospects. No luck. We were just about finished our tour of the entire hall when we rounded the corner and came across a woman who'd scored an incredible endcap double stall: 'Treemoreland Farm Antiques' proprietor Lorelei Stoneton. She was based in Waverly-on-Sea and stood in the middle of her booth, surrounded by gleaming dining room tables, low-slung chaise lounges, and an assortment of French gilded clocks. What really caught my eye were the two watercolor paintings she had hanging over a mantlepiece she'd somehow gotten crammed into the stall as well.

We made our introductions.

"So you're here with Ewan?" Lorelei asked.

"Helping out as best we can and also doing some research of our own," I said.

"We need some help with our late aunt's watercolor painting," Gertie explained.

"I see. What exactly are you looking to research?" Lorelei asked.

I hauled out my phone and brought up the picture of the watercolor. "Here it is. It's a painting along with some clues for a treasure hunt."

"How exciting," Lorelei said. "Do you have the provenance of the item?"

"Oh dear, no, I haven't. I just assumed she purchased it from a gallery," I said.

"We should explain. Our aunt was Lady Edwina Greymore, of Greymore Hall. The big house has quite an art collection," Gertie hastily added.

Lorelei took a closer look at my phone, expanding the photo in all areas using her thumb and index finger. She frowned and next focused on the top right picture corner. Then she tapped it with her finger. "Have you ever looked at this part of the frame?" Her eyes were curious and bright. She had yardstick-straight silvery blond hair with a fringe, and it suited her well.

"We thought that maybe the frame was distinctive. It does have some kind of scrolling etched into it," Gertie explained.

"No dear, not the scrolling. But this little mark here at the top. I've seen it on a frame before, but I can't quite remember where. It must've been during one of my antiques fair travels," Lorelei said.

Gertie jabbed me in the ribs, making me jump. "So you know who the artist is, then?"

Lorelei shook her head. "Not the painter, but the frame-maker. And he had quite the reputation for hiding things inside framed artwork."

"Like a secret compartment?" I asked.

"Exactly. If I were you, I'd go back and check the original painting to see if there's anything hidden in between the frame back and the mounting board. That could be the answer to your treasure hunt."

"Wow, thanks, Lorelei. That's a fantastic clue," I said. Inside my head I was doing cartwheels.

"Glad to help. Now, if you know anyone looking for a fabulous dining table, send them my way, please," she said.

"Shall do," I said, returning her bright smile.

Gertie and I practically bounced out of Lorelei's stall on the way back to see Ewan. He was deep in the midst of conversation with two prospective customers, haggling over both the side cabinet plus a set of candelabras. Ewan raised his eyebrows in a quick hello to us and then got right back to business with the men in front of him. We didn't want to disturb him and had also spied the cafeteria halfway down the other side of the building.

We made a beeline for sustenance.

"I would love a cuppa and a snack. Something sweet, like a cinnamon bun or a danish," Gertie said. "I can feel my blood-sugar level drop. This o'dark thirty stuff in the morning isn't good for my constitution."

I shot her a disapproving look. "Are you kidding? Early morning has the best light for painting, ever. I've lost track of the times I've been up at 4:30 a.m. to catch the sunrise and did a beautiful painting as a result."

We continued to walk, passing a lot of the vendors we had already stopped to visit. This really was a friendly bunch of people, and we even got waved at by some of the dealers who had tried to help us with our watercolor mystery. The show floor was busy, with probably at least five-thousand visitors today. Everyone was looking for a deal. Some clutched attic finds, convinced they'd be millionaires by the closing gong.

The jolly lady behind the cafeteria's counter was one of three people working to keep up with thirsty fairgoers. The line was three rows deep, and one could order tea and coffee, hot cocoa, bottled water, and an assortment of pre-wrapped pastries and sandwiches. Napkins were plentiful, and one certainly needed them for all the sugary delights the cafeteria was selling. The fair's owner, a large corporate conglomerate, had figured out that deals were best made when caffeine and sugar freely flowed through attendees' veins.

We loaded up with recyclable take-out trays, sugars, milks, and napkins, then headed back towards Ewan's stall. He was just waving off the last customer. "Ladies, you come bearing gifts, I see," he said.

"You bet, this should help. It's been a full day," I said, pressing a large danish and tea into his hand.

"Brilliant, cheers," he said, pretending to clink glasses with both of us.

We both hopped up on his rented barstools and sipped the hot liquid for a moment, neither Gertie nor I daring to ask why the velvet ropes on the antique chairs were undone. It was simply marvelous to take a load off one's feet after such a long walk around the arena.

"How is business?" Gertie asked.

"Really good," Ewan said. "I've sold about twelve pieces so far. That's why I come here every year. You cannot beat the level of expertise or business opportunities."

"We've found a dealer who thinks Aunt Edwina's painting may have a hidden message sandwiched in the back of the frame."

Ewan quickly swallowed a bite of danish. "Really? That would be quite a find. Maybe Aunt Edwina had a spare copy of the Magna Carta tucked away." He grinned.

Gertie snorted. "Hardly likely. It's not like she needed the money for a rainy day. She was well provided for as Lady Edwina."

He looked a bit sheepish. "Okay, then at least let's hope for some family letters, something juicy."

"I would settle for the full name of 'E.E.'," I said, finishing up my cinnamon bun. I could feel Ewan's eyes on me, and he pointed to his mouth. I frowned, then realized he was politely pointing out a bit of icing on my mouth. I wiped it quickly, and he nodded.

"Are you enjoying the fair?" he asked.

"We like the variety," Gertie said, jumping in, eager not to be the proverbial third wheel. Again.

A large gong sounded over the loudspeaker, followed by the announcement: "Sixty-minute warning, exhibitors, sixty-minute warning."

Ewan smiled. "Management knows we're long talkers, especially when we're haggling over the price of a side chair or a silver spoon. That's why they give us an hour to wrap things up. I've almost got my two chairs sold, but he's a Nervous Nellie buyer. Had to go check with his boss."

"You mean his wife," Gertie said with a grin. She looked around the stall. "You just leave everything here overnight?"

Ewan nodded. "Pretty much. I do trundle back and forth any small items that are easily lifted such as jewelry, hat pins, and snuff boxes, but the heavy items stay on site."

"They've got good security here?" I asked.

"That man in the high-visibility vest as we drove in? There's about thirty more of him crawling the grounds. The fair's management also hires some off-duty police, undercover folks, to be on the prowl for the light-fingered lot. It unfortunately happens in our trade, so we all watch out for each other. Stolen from one means likely sold to another, and no one wants to deal in stolen goods."

"Mr. Kilburn, I have a question for you about silver," Gertie said to Ewan.

"Did something catch your eye?" he asked.

"It was a silver coffee pot, and it was only £200 because I think the dealer believed it was just silverplate. However, I looked at the hallmarks on the bottom, and I think it's solid."

Ewan's eyebrows went up. "I didn't know you were into antiques, Gertie."

"I've dabbled over the years. Plus, in my former line of work I got to see a lot of silver. You know, up close in the biggest houses of them all."

"What did the hallmarks read?" he asked.

"It had an uncrowned lion, broken anchor, and the maker's mark H and T."

"That's for Hefner and Tilford in Mossmarleigh. They made lovely silver items. The uncrowned lion, full body, is the silver standard mark for .925 purity. The broken anchor stands for Mossmarleigh. The lower case 'e' stands for the year—there are charts you can find, and they change every twenty years or so—I have a guidebook here." He rummaged in his briefcase and looked up the letter, then showed Gertie the exact page. "Did it look like this?"

She nodded. "That's the one."

"Good. Then it's early nineteenth-century vintage." The way it all just rolled off his tongue was pretty impressive.

"You're sure?" she asked.

"Positive."

"Right, if what you're saying is true, then there's money to be made." She got a wild look in her eyes. "I'll be back before closing."

"Fancy that, your cousin having an eye for silver," Ewan observed as Gertie hustled away in search of her coffee pot.

"Gertie is surprising in many different ways," I said.

True to her reputation, Gertie was back in about half an hour, clutching a highly ornate, fluted silver coffee pot covered in a design of swans. She handed it to Ewan with a serious look on her face. "Tell me if I just wasted £200 or not. Please. Put me out of my agony."

"Well, let's have a wee look here," he said, taking the coffee pot from her and carefully turning it over in his hands. "It's in wonderful condition. Now, the rule is that every removable part needs to be properly stamped. The lid and the base are both stamped with the exact same markings, so that's a good thing. We're not looking at a piece that has a replacement lid, for example."

"What do you think it's worth?" she asked him.

Her question set Ewan back on his heels a bit. "Well, I'm no silver expert, but I do know this Mossmarleigh silversmith. I have seen this particular maker's swan design on some other pieces, but they were pincushions and salt sellers. This coffee pot is more of a larger item, up there with the platters and the tea services. Looking at how nicely the swans are engraved, and condition, well, probably £4,000 to £5,000."

Gertie looked at me, frantic. "Where's our vehicle? We should leave before the dealer realizes—"

Ewan wasn't finished with her yet. "Now, mind you, it would likely be worth £15,000 if you had the matching teapot, creamer bowl, and sugar bowl. This is probably part of a set. I take it the dealer had no other pieces?"

Gertie's face fell. "The complete set would've taken care of all of them."

I saw Ewan's face go quizzical.

"Her two-pounds donation to every one of her active churches in England," I explained.

"Ah, yes. Gertie's donation box penance is calling," he said. "Well, you're partway there with that coffee pot of yours."

She sighed. "Yes, and beggars can't be choosers."

***

6:00 p.m.

We stopped at the supermarket on the way back to Ewan's shop in Plumsden. Gertie, Ewan, and I then sat in the sloped alcove of his tiny office and munched on meat pies and spice cake. I'd been the one who'd insisted on a small tub of Greek salad to share amongst the lot of us, ensuring there was some semblance of vegetables in this hasty meal.

"Well, ladies, that was a long day, especially when you have the drive on either end of it," Ewan said.

"Thank goodness for your mountain men to help unload the big pieces. My back would not have taken that," Gertie said. This time she was perched on a low beach chair, the kind that got all tangled with wood and canvas. She'd spotted it at the back of his shop and claimed it with glee. The padded shoe inserts were not one hundred percent effective to stave off the effects of all the extreme standing and walking we'd done today.

Ewan stared down at his meat pie. "Well, it's not exactly the height of elegance, but it is food."

"I just had elegance. Aunt Edwina was the one who liked fancy parties and catering. Quite honestly, it's not my thing," I said.

"So we're bucking family tradition here?" he teased.

Gertie emitted a giggle. "Aunt Edwina was always trying to cram us into dresses and heels, kitting us out like debutantes. Much to her chagrin, we turned out to be a scruffy painter and a defrocked priest!"

None of us could stop laughing at that one. Especially not when Gertie's deck chair collapsed and turned her into a human sandwich, she the limp lettuce in the middle. It took all of us to extricate her into a sitting position again. It was like she'd suddenly grown three extra limbs.

"I thought I was a goner. Thank you for rescuing me," she said with a gasp.

"Oh, I nearly forgot," I said, after my next mouthful of Greek salad. I retrieved the five photos I'd purchased at the fair from my satchel. "What do you make of this lot, Ewan?"

He looked through the photos with a great deal of thought, hovering over the one of the sweet child, and then putting it side-by-side with the young woman. "My guess is that this is the child's mother. See the flowers in the background? They're the same. And the father was away serving in the military. You'd need an expert to tell you more. Try searching online for 'British Military Uniforms' and then attempt to date the photo that way."

"I just find it so sad. I had to rescue them. They were there by themselves in a box of postcards, somebody's family memories for sale," I lamented.

He emitted a polite cough. "I hate to tell you this, but there are thousands if not tens of thousands of photos just like this that never do get rescued. The younger generations tend not to see the relevance if their elders haven't labeled them properly."

"I didn't think you were supposed to label photographs," Gertie said.

"You're not," he said. "At least not with ink, pen, or marker. Lightly write on the back with pencil, scan them, and then put captions online. That's how you label photos as well as save the information for generations to come."

I shrugged. "Well, these particular photos are going to be on my personal mystery tour. I'd love to reunite them with their owner."

And thus we sat around munching our cold dinner, staring at our tired feet, and contemplating our busy day. Gertie's new silver coffee pot sat in the place of honor, front and center on Ewan's desk. My tired mobile phone was sitting right next to it, having shown literally fifty dealers Aunt Edwina's painting today. We planned to have a really good look at the original once we got back to Holgarth Hall tonight. We broke up our tiny gathering about 7:00 p.m., with promises of 'same place, same time' the next morning. There were at least fifty more dealers we could go talk to, hopefully in a less frenzied fashion.

Athena wearily trundled Gertie and I back. All was quiet at Holgarth Hall, and we were glad to see the latch on the petting zoo in place, all residents where they should be, quietly munching on the food properly assigned to them.

Chapter 19

——

"And now for the moment of truth we've waited for," I said as Gertie and I sat on one twin bed, Aunt Edwina's painting on the opposite one. The painting mocked us, daring us to find out more of its secrets. I held it up and looked closely at the wood tooling in the top right corner of the frame. "You know, I think that dealer was right. There's a very fine line that could be concealing a hidden compartment. It could also be just for the frame's joinery, but it's a little bit off corner, so that makes me wonder."

"I'm surprised Lorelei picked up on it," Gertie said. "It's hard to see something that fine on a picture, no matter how big it's blown up."

"I need something small to pry this apart. Nail scissors, a file, hairpin. Something flat and tough."

Gertie handed me a pocketknife, handle towards me, sharp little blade on the open end pointing towards her. "Give this a go," she suggested.

Gertie's pocketknife worked perfectly. The frame pried apart with a little bit of twisting, and we soon set our eyes upon the various parts of the sandwich that made up a framed water-color piece of art. Our new dealer friend's hunch was right. Out from the stack of thin card, paper stock, and glass fell three envelopes tied together with thin, pink ribbon. We both gasped. Another stereo moment.

"It was hidden behind the mat so no one would see them," I said.

"Do you think Aunt Edwina wanted us to find them?" Gertie asked.

"Hard to say. But knowing Aunt Edwina, they'll have something to do with her mystery and the treasure hunt." I turned the small packet of letters over in my hand and saw a faded kiss stain in a mid-tone pink lipstick on the envelope. It was just the color that a young lady would wear, not siren red, not pale and uninteresting. Beneath the kiss stain were three words: *treasure us always.*

"I think Aunt Edwina knew the secrets and wanted us to find them. Why else would she give you the very painting that's concealing the letters? Do you remember when you first saw this painting at her house?" Gertie asked.

I shook my head. "I hadn't seen it before the wedding. And I would've remembered because it's got distinctive brush-strokes." I peered at it closer.

My hands were nearly trembling as I pulled at the thin pink ribbon and undid the limp bow squashed flat over time.

When the three letters came tumbling out of their ribbon, we saw that each one was stamped on the address side as *'Undeliverable. Please Return to Sender. 1946.'*

"Are you going to read them?" Gertie demanded in an impatient voice.

I handed her back the pocketknife after slitting the envelope tops. "Yes, and we should be prepared for a host of different things. Letters hidden this long usually contain deep family secrets."

Someone had treasured these letters, treasured the sender and the recipient, yet one of them never received the other's correspondence. I carefully opened the first letter and read aloud from Aunt Edwina's distinctive, fine handwriting:

June 1944

Dear E.:
You feel like a million miles away, yet I know our
hearts are still right next to each other. Be safe, be
calm, and remember I'm always here waiting for you.
The light in my life turned on when I met you.
All my love, E.

I had to comment. "If these were written by Aunt Edwina, then she was quite young."

We both read the letter again. Gertie and I looked at each other and didn't really know what to say. I opened the next one:

July 1944

Dear E.:
I sat under our oak tree at Greymore today and saw
where you carved our initials in the bark, a lasting
testament to our love and commitment to each other.
I miss you with all my heart. I am waiting for you,
even though you said not to. It's the least I can do
to repay you for the bravery you give in our coun-
try's service.
All my love, E.

There was one final letter and I opened it in haste:

August 1944

Dear E.:
I miss you, my love. My world stopped turning since
you left two years ago. Do you have any news of when
you're coming home? Christmas leave would be so
wonderful. I don't mean to cause you anguish, but I've

had no news for so long, and I do worry about you.
Did you get the socks, chocolates and toothbrush I
sent to you?
All my love, E.

"Granddad's first name was Bruce," Gertie said. "I wonder if 'E' was a friend or even a tenant on the Greymore estate." She picked up one of the letters and held it against her heart. "Frankly though, I think these are love letters Aunt Edwina sent to someone before she married Granddad."

"So why not let sleeping dogs lie? Why would she want us to find these and perhaps risk upsetting our family?" I asked.

"Confessions from the grave? Maybe enough time has passed that it doesn't matter anymore?"

Gertie made two good points. I had another, much better, reason to offer. "Or maybe this is something of a mystery that she couldn't figure out during her lifetime, and she's passing the torch to us. Those Christmases, all the time she played riddles with us, getting us to figure out the anagrams ... she was seeing if we'd be up to it when we were older."

Gertie gave me a steely eyed stare. "Then I suppose, cousin, that we passed the test."

"Exactly. All we need now is to figure out who 'E.E.' is." I sighed. "Plus whatever Aunt Edwina's 'H.P.' key opens in Plumsden. We're no closer on that front."

"What did the riddle say?" she asked.

"Go to the most knowledgeable person. In England, that's either the priest, the postmaster, or the pub owner. They know everything about everybody."

We both had the same idea at once and exclaimed in unison: "Clint at The King's Arm pub!"

We went to sleep that night and my head was spinning. My brain swirled with the endless possibilities of what lay ahead based on the road we'd just dug up from the past.

Chapter 20

———

Waverly-on-Sea Antiques Fair. Next Day.

We caught the light-fingered woman red-handed. And boy, did the thief have a good disguise. He'd cleverly made himself up as a heavyset elderly woman using a walker. Everybody gave 'her' a wide berth as she walked up and down every aisle of the antiques fair. She wore a heavy overcoat, despite it being a bit of a warmer day without rain. Nobody ever questioned her leather handbag or the fact that she sometimes stopped in the middle of the stall to sit down on her walker's seat as she panted, trying to catch her breath. The thief played on the fact that everyone had sympathy for the elderly and double that for someone needing a walker.

Except this individual wasn't elderly, nor did he need a walker.

It burned me right up seeing the clever scam.

I happened to be walking past when I saw the person sitting on her walker, brakes on, laboring away with her breathing.

It wasn't that which caught my eye. It was the fact that the cuffs of her overcoat were so wide, and one got caught in the brake handle of her walker. I nearly went over to help her but then saw a tiny brass ornament fall out of her sleeve. Once I saw hairy arms, I knew what was going on. I quietly flagged down a man in a high-visibility vest and told him what I'd just observed.

"Thank you, ma'am, there's been a ring of them here operating for a couple of years now. We've been trying to break it up but just can't seem to catch them," he said. He spoke into the radio attached to his shoulder.

A garbled response came back; all I understood was 'ten-four'.

"If you need me again, I'm over at Ewan Kilburn's stall," I said.

"Very good, ma'am. Thank you for stepping forward as a witness. It's good citizens like yourself who prevent the ruination of these fairs for the rest of us."

I raced back to Ewan's stall and told him what I'd seen, recounting it in a slightly breathless version. He looked at me, his eyes open wide with amazement.

"I lost three hat pins this morning. I'd be curious to know what's inside her leather handbag. Imagine tripping around gaining sympathy when you're really pilfering sellers' wares. Disgusting," he said.

"After having just lost my dear grandmother, it bothers me even more that he's impersonating an elderly woman. I'll bet he's thirty years old and wearing a bunch of cosmetic prosthetics," I said.

Gertie suddenly reappeared, a swan-embossed silver creamer jug in her hand.

"Well, you certainly look full of the joys of life," Ewan said. "Is that another solid silver find?"

She nodded. "I'm on a quest now."

"What are the hallmarks on that one?" I asked.

"Same as the coffee pot. The lion, the broken anchor, the H and T, and the lower case 'e'."

"I think she's on a roll," he said. "Hello, hello. Clive, what have you got there?"

Clive was apparently the largest security man on site; he was bursting through his high-visibility vest. Tight in his grip was the thief disguised as an elderly woman, wig and overcoat now off, and leather handbag slung haphazardly over the burly guard's shoulder. Clive looked like an official who'd gone dumpster diving behind a designer fashion shop.

"You said you were missing three hat pins? Are these the ones?" he asked Ewan. Clive rummaged through the thief's handbag and brought out a handful of them.

"Yes, those are the ones. And add me to the list of people who want to press charges against this thief. It ruins business for all of us," Ewan said. He gestured for Clive to keep the hat pins as evidence.

The thief, a mid-height, muscular man, wore a skin-toned bodysuit to give him extra midsection weight, thick calves, and a back hump. He scowled at Ewan. "You lot have just ruined my children's birthdays," he said. "I could have made close to four-hundred quid on this stuff. Now I can't afford to buy them gifts."

"I doubt it. More likely that loot was going to pubs and racetracks," Ewan shot back. "What about all the dealers who depend on their sales to put food on their own table? Your argument holds no water, mate."

The police arrived and started talking to Clive and the thief.

Gertie stepped forward. "Would you mind taking your shakedown somewhere away from our stall? We're trying to run a reputable business here."

The police and Clive apologized, then complied. After the thief was handcuffed, they headed towards the exit where a police van already had two other suspects inside.

"Well, imagine that. Fresh off the heels of her wedding, and Julie's already a world-class crime fighter," Gertie said with pride.

I caught the hurt look in Ewan's eyes. "I didn't know you were married, Julie," he said.

"I'm not. She's just teasing you," I said.

The poor man looked even more confused. He shot a darting glance at my left fourth finger and seemed to breathe a sigh of relief when he saw there were no rings encircling it.

"Your ribbon? Where did that come from?" I asked him. He had a long, fancy ribbon with streamers hanging off his sports jacket pocket.

He slapped a hand over his chest. "I almost forgot to tell you. Our stall won Best in Show."

"No kidding," Gertie said. "I must've missed the judging."

"The judges come around before the gates open to the public on the first day of the fair. That way, everyone's still got full inventory plus the stalls are at their finest."

"Do you get a write up for publicity?" I asked.

He nodded. "We'll be in the local paper as well as in the dealers' magazine that goes out all over the UK next month."

"Well done, Ewan," Gertie said. "I think you should wear that ribbon all week." It was a bit of an ask, considering the ribbon was two feet long and made up of a combination of red, blue, and white streamers all terminating in a rosette that was wider than his head in diameter.

"I think we need to change the subject," he said with a grin. He turned to me. "Thanks. You've done the industry a great service today, Miss Fincher."

I noticed how he emphasized the *miss* on my name. It made me feel warm inside. I was now used to having the gentle

Scottish man around, sharing ideas, jokes, and interesting finds with him. What a change it was from walking on egg-shells around my faux husband. It was a genuine—correction, wonderful—relief and quite frankly, I didn't want the coziness or the feelings of safety and belonging to ever end.

***

Plumsden. 11:00 a.m. Tuesday, the Following Week.

We gave Ewan the Monday to get settled back in his shop and unpack from the antiques fair in Waverly-on-Sea. But bright and early on Tuesday, we were there with bells on, as my father liked to say. Today was the day we were going to see Jalaal Kahanis, Ewan's painter friend. The nice thing about having one's own antiques shop was that the hours were fairly flexible. Everybody knew it was a small business with eccentric clientele and frequent visits to far-flung estate sales. All Ewan had to do was change the voicemail, put a sign on the door saying 'early closing day', set the alarm, and we were good to go.

We pulled into a tidy little farm about ten miles away in the village of East Tysonford. There was a large weeping willow in the front yard hiding a charming, whitewashed English cottage covered in mauve wisteria. Athena crunched over the gravel as she looped around the circular drive and pulled up near the front door.

"What a lovely place!" Gertie exclaimed. "I used to have a cottage like this before I lost my black gown."

Ewan shook his head and grinned. "Your black gown? Seriously?"

"Come on, you two. Let's not keep Jalaal waiting," I said.

It was a bit like unpackaging Julie-the-human-pretzel consigned to Athena's third row. In the scramble to get Norris out of the van, one of his paws had scratched a long line in the second-row bench seat. Lance had insisted on sending it out for repair, and as it was a rare 1963 vintage, we had no idea when we would get the bench seat back for the van. So Gertie just told all her passengers to mind the gap.

Because it was a wide one.

I had Aunt Edwina's watercolor painting in hand. Ewan stepped forward to the cottage and rapped on the door, using the iron knocker in the shape of a ram's head.

I was about to ask about the choice of door hardware, but the bleating of a rather large herd of sheep in a nearby field answered my question.

The sound of a madly barking dog punctuated the near proximity.

The door was snatched open, and there he stood before us: Jalaal Kahanis, round glasses askew and toes sticking out of his knitted slippers. His jeans were faded and torn, and his lumberjack shirt nearly swallowed him up because it was two sizes too big. The paint splashed all over his shirt made me feel right at home. The house smelled of oil, turpentine, and other mineral spirits. When we walked in, it was immediately obvious why. He had filled the entire front sitting room with newly painted, drying portraits of brown-and-white Springer Spaniels.

His model, having performed her greeting duties, retreated to the comfort of her cozy wicker basket.

"Ewan and company!" He said it with a warm tone in his voice, as he stood aside like a gallant man and ushered us further inside the house. "Come in, come in. Welcome to my humble abode. Don't mind the paint pots. Oh, and please don't sit over there because you'll disturb my brush-cleaning assembly line ..."

"Thank you for seeing us, Jalaal. I know you're very busy," Ewan said.

"Busy? That's an understatement. Do you know I have five commissioned pieces to finish by the end of the summer? Five. Count them, five."

"I can see that. Interesting subject matter," I said, my eyes looking over the dog subjects he had on easels surrounding us. The dogs were all in different poses, some outside paddling in a lake, one posed in the studio, one out on a walk, one running in the woods. It was almost eerie seeing so much of a repetitive subject that was, well, canine.

"I know. I have a massive order from the owner who lives in a drafty old castle up in Scotland. He bought a few of my landscapes from Ewan, and that's where I got the referral." Jalaal slung his least paint-splattered arm around Ewan's shoulder. "I'm very obliged for the work, starving artist and all, etcetera. Anything I can do to repay the favor, just ask. Please."

"Thanks, we're looking for your help identifying a mystery artist. He has the initials 'E.E.', and he works in watercolor," Ewan explained, stepping over to take the 'E.E.' painting from me.

"And you'd like to know if I'm familiar with this scene?" Jalaal asked. "Easy. This scene has been painted by hundreds, if not thousands, of art students in the area as a component of their first-year studies. It's classic reflective pond stuff. Instructors like to show them reflection concepts and how to capture water movement with various types of foliage surrounding the pond."

"Okay, thanks. Do you know who 'E.E.' was?"

Jalaal took a close look at the painting. Gertie and I had re-sandwiched the contents and cobbled the frame back together once we'd retrieved all the letters. "Hmmm. This is better than most, I will say that. When did you say this was from? The 1940s?"

"We didn't say. You have a good eye." I gave him an encouraging smile.

Jalaal continued. "The reason I assumed it was the 1940s was because he's written that in one of the trees. See, look here, it's painted as a bark striation and knot in one of the tree branches."

We all crowded round to see what Jalaal was pointing out.

"He's right. I can see it!" Gertie said.

Jalaal continued his analysis. "So, you've got a mysterious painter who likes having fun with his audiences by hiding things in his paintings. Do you have any more?"

"I think we will come into possession of some of them soon," I said.

"His style is unique, and he's also very good," Jalaal said. "I think I have a book here somewhere on famous anonymous painters. Let me rummage for a moment. I'll go check in the back."

Jalaal didn't say whether we should follow or not, so we all trooped along behind him. We went down the hall where various oily rags and smocks were hung on coat pegs. Out back we could hear a parrot squawk, and in the midst of us going down the hallway, we heard the sheep bleat again.

This artist had a small art-supply mail-order business at the back of the cottage. This was my jam. I zoomed right in on the elusive sable hair brush set I'd been coveting for months but could not find anywhere, including online. "I've been looking for one of these for so long!. How much?" I was a child in a candy store.

"Those ones ... wholesale price should be on the back. I make fifteen percent markup, but for you I'll take zero commission just because you're with Ewan."

"Jalaal, that's very kind, however, I wouldn't dream of taking away your livelihood here," I said.

He looked up from the pile of books in his shop and grinned. "Don't think twice about it. If Ewan hadn't put me onto the dog man, I wouldn't be in this cottage, let alone have enough to eat every day. They're yours, wholesale from me to you."

"Well, that's awfully generous, thank you," I said.

"Aha! I knew I had it here," Jalaal murmured. He held up a book still in its shrink-wrap. It was called *Anonymous & Timeless Watercolorists of the Twentieth-Century*.

Jalaal tore off the plastic wrap and went straight to the index. We all read it, in black and white: The painter 'E.E.' was profiled in chapter one and was also mentioned in the introduction plus the epilogue.

"Looks like he was pretty well-known," Jalaal said. "Like I said, unique style, and I like his work. It's a shame he didn't go public when he was active."

I scanned page one of the first chapter as I read over Jalaal's shoulder. I gasped and then read aloud. "Anonymous painter

'E.E.' was only active from 1937 through 1941. It is assumed that he perished in World War Two."

Gertie and I made eye contact.

"Those lovely letters? Aunt Edwina was sending them to a dead man," I whispered.

***

The King's Arm Pub. Plumsden. Midday.

Plumsden's pub was a popular spot with the locals. It was a black-and-white, timber-framed building, done in the Tudor style that was favored by tourists. This one, however, really was built in the 1500s and had the sagging eaves and doorframe to prove it. The little blue plaque to the right of the front door denoted it as a listed property, meaning that the owner would have to get planning permission to change a single flagstone on its front steps. I always thought that this was the way it should be, as did Gertie and Ewan. England's heritage had to be protected for us as well as for future generations.

The pub sign was maintained with great reverence. Oddly, it showed a grinning medieval king flexing his bare bicep, hence, 'The King's Arm'.

"Before I learned its peculiar history, I always thought this pub had a spelling mistake on its sign," Ewan said.

"Ah, but you soon found out that was wrong," I said.

He nodded. "A medieval king once challenged his favorite knight to an arm-wrestling contest here. Hence, the arm. Singular."

Gertie grinned. "I think it's hilarious. The rest of similarly named pubs are called 'The King's Arms' meaning a heraldic suggestion and reference to something the king did for the village, such as grant it a market."

"Look at you, just a fountain of historical facts," Ewan teased.

"She has to be, to keep up with you," I said back in jest.

The three of us headed for a booth way at the back, away from the noise and darts game up front. The plastic-encased menus were on the table, and I quickly typed in an order on my phone and texted it to Gertie. Ewan did the same. Gertie then went over to the bar to place our order. For efficiency's sake, there was only table service to deliver food, not request it. Ewan and I watched her engage the bartender in animated conversation. Clint Yamamoto was a middle-aged man, slightly portly, with salt-and-pepper hair. He wore a fashionably untucked men's shirt plus jeans. He was well-known in Plumsden, having owned the pub for over twenty-eight years.

"What do you think those two are talking about?" Ewan asked me, looking at Gertie over at the bar.

"Probably asking if Clint knows anything about the value of a silver coffee pot and creamer set," I joked.

Ewan leaned back in his seat and laced his fingers behind his head. "My goodness, ever since I met you two my life has taken some unexpected turns. What with a mysterious painter, taking down a thief at the antiques fair, riding in an ancient— sorry, vintage—van, wartime love letters, and learning all about a defrocked priest. And that's just this week!"

"At least with Gertie and I, you can't ever say it's boring."

We looked back over at the bar. Gertie was busy regaling Clint with some joke, and he roared with laughter as he filled a glass with dark ale. We saw her bring Aunt Edwina's brass key out of her pocket and put it on the counter, as she was busy telling him her story.

Clint stopped laughing. He looked at the key, then put down the glass of ale with its frothy top. He looked her straight in the eye. They exchanged a few serious words, and then Gertie turned around, motioning us up to the bar.

"You two are never going to believe this," Gertie started. "Tell them, Clint."

The bartender put his hands on the counter and leaned forward, almost as if he was sharing a conspiratorial secret. "Folks, it's like this. Lady Edwina Greymore was a regular in my pub, the third Saturday of each month. She sat in that large booth over there with four of her friends, all the high-society ladies who do good things for our community. She always told me that they didn't want to meet at a fancy restaurant because that would defeat the purpose."

"The purpose of what?" I asked.

"The purpose of their monthly Sherry Club," Clint answered. "Most of the ladies were from grand houses, and they had their own private stock to drink while they were here, no doubt acquired on their global travels. You see, the brass key that Lady Edwina left to you opens her private liquor cabinet here at my pub. I'll show you."

He took us into a locked room at the back, one that had thirty different substantial private cabinets, each with two doors inset with elegant, diamond-paned glass. He slid the key into Aunt Edwina's cabinet and turned it. The small doors easily swung open, and inside we saw three unopened bottles of fancy sherry, an envelope, plus a watercolor painting. We opened the envelope propped up beside the bottles and found another clue and key inside. Upon closer examination, we noted that the artist 'E.E.' had signed the watercolor painting.

Chapter 21

——

Next Morning.

Her Majesty treads its lumber most days in her lair
This town built strong arms to protect her with care
All the craftsmen print runners, fine ones, they'd say
But their horse's color wasn't known until the day
Large hands and strong backs meant a sure success
A seven-color man gave his wife a gorgeous dress

"This riddle's a bit tougher," Gertie said over breakfast. This morning she was clad in a seafoam-green floral dress and wore a darker eyeshadow. Her hair was clamped back in a severe bun.

"I don't know about that makeup, Gertie," I said.

"It's a smoky eye. All the rage with the fashion models."

I shook my head. "It looks like a black eye. People might think we've been brawling."

"Piffle." She went on studying her vintage map book. "Large hands and strong backs. Hmmm. Perhaps a place that made war munitions, tanks, or airplanes. Aunt Edwina's age group would mean a big factory in World War Two."

"And look at the craftsmanship she describes. A horse's color not known until the day. What do you suppose that means?"

"Printing runners. Tablecloths for a special dinner, perhaps?" Gertie asked.

"For horses? Look, it mentions horse's color not known until the day. The day of what?"

"She describes the craft in the final two lines: large hands, strong backs, seven-color man ..."

"Gorgeous dress. It's fabric printing of some kind."

She thought on it and searched a few things on her phone. "Seven-color man: note man, not machine. This is a craft, and a precise one at that if he was handmaking something good enough for his wife to wear."

"Printing runners? How about physical runners, like race-horses?" I suggested.

She nodded then turned her phone to me. "The annual derby for racehorses. The silk printers had the stock scarves ready to go, all except the color of the racehorse in the center. They didn't print that until the winner was announced on the wireless."

"You're kidding." I read exactly what she'd just described on her phone. "That's amazing. Who would have thought they went to all that trouble, way before our age of automation and just-in-time inventory?"

"It was a different world back then."

"I completely agree," I said. "So what town made armaments and had craftsmen doing silk printing back in World War Two?"

Gertie typed furiously on her phone once more. A few more taps, a minor cough as she scrolled, and then the answer popped up: *Ludring*.

"Isn't that near Bexleyheath?"

She nodded. "The town where a famous fabric designer built his home."

"So that's all well and good, but what about Her Majesty stepping the boards? A theater?"

"It says 'treads its lumber'," Gertie corrected. "Likely it supplied wood used in one of the royal palaces."

This time I got out my phone and tried to find the proof. It was amazing what tiny phones could locate. "You're right. Ludring did have a lumber industry."

"The world continues to get smaller, with every corner we look into." She grinned.

"How far do we have to go this time?" I asked.

Gertie checked. "According to the search engine, about an hour north and slightly west by car. Vintage van, in our case."

Her plate was clean, and I just popped the last bit of toast in my mouth. I had so enjoyed the homemade jam that Holgarth Hall offered. It would be hard to leave this place, mainly because of its eccentric owner and his sidekick.

"Come on, then," I said. "We should get on the road and try the next key."

***

"I'm going to miss the menagerie at Holgarth Hall," I said to Gertie as we packed Athena.

"Me too. Oh, Lance told me that guests number fourteen and fifteen arrive tonight."

"I'm sure they'll get a warm, yet odd, welcome."

"We survived Lettucegate. Maybe the next guests will have Carrotgate," she said.

"Or Beetrootgate," we heard behind us. We both turned to see Lance there, wearing a housekeeping apron and holding a feather duster. "I've come to get rooms ready for the next guests. Not to rush you, mind," he hastily added. "It's been loads of fun having you here at Holgarth."

"Will you survive without us, Lance?" I teased.

He saluted me. "With a stiff upper lip, Miss Fincher. You have my word."

We had a good laugh.

"Algy's doing a video chat with some horticultural subcommittee, so he asked that I see you off."

"It was good of him to think of us," I said.

"Of course." He caught us staring at his apron and duster. "Not exactly the look I should embrace."

"To each his own, my friend," Gertie said in a jolly voice. "Shoulders back, head held high, and soldier on."

Lance looked glum. "About the only thing I can do with Algy in command." He visibly brightened. "I nearly forgot!" He reached into his pocket, took out a folded brochure, and handed it to me. I saw it was an ad for a military memorabilia shop in London.

"If you have time, go and see them; the owner's son is a mate of mine. Or you could email him those photos from the antiques fair and ask him to date them for you. Just mention my name."

"Well, that's very kind of you, Lance. Thank you," I said. "I would love to get these pictures back into the correct family's hands."

"Best of luck," he said.

And then it got rather awkward, because Lance was obviously no good at goodbyes. Actually, he wasn't good at many things according to Algy, but Gertie and I both sensed that the older brother overemphasized that more than he should.

Lance politely put out his right hand but was quickly enveloped in a hug by Gertie.

"We'll tell all our friends about you, and we hope that your bed-and-breakfast is a smashing success!" she said in her jolliest voice.

Lance looked slightly soporific, but hugged her back with a firm hold. I offered him a hug as well.

"Right, now we're off," Gertie announced. She was always good at making a situation final when nobody else really knew how. I suppose that was the priestly training in her.

Lance waved his goodbyes, and we trundled down the road.

We were already going less than a crawl, but Gertie slowed down even more.

I looked at her sideways. "Okay, what did you forget in the room?"

"Nothing. I'm just wondering if Aunt Edwina is playing tricks with us. She knew we would go after the riddle first, and just assume that the painting would go along with the riddle. Do you think that's how it works with all of her clues?"

I had already taken a picture of the painting on my phone in case we had to do the tours with the second watercolor just as we had done with the first. I brought it up on screen and studied it. I saw an aerial view of a large factory, with many intersecting roads in the southwest corner of the painting.

"You know, I think it is true to the riddle," I said. "She's guiding us towards something, so why would she want us going in two different directions?"

"Just checking. I tend to agree, but reserve the right to change that opinion if we find some more mysterious numbers hidden in that painting," Gertie said.

I peered super close at my screen. Looking for hidden numbers wasn't something I'd gotten around to yet. "Good call. I did miss something." Right there on my phone were sideways digits hidden in the corrugated tin roof on one of the buildings. It was faint, almost too small to see, but it was there. No, it wasn't a secret message to the invading Axis powers, but rather the artist's own code to the woman he painted for: 42-03-29.

I read the numbers out to Gertie, and her eyes grew wide.

"What do you reckon they mean?" I asked. "Could it signify the day they met?"

"Or the day he left for war?" she asked.

"Or the tail number from his airplane or serial number on his uniform?"

"I like tail number. That's a good one," she said. "I'll bet that Ludring has its own Maude Livingstone and Family History Society. They're our best bet when we go hunting for the key's lock."

"Sounds a good plan. We should also take apart the frame on the second watercolor."

"You must be joking!" Gertie said, astounded.

"I'm dead serious. There's the same join in the frame's wood as with the first watercolor. I think there are more goodies inside this painting for us to discover."

Gertie pressed down on the accelerator.

Chapter 22

Singed Pie Cottage, Ludring.

The fiftyish woman at the bed-and-breakfast's front counter looked like a sloth. She moved just as slowly, and her stringy, sandy-colored hair framed her face like an overgrown bowl cut. Her nails were cut right to the quick, and her lip gloss was the palest of pale. Her porcelain skin was so light that she appeared to be a translucent ghost.

"One room, two twin beds, yeah?" she asked in a non-hospitable, non-Ludring accent; perhaps she was from an industrial area.

"That's correct," I said. I'd left Gertie inside Athena guarding our belongings out in the parking lot. The house sat at the bottom of the street in a dark dip, a back road. The town was bustling and gave off a can-do vibe. Unfortunately, our host did not. She was of the cannot, won't, and tell-somebody-who-cares variety.

"£89 a night plus tax. Breakfast is seven till ten each morning. No pets allowed. You don't have any pets with you?"

This perfunctory, pablumy welcome was so different from the warmth that Algy and Lance had exuded. This woman was showing us all the hospitality of a damp cardboard box.

"No pets. And where is your parking, please?" I asked.

She jerked a thumb behind her. "Around back. £10 per night extra."

I could see her actually ringing up the parking charges in her mind. It wasn't a fancy house by any means, certainly not a manor home. This was just a single-family home, probably an empty nest with a couple of rooms to rent out because the children had all left.

Bed-and-breakfasts were wonderful places for people to make a little extra income. But for the side hustle to really be successful, the proprietor had to genuinely want people in her home. This woman appeared to be oblivious to all but the money exchanging hands.

"Rooms are cleaned once a day sometime between noon and four, so if you could please be out of the room at those times, it is best all round, yeah?"

Yeah, you are a drip!

Fortunately, I had enough self-control to stop myself from saying it out loud.

"Very well. We'll park around back and get settled, then," I said.

I doubt she would have noticed if I sent a herd of monkeys up the stairs followed by a boisterous unicorn.

She looked up from her rock-climbing magazine. That would explain the faded scars on her knuckles. "That suits."

"Oh, do you climb?" I asked.

"I used to, before my accident." The chill slightly improved in the room.

"Oh, I'm sorry you're unwell," I offered.

She shuddered. "The line broke, and I fell fifty feet. Luckily I was wearing a helmet."

What does one say to that? I felt very awkward indeed. "Well, at least you're still standing here today."

She nodded and went back to her magazine.

I beetled back outside to Athena as fast as possible.

＊＊

Once we'd brought our luggage into our room, I told Gertie all about the front desk clerk. "It was like I couldn't say anything right at all. I tried to show interest in her rock climbing and obviously that just reminded her of bad memories."

Gertie gave me a steely gaze. "When I was preaching, there were a few people I just couldn't reach. It didn't matter how much I tried, some were just outside the realm of reason. Off in their own little worlds, and it was sad, because some of those worlds were chockablock with sorrow and grief."

"So what does one say to people like that?" I asked.

"Let them wallow in themselves for a bit, and hope they turn turnaround. The really tough cases simply walk away, and you don't ever see them again."

"That's sad." I pulled out the mysterious family photos I'd bought at the antiques fair. "I wonder if this family was in disarray and that's why these photos were discarded."

Gertie put an arm around me. "Do buck up, dear. You don't know that's the truth yet. Plus, it's a lovely, warm day outside. Carpe diem and all that!"

I smiled at her. "I do appreciate your positive enthusiasm."

"And you can have more of it as soon as you put the kettle on. Do I spy some Scottish shortbread over there on the side table?"

"I'll split it with you."

"After my shower." She muttered something about the hot sun beating down on her through Athena's vast windscreen as we drove.

Sixteen minutes later we sat at the desk, Gertie in the comfortable easy chair and me at the desk chair, munching on shortbread and contemplating our next move. I set my eyes on the watercolor painting and, without a word, Gertie pulled out her pocketknife and handed it to me. I went to work prying the frame apart at the little line where we could see the join. Sure enough, as the sandwiched parts in their frame came apart, we were rewarded by two items that fell out onto the desk. The first was a small scrap of calico fabric. This particular design was an intertwined set of stems and flowers. The next item that we were bestowed with was a letter, postmarked 1942, in an envelope marked *To Edwina Greymore, Greymore Hall.*

"Could this be what I think it is?" I asked.

The envelope was already slit open at the top, and I pulled out the folded letter inside. I read aloud:

1942

Dearest Edwina.

Seeing you when I was on leave was the highlight of my time away from the airfield. Our time together was much too short. But the defense of our country is paramount. The defense of this very bedrock upon which our island rests must come first and foremost above any personal desires.

I shall write to you as often as I can, as often as the censors allow. For now, I remain in your heart as you are in mine.

Love from E.

"Okay, so not 'E.E.' He just called himself 'E.' Why drop the second vowel?" I asked Gertie.

"Likely because it was his last name, and they didn't need to use it. It's from 'E' to 'E.'"

"It could've been short for a nickname too, you know. And why the calico?" I asked. The piece of fabric was heavier and of quality. The printing on the fabric was perfect, and the bold pattern really stood out against the wood grain of the desk.

"The riddle implied silk. Maybe the business also did calico and other fabrics," I said.

"What do you want to do next?" Gertie asked.

"Go to the post office and ask about this key." I checked my watch. "They clean the rooms here sometime between noon and four each day, and trust me, it's not a good idea for us to be here at that time."

"A warning from a recalcitrant front desk clerk?" Gertie asked.

"Indeed. She's very odd. Kind of like the girl in school that you want to make friends with because she's all by herself, but you really don't know what to say."

"Maybe that's why we should try harder to talk to her," Gertie said.

"I don't know about that. She's pretty firm on where she thinks the world should be."

"Okay, so we'll take the key and go to the post office?"

I picked up my coat and looked around the room. Slight panic. "Wait a minute. Where is the third suitcase, the one with all the money?"

"I left it in Athena," she said.

"Gertie, that's a lot of money."

"There is no way they'd make a fast getaway lugging all those coins. This place doesn't even have a bell cart like Holgarth's or the Fizzleywick Hotel."

I picked up our room key and put it on the same ring as the key from Aunt Edwina's envelope in Plumsden. "You live dangerously, cousin."

She shook her head. "Not as dangerously as someone who's about to leave the room without street shoes on." She sniggered.

I looked down. Then I rolled my eyes. "I'm still breaking in my latest sandals, so I put on my cheap flip-flops when I got into the room." I liked flip-flops because they protected you from whatever germs were on the carpet or the bathroom floor. I even wore them in the shower. Problem was, one had to be super careful when the water was running because it got very slippery if there was no anti-slip surface at the bottom of the stall. I'd once narrowly avoided a pretty scary back injury by yanking half the shower curtain down from its rail because I'd skidded on the slick surface. Never again would I be that foolish.

But proper street shoes for our next excursion would be a good idea.

Shoes donned, we clambered back into Athena and trundled off to Ludring town center, using the route to Dartford. Gertie found a skookum parking stall and grabbed it before somebody else struck gold. Parking anywhere in England was always a challenge. It just wasn't designed for so many vehicles, nor for ones with engines. Little villages and towns grew up with horse-drawn carriages, carts, and wagons; the advent of the motorcar era brought a whole new set of challenges to everyone and everywhere on our lovely island.

The Ludring post office was one of the largest in the county, offering banking, mail, bill payment, licenses, and money-sending services. It also dabbled in travel insurance and tickets. A thin, nervous woman in her sixties, waist-length hair in a thick braid, was alone at the front counter. Her counter's brass sign read 'Miss Primrose Smears', a rather unfortunate name if one ever did exist. The line below her name read 'Postmistress', so Gertie and I both knew she was the woman we needed to see.

"Good afternoon," I said, striding up to the counter with Gertie beside me. I saw Primrose sit up ramrod straight, stiffen her back, and literally lean away from us. I couldn't fathom why because I was smiling, not frowning, like Aunt Edwina always insisted. Then I remembered. *The smoky eye.*

I looked over at Gertie and saw that the warm sun had now melted some of her fresh dark-grey eyeshadow, which now ran down the creases of her eyelids, over the corners of her eyes, and into a couple of tiny rivers leading down to her cheeks. Gertie looked like a Halloween partier with a hangover, not someone emulating a supermodel's fancy eye makeup. In fact, it now looked like she had two black eyes, and I could see that Miss Smears was contemplating whether they were self-inflicted or if I had something to do with Gertie's apparent injuries.

I stood in front of Gertie to block the view. "Good morning, we're wondering if this key opens a box here." I placed the key in my open palm, now separated from our room key.

Miss Smears took the key from me with very guarded fingers. I'm sure by this point in time she was extremely grateful that she was sitting behind a shield of bulletproof glass. She couldn't help but look around me and get another glimpse of Gertie, all eager and leaning forward, yet completely oblivious to the shiners on her face.

Miss Smears cleared her throat. "Well, I don't recognize this key. All of our post office keys are much smaller. This one looks like it opens a padlock of some type, not something that would be on the door of one of our boxes." She spoke in a shaky, nervous tone.

"Oh dear." I sighed. Then Gertie came around to face the counter herself.

"Do you any idea where we could find something that it would fit into?" Gertie asked.

Miss Smears took one last look at the key before handing it back through the small opening where one normally passed credit cards or bills. She shook her head. "I am sorry. You could ask someone at the Ludring DIY store, perhaps? They might be able to assist." She made a big show looking around both of us to see who else was waiting in her queue. Luckily for her, there were three other people, one of whom was clearing his throat as if he wanted to get on with his day.

"Well, thank you. I suppose we'll be on our way." I scrambled to put the key back in my purse and managed to get it caught on my combination wallet/phone case strap. Out it came, and because I'd left it half unzipped, the phone came loose, somehow turned on, and clattered out onto the counter, skittling under the partition and ending up right under Miss Smears's nose.

She saw my phone's unusual screen background: the second watercolor.

Miss Smears issued a brief smile. "Oh, that's the old armaments factory that was once here in Ludring. Are you a social historian?" There was something about the way she said 'historian'. Something about days gone by obviously piqued her interest.

"Um, sort of. It's a watercolor painting my aunt left me as part of a treasure hunt. You said it was an armaments factory?"

She picked up my phone and looked closer. "Oh yes, definitely."

"Do you know the firm well?" I asked.

She shied a bit. "My grandfather worked there during the war. Terribly dangerous work considering how frequently the enemy tried to bomb the factory."

"Do you happen to recognize the artist? He signed his paintings 'E.E.'"

"I'm afraid not," she said.

Gertie and I nodded our thanks and left. We took a good spy at the post office boxes on our way out, and Miss Smears was quite correct: our latest key would definitely not fit in any of them. I supposed she also had no safety deposit boxes hiding at the back like Roger the Mustache did in Plumsden.

Pity.

I ended up walking behind Gertie back to Athena. I got a full view of her from behind and was amused to be following a perambulating floral dress, sensible T-strap shoes, a black leather jacket, and red hair frizzing out of its bun in all different directions. She looked very odd indeed.

I rushed to walk beside her. "Gertie, you need to fix your hair."

"This from the woman who arrived at the fanciest hotel in Carlingheath looking like a human version of a painter's palette?"

That stopped me. I shrugged. "Okay, touché. But I think a mirror would be a good idea."

"It can't be all that bad," she said. She acted a bit annoyed as she climbed into the driver's seat inside Athena. She reached up and angled the rearview mirror at herself then peered into it. It was like an electric shock coursed through her as she sat bolt upright and flattened herself back against the headrest. "Good grief! Why didn't you tell me I looked like I was just in a prize fight?"

"I was still trying to figure out if you'd won or not," I said with a grin.

"Well, I'll do the best I can to fix it, but in this heat, I just don't know ..." Gertie muttered as she took a tissue and tried to wipe off as much of the melted eyeshadow as possible. "I really need some makeup remover and warm water. Is there a chemist's around here?"

"I can do you one better than that." I handed her a small bottle and another tissue. "Use this. That'll get rid of the makeup."

She looked at me with a suspicious set of black eyes. "This isn't paint thinner, is it?"

I bristled. "Of course not. It's eye-makeup remover, fragrance free, about as basic as you can get. I had it in my purse left over from the wedding."

Gertie delicately dabbed at her eyes and the stuff actually did start to come off. I helped her rinse her eyes with some water from my reusable glass bottle.

"There, much better," I said. "You were beginning to scare me."

"I decided it would be better to try and outrun the past," Gertie said. "But I've learned that it has a funny way of catching up with me, no matter where I am."

I crossed my arms and looked at her. "Well, your face looks fine, but your hair is still a rat's nest."

"Thanks for that."

"I can see if I've got a comb or some hairspray ..." I rummaged in my purse some more.

Gertie held up a hand. "Don't bother. I know what's causing the problem, and it won't be fixed until we leave this town."

I looked at her, surprised.

"Oh yes, go ahead and smile, you of the still-silky locks. Remember how I took a quick shower when we arrived?"

I nodded.

"Well, the River Cray runs over chalk beds right beside Ludring. This makes for very hard water, so hard I can't even get a comb through my hair after my shower. Had the same problem when I was in the area last time doing some sermon auditing. I should try some swimmer's shampoo to strip away all these minerals clogging my hair shafts."

I had to laugh. "I cannot believe we're talking about shampoo and eye-makeup remover. When we were little, you had zero interest in any of this stuff, including during our teenage years at boarding school in America."

She gave me the side eye. "It's just a disguise to throw them off my trail. You'd want a disguise too if your karaoke video went viral."

We headed back towards our bed-and-breakfast, following the new route our phone app showed us. Somehow, we ended up in the midst of a retail strip mall.

"Are you sure this is the right place?" I asked as we trundled down a small alley.

"You bet. It's near the site of an old silk-printing factory. In World War Two the armaments factory took it over," Gertie said.

"So what are we looking for?" I asked.

A newish car park was visible to our right.

"Look, there's a place I can get some of that swimmer's shampoo. We've hit the jackpot: coffee shop, burger joint, plus a plastic and gimmicks shop! Do you know how cheap their dish scrubbers and desk organizers are there? They're fantastic!"

"And just what does all this have to do with finding what our key opens courtesy of the watercolor painting?" I asked.

She looked at me and got a very sweet smirk on her face. "See that back alley over there, the one where the dumpster's parked near that bank of storage sheds?"

"Yes, but ..."

"But nothing. I spy an older, wizened man who's doing maintenance work over there. He's likely the best person on the planet to ask about the details of this complex."

"Method to her madness. I like it," I said.

"Just like Aunt Edwina used to say. There's no sense getting old if you don't get crafty."

We both grinned.

***

Gertie was right. The senior, wizened man, Stan Trentworth, started working on site during this industrial estate's redevelopment. The place was comprised of six main parcels of land, each one being modernized by the borough to improve traffic flow and employment for the local area.

Stan was the general expert, someone who'd seen the old replaced with the new, yet was still aware of the little hidey spots, remnants of the past. He wore a greasy pair of overalls and looked to be in the middle of taking apart the gear works of a diesel engine in one of the sheds. There was a row of about ten sheds, all of them padlocked except the one he was working inside. The sheds were the transition barriers between the newer strip mall and the automotive industrial area behind. We approached with a spring in our step and hope in our eyes.

Stan turned out to be super helpful. "Well, ladies, you're correct. When calico and silk went out, armaments came in. My grandfather and father both used to work there. They told me countless stories about the workers getting bombed out of their own homes nearby during the blitz," Stan said.

"It must've been quite an armaments factory," Gertie said.

"It certainly was. Lots of the men were away fighting for this island of ours, and a lot of women got their war work here. Many of them didn't want to go back to the kitchen when the war was over."

Gertie gave him a knowing look. "After the excitement of your own paycheck and helping to save your country, who would want to go back to cooking Sunday dinner and washing dirty socks?"

We all had a laugh over that one. Stan wiped his greasy hands on a shop rag and took the key from my outstretched hand. "And you're wondering if there's something here on site that this opens?" He'd obviously been here since early this morning because he sported a late afternoon shadow. His whiskers were coming in as white-grey. Two men who passed him gave Stan a courtesy wave out of respect.

"Yes, that's the idea," I said. "We thought you might have worked here for a while."

"Because I look old or because I look competent?" he teased.

"To be honest, both. And I call it seasoned, not old," Gertie replied. Her hair was somewhat tamed, and now that she didn't look like she just came from the boxing ring, we had a better chance of being taken seriously.

"How on earth did you get here?" he asked.

Gertie pointed to Athena.

"No, not your vehicle. I meant how did you find this car park?" he asked.

"We followed the history based on the watercolor painting our aunt left to Julie, my cousin here. Then your postmistress helped. The fabric works turned into armament works, which led us here, which then led us to you."

Stan grinned. "So I'm the prize, then?"

Gertie gave him her best smile. "As much as you can stand it, all day, every day. Right now we're both imagining you wearing a first-prize ribbon and holding up a silver trophy."

He waved off her joke and then got serious. "I think you came to the right place. Do either of you know Lady Susan Marcelon of Ludring?"

We both shook our heads no.

"Well, about six months ago, Lady Susan came to me on this very spot. She was wondering if she could rent one of the sheds. Very particular about the fact that it had to be one of these sheds, on this specific parcel of industrial land. I had a couple that were not being used at the time, checked it out with the landowner, and we started up a little rental business on the side where we split the profits."

"And this Lady Susan, she's a relative of yours?" Gertie asked.

"Oh, heavens no," Stan said. "She's one of the richest ladies in the county. If we were related, do you really think I'd be standing here messing about with an old diesel engine in my seventies?" He looked over at Gertie with a curious smile. "I have a better chance of being related to the Duke of Wellington."

"So I take it Lady Susan's a friend of yours?" I asked.

"She's a client. Nothing more. But she did rent a shed, and the key on her padlock is quite distinctive. It's one she brought herself, and it's very, very similar to the one you have in your hands there, Julie."

I felt my enthusiasm and excitement dial up tenfold. I held the key aloft. "Can we try it?"

He looked over his shoulder, checking that we were out of anyone's earshot. "That's why I asked if you knew Lady Susan. Because when she locked up her belongings, she told me that one day a young lady would be along to open up the door. I was to ask her two specific questions and, if she answered correctly, guide her to the right shed. After that, it's completely up to the key holder as to what they do next."

"Oh good, a puzzle! We love those," Gertie said with jolly giddiness.

"Just give me a moment." Stan went over to his battered toolbox and opened up a secret compartment down at the bottom by removing a tool tray from overtop another one. He pulled out a folded piece of wax paper inside which there was a folded note. He read the note to us:

1. *Where was Edwina born?*
2. *What came first: London's Great Fire or the Great Plague?*

"The first one is dead easy," Gertie said. "Aunt Edwina was born in Oakhurst."

"And the second?" he asked.

Gertie looked at me. "You're the big cities history buff. What do you say?"

I nodded. "The Great Plague hit London in 1665, and the royal family was evacuated to Oxford before that time. The Great Fire of London, which actually came as a blessing because it burned up a lot of the fleas that spread the disease, occurred a year later, in 1666." I was now well into my stride. "Did you know that King

Charles the Second and his brother James were both out there on the banks of the River Thames, personally filling up buckets with water to help fight the flames?"

Stan rocked back on his heels, listening to my history lesson. He scratched his head. "That's pretty impressive, young lady."

I took a tiny bow. "Thank you. I always enjoyed my history lessons."

"And that's 'Open Sesame' as far as I'm concerned," Stan said as he checked off the questions on his list. "It's shed number sixteen over here."

"I thought you said there were only ten sheds?" Gertie asked.

"There are. We just started numbering them at eight." He shrugged.

I fitted our key into the well-oiled padlock for shed number sixteen, and the lock turned like butter. The heavy weight at the bottom came apart from the U-shaped metal going into the lock. Stan stepped in and handed the padlock to me. He motioned for us to move back a bit because the doors swung open as opposed to sliding to the sides. Inside it looked like there was a large vehicle under a tarp, as well as various shelves holding a few dusty items.

Stan went over to the tarp and yanked it off with one swift pull. After the dust had settled, we gasped. We were looking at a fancy touring sedan from the 1950s. It was a silvery grey, with polished wood and leather interior. Fully restored and impeccably clean. Elegant to the hilt, right down to the polished and chromed spare spoked wheel mounted just above the back bumper.

"Well, well," he said. "I had no idea she had one of these inside my shed. Wonder why she didn't keep it up at her big house? They've got garages up there for dozens of cars."

I went over to the car and saw that there was an envelope on the passenger seat in a plastic pouch. This time the stationery was from Marcelon Manor near Ludring. I held it aloft and smiled at Gertie.

I broke the seal on the envelope as Stan and Gertie watched. The note inside read:

Dear Julie:

Congratulations on making it this far. I knew you and Gertie had it in you. Switch cars and take this one instead of whatever you're driving. Lock your vehicle in here so it is hidden while you run around town.

Mind how you go with Chris. I have my suspicions but don't want to interfere. Just know I've already arranged my legacy gifts to stay out of gold-diggers' clutches.

Please visit Lady Susan and return her car. That is the confirmation she awaits in order to help you with the next stage of your quest.

I hope you are finding this as fun as I did setting it up.

Love always,
Aunt Edwina

I silently handed the note to Gertie.

"You're welcome to look around," Stan said. "My instructions were if you answered the two questions then it was carte blanche. Now, if you will excuse me, I've got an engine to work on. Just lock the shed door when you leave, please."

"Thank you so much for your help. This family history quest is getting more and more interesting," I said.

Stan went back to tending his diesel engine.

I looked at Gertie. "Aunt Edwina was very perceptive. She already had her suspicions about Chris. When Chris and I got engaged, I was living off my bank account's overdraft. My father and his siblings are all still alive, so I never anticipated any large inheritance from Aunt Edwina."

"I think it's safe to assume Chris believed different, that you were soon going to be a wealthy woman," Gertie said.

l was saddened. "l trusted Chris. I said we didn't need a pre-nuptial agreement. Come to think of it, he did look a bit too pleased when l told him."

"But you didn't know what he was really like back then," Gertie said.

"True. And to my credit, this was all arranged long before l knew he was flat broke. Truth be told, on our wedding day my paintbrushes were worth more than the equity in his sportscar."

This situation got more curious by the minute.

"Turning to much more important things than a deadbeat, how do we know this car's going to run properly?" Gertie asked.

"Do you really think Aunt Edwina, with all her money, would leave us with a broken-down vehicle?"

"But it didn't sound like Stan had ever seen anyone come into the shed. And don't forget the dust all over the tarp."

"All window dressing. Trust me. Aunt Edwina had it serviced somehow. Maybe on Stan's days off. l trust her. We both need to trust her."

Gertie shrugged. "All right, agreed."

We proceeded to examine the rest of the contents of the shed. In the back we saw something hopeful: a chest with a hasp that wasn't locked. However, once we opened it up, all we found inside were rags and car wax containers.

"It looks like that's all there is to find, cousin," Gertie said. "That chest looked hopeful, but no dice."

I eyeballed the parking space inside and determined that there was plenty of room for Athena once the fancy sedan was moved. We could do the switch no problem, yet as soon as we started, another secret revealed itself in a most unexpected manner.

Chapter 23

—

Neither of us expected to find something *underneath* the vehicle. Heck, what with the grand touring sedan taking up most of the shed space, we'd only looked on the shelves that surrounded the vehicle.

We missed the trapdoor underneath. The metal handle was sunk into the floor, flush with the concrete surface. This meant there was no damage to the vehicle as we drove it outside. The sedan had started perfectly, her engine purring just like a contented Persian cat. We then shut off the engine to momentarily re-tarp the sedan so she wouldn't attract any curious onlookers. Next, we examined the trapdoor in the floor. I pulled on the handle, and it easily lifted up on well-maintained hinges. There was a tiny metal compartment underneath, and it contained one small tin box that bore two metal latches and a handle.

It was an ancient lunch kit.

I looked at Gertie. "Do you think we've already found the key for the next town? I thought we had to go and see Lady Susan first?"

"That was my understanding too," she said.

We both peered down into the small hole and looked at the metal box that awaited us. I reached in and picked it up, bringing it to the surface. Underneath the box was an old newspaper, yellowed with age, from 1941.

"Maybe this is a clue to 'E.E.'," Gertie said with excitement.

"Could be," I said, opening up the full-sized newspaper and starting to flip through the pages. There were several articles about the war, interspersed with various ads for blackout-curtain designs, a substitute for silk stockings, and bomb-shelter delivery schedules for various neighborhoods. Towards the back were a couple of pages filled with want ads, both recruiting for the military as well as for the homefront factory workforce.

Gertie picked up the small tin box and slowly rattled it. A couple of things moved back and forth inside, but we couldn't tell what they were. She set it down on the floor of the shed, flipped open the two metal latches and wrinkled her nose. Next, she pulled out an old thermos and something wrapped in more newspaper. She unfolded it and wrinkled her nose even more. She held it up towards me. "Fancy a sandwich?"

"Are you serious? It looks mummified," I said.

We both crouched down to look at it. The bread was rock hard, the lettuce melted against it, and whatever meat and cheese used to be in there were now congealed into a dark, leathery mass.

"The lunch kit was obviously airtight, that's why it hasn't gone moldy," I said.

"Don't think I want to touch that sandwich. It can go straight into the compost bin." Gertie picked up the thermos and unscrewed it, holding it away from her as the lid came off. She looked inside when she'd plucked up the courage, then emitted an unexpected wide smile. She tilted the thermos sideways so I could also see what was inside. At first I backed away, then I totally relaxed. There, in a big roll, were loads of modern £50 notes. Gertie pulled out a simple piece of Greymore Hall stationery. It read:

> *Bonus find: fun money! Love Aunt Edwina.*
> *PS: the historical sandwich really fooled*
> *you at first, didn't it?*

"She thought of everything," Gertie said. "It's just like Aunt Edwina to make sure we're taken care of."

"So let's make her proud," I said. I waved at Stan and motioned him over. He helped us back Athena into the shed—Gertie made sure she slipped a £50 note to Stan for his trouble—and relocked it again with the same padlock. Stan had one key, and we had the other. He told us we could be back tomorrow or in four weeks or four months, it made no difference to him. He gave us a wave as we drove away in our new loaner vehicle. I felt so fortunate we'd found such a nice man who treasured the past as much as we did.

***

Ludring's residents all knew where the large manor house was located a few miles beyond the town, in a more rural area. We stopped at the bottom of the drive to take a look. Mentally, we had to admit we were comparing it with Greymore Hall. Marcelon Manor was rather a hodgepodge design, a mix of a box-like Jacobean Castle merged with two turrets from a medieval French stately home. My phone had yielded information that Lady Susan's now-deceased husband was descended from a long line of French counts, one of whom had won Marcelon Manor in a card game held in France in 1830. He moved here, sight unseen, to take advantage of the prosperous local silk trade as well as to escape the second French Revolution.

In 1831, the two turrets had appeared. Perhaps the French count considered himself needing an ode to Versailles Palace, because apparently the house contained its own, albeit smaller, hall of mirrors plus enough gilt furniture to fill both great halls. The house sat on thirty-nine acres and was surrounded by trees and a large field of sheep. We drove down the asphalt entranceway, feeling quite posh in the fancy sedan. The front entrance was exceedingly grand: a porte cochère with arches and the family crest up high, announcing itself to the world. A few humongous oak trees shaded the front lawn, and around the side were low stone walls made of the same beige-colored stone material as the house. One could tell that modern thought was in use here by the fluorescent 'Grandchildren at Play' signs on the driveway limiting us to five miles per hour. The house was quite imposing with its red-tile roof and second-story balcony that hid behind hundreds of balustrades.

Two staff saw us arrive and followed us to the front entrance. One wore a grey chauffeur's uniform complete with shiny black boots, white-cotton gloves, and cap. The other man was in overalls and looked like he was a greenskeeper on his way to mow the lawn. They both issued us welcoming smiles as Gertie pulled up and parked. Both of our doors were swiftly opened moments after Gertie stopped the car.

The chauffeur spoke first. "Welcome to Marcelon Manor, ladies. You are most welcome. It's lovely to see Lady Susan's touring sedan back." He gave it a once over, as if he was checking for scratches and dents that we may have put in the paint.

Gertie reassured him with a cheery voice. "We thought she belonged to our Aunt Edwina."

The chauffeur ran a caring hand down the car's hood. Then he shook his head. "No, miss. This vehicle firmly belongs at Marcelon Manor. But Lady Edwina and Lady Susan were close friends. Shall I take your bags inside to your rooms?"

"Rooms? We're staying at a local bed-and-breakfast," Gertie said.

"Oh dear. I don't think Lady Susan will like that. Please go inside, and we'll sort this out later." He appeared eager to get the sedan back into its garage and start polishing it.

The greenskeeper said nothing except to tip his flat cap to us and follow the chauffeur's lead. A housekeeper appeared at the front door and stepped aside to let us walk into the house.

What the internet had told us about the gilded furniture was nothing short of an understatement. One's eyes literally had to adjust, as the gleam of the furniture bounced off every wall and mirror. To our right was a formal parlor with a bay window that had a three-story-high set of paned glass, in the middle of which were two large stained-glass artworks. One showed a poker hand's full house; the other depicted a pastoral scene with Roman-nosed sheep in a field.

We were led into this formal parlor and invited to sit down on an ornate gilded sofa, done in newish cherry-red upholstery, set in a square arrangement with three other pieces of furniture right underneath the stained-glass bay window. The high ceilings were covered in ornate, white plasterwork, with gold leaf smattered about on appropriately placed fig leaves adorning various Greek figures. Double rows of ancestral portraits hung on the wall, interspersed with small hunting scenes and a couple of mantlepieces down below.

This was a busy room, also crammed full of side tables, a display of antique crystal decanters, plus two rows of photos, presumably of the lord and lady's son, daughter, and five young grandchildren. There was also a pile of somebody's avid quilting hobby supplies. Below a portrait of Cardinal Wolsey from Tudor times hung a sixty-inch screen television playing a 1930s black-and-white movie at a low volume. There was a pair of fuchsia, feathered, slide-on slippers at the foot of the modern leather recliner right in front of the television.

Apart from the handsome movie star on screen, there was no other sound in the house. It was like we had walked in on somebody who was relaxing yet had left in a hurry. We sat on the sofa, like two bumps on a log, wondering what to do next. We actually got enthralled by the movie, because it was made at a time when the world wasn't so frenetic, and people were much kinder.

The silence was broken by a silky, smooth voice. "Please accept my apologies for leaving you here to your own devices. I'm Lady Susan Marcelon, and welcome to my home," she said. Lady Susan was a tall, elegant woman dressed in an extremely bright, multicolored paisley caftan, a headscarf wrapped around her thick grey hair, and bright-purple painted toenails on her very bare feet.

That would explain the orphaned feathered slide slippers near the recliner.

She shook our hands with firm alacrity. "Were you offered refreshment yet?"

We said no and then Lady Susan reached over to the side of the room to pull a tasseled, braided silken cord. The housekeeper we first set eyes upon only a few minutes ago reappeared and was instructed to provide sandwiches and cakes out on the back terrace.

"And of course you *absolutely must* stay with me. I'm told you're at a bed-and-breakfast in Ludring?"

"That's right," I answered. "It's clean enough, but the owner is not, well, how do you say, overly enthused about her role and her guests."

"Well, we are, and you *must* stay here. I can send my driver immediately for your bags if you wish. He'll take care of the room charges as well."

I could tell Gertie was doing the exact same thing as I— methodically going through each square foot of the room we were staying in right now and figuring out how much of a mess we had left. We both shook our heads at each other, deciding it was inappropriate to have a random chauffeur walk in on a room that we hadn't left in a fully conservative matter. There was just something wrong about showing a stranger one's undergarments mid-drip-dry.

"That's fine, if he could just give us a lift back so we can pack, and then we'd be happy to come and stay with you."

Obviously the right thing to say.

Lady Susan gave a sigh of relief. "Well, that is excellent, dears. I'm thrilled that Edwina's nieces have figured out her clues and brought my late husband's sedan home. Of course, Edwina's death means the end of so many fond traditions. Quite sad, indeed. I shall miss our family history research discussions. That was the main topic of our Sherry Club meetings, after we had finished arranging good deeds for the community."

"Just before she passed, Aunt Edwina reminded me of the importance of keeping good family photographs," I added.

"Of course, you must. You absolutely must!" Lady Susan said. "I'm much younger than Edwina and value all she taught me about family history. You must both really miss her." She gave us a look with her vivacious eyes. "Look at me! Monopolizing the conversation again! Now where are those sandwiches?"

Lady Susan hadn't even sat down yet. She strode over to the side of the parlor adjoining the front hall, stuck her head out, looked both ways, and then decided it was time to move. Her eyes caught the stained-glass window as a particularly fierce sunbeam shot right through and lit up all the different colors. "Ghastly, isn't it? My late husband said if I was to have my sheep, then he was to have his poker cards. I suppose one could call it a good compromise in a marriage, but my staff certainly have their doubts."

We followed her like dutiful puppies out to the back terrace. It was a lovely area, done up with square paving stones interspersed with bushy bits of green grass connecting them to each other. A large trellis covered with wisteria was on one side and made a wall framing the outdoor cooking appliances. Various sturdy swing sets and toys were in a neat grouping off to the side for her grandchildren's visits.

We sat on candy-cane red-and-white-striped poufy cushions placed on top of sturdy metal deck furniture. The housekeeper soon brought out our luncheon: five different types of sandwiches with their crusts removed and a smaller platter of cakes. She followed it up with a pitcher of lemonade and a pitcher of ice tea, plus glasses and utensils for us all.

"Your sedan drives like a dream, if I may say so," Gertie said.

Lady Susan smiled and toasted us with her lemonade.

"May I ask why we were critical to get your car out of jail?" I asked. It seemed like a question just begging to be asked.

Lady Susan laughed. "I'm sure you both think it's just some funny women's wager, correct?" She didn't wait for our reaction. "In a way, I suppose, it was."

Chapter 24

———

"Edwina and I founded our Sherry Club well over thirty years ago. It started as a group of titled women who wanted to do good things for the community. It soon took on a bigger role when we were approached by a couple of family history researchers who thought they were related to my line a few generations back. We did all the right things, encouraged them, gave them access to our family archives, and I even had them stay with me here at Marcelon Manor. Gave them the full run of my library and office, including free photocopies," Lady Susan said.

"And?" Gertie asked. "There's always an 'and'. Or a 'but'."

Lady Susan got a faraway look in her eyes. "And we found out that these two researchers were nothing more than scam artists looking to steal the family silver."

"That's terrible," I said. "What did you do?"

"The police were involved and caught them departing with my collection of eighteenth-century bronze figurines. In anger, one of them chucked a figurine at the house and broke a front bay window. That's how we came up with the replacement stained-glass windows you've just seen."

"Off in the police van it was, hey?" Gertie said.

Lady Susan nodded. "It was a valuable lesson. And one that we thought other ladies should learn. We all vowed to protect each other in this modern world gone mad. You see, sometimes family is only after the money, not the respect, not the family name that's been so cherished and protected over the centuries. That's when we made our pact."

"A pact?" I asked.

"To protect our estates. To protect them from destruction, demolition, or from being turned into a garish fun park that makes a mockery of everything our ancestors had achieved."

"Some people like the bright lights, terror rides, and the arcades," Gertie said.

Lady Susan smiled. "Of course. In my younger days I was the first one to jump on the ferris wheel or whatever other terrifying ride was on offer. But not at a manor house. At least, that's how our group felt. We wanted history to be preserved as it was, so future generations could appreciate it. Tomorrow's successes depend on yesterday's learnings."

Lady Susan set her eyes on me. "And how do you feel about all that, dear?"

I shrugged. "I agree with preserving history and not squandering a family's fortune on ridiculous things."

Lady Susan took an elegant sip of her beverage. "Such as poker cards in a stained-glass window?"

"I didn't say that," I said.

"You didn't have to, dear. But that's all right. You're honest, and that's good."

"Who are the other members of your Sherry Club?" Gertie asked.

Our hostess leaned back in her chair, seeming comfortable. "Well, there is Maude Livingstone at the Plumsden Family History Society, the owner of Petford Grange, a huge estate home that she rattles around in all by herself."

"We met her. She was extremely helpful," Gertie said.

"Indeed. There's also one lady who emigrated here from France. Her ancestors had something to do with Versailles, but I'm not quite sure if it was on the guillotine side or not. Finally, there is one lady from Devon."

"The group met once a month at Plumsden's The King's Arm pub?" I asked.

"That's correct. Edwina said you were smart, and I see she was right. When she asked for help setting up this quest, I was only too happy to help."

I was confused. "I'm afraid I don't understand. We found what the key opens, and we exchanged vehicles like the note said to do. We even found the bonus money in the floor locker. But what's next?"

"Did you look at the last watercolor closely?" Lady Susan asked.

Gertie nodded. "The dates. There was a series of six numbers hidden in the corrugated tin roof of the armaments factory. We couldn't quite figure out what it was."

"What were the numbers?" Lady Susan asked gently.

"Forty-two, oh-three, twenty-nine. We thought it was either a date or the tail number of an aircraft."

"Add each digit to the others, and they total twenty. Room number twenty is the one you're staying in tonight, Julie. A series of three digits can also mean a combination to a safe."

"You mean in my room?" I asked.

Lady Susan nodded. "It was the final bit of help I offered to Edwina. She said if you got this far, then the stakes could go up."

"And here we were thinking we'd figured out the date when Aunt Edwina met her first love," Gertie said, chagrined.

"Come, come, ladies. That would have been too easy. Edwina spent months plotting this out and was quite pleased with herself. None of us Sherry Club ladies knew the entire plan, only our specific role in it. Once you found the sedan and brought it here, and then repeated the safe's secret combination, my job was done. You need to figure out what to do with what's inside the safe. I can't help you because I have no idea what she put in there. I didn't even know the combination until you told me."

"You mean Aunt Edwina put something secret in the safe in your own home, and you don't even know what it is?" Gertie asked.

Lady Susan nodded. "Edwina has a safe just like it in her summer home in Devon. She made sure she returned the same favor to me."

***

It was like Christmas with an impatient set of seven-year-olds as we trooped back to the bed-and-breakfast, packed up our bags, and checked out. Lady Susan's chauffeur, Alfred Meadows, was most dedicated with his assistance. On the way back to Lady Susan's house, we asked him a couple of things about the local area.

"We found the sedan at the old silk and calico works, later the armaments factory site," Gertie said.

"Yes, miss. That factory helped keep Churchill well-supplied with fighting gear against the enemy. There was another large silk printing works here in town, founded in the early nineteenth-century. Long gone now, though. One of the silk printing company owners really won the day for Ludring. He entered an elaborately printed shawl at the Great Exhibition.

It was a wonderful swirl of fern leaves and flowers, all painted in vivid blues, yellows, pinks, and greens. It took home a gold medal for Ludring with the distinction that Queen Victoria herself was fascinated by it."

"Where is the shawl now?" Gertie asked.

"In London's Victoria and Albert Museum. We're very fortunate it survived all these years," Meadows said.

He drove us up to Marcelon Manor and promised to bring our bags up shortly. It was more agony waiting for him to do that while we stared at the portrait of Admiral Sir Leonard Byron Gyntonne, a great naval man from the Ludring area, hanging on the wall in my room. He wore a splendid coat decorated in heavy gold braid, had an elegant white cravat, and carried a telescope in his right hand. His expression was one of firm confidence, with deep, weather-induced jowls belying his vast experience at sea. Lady Susan had told us that this was the painting in front of the safe, and we dared not swing it back before we were ready, lest getting ahead of ourselves with excitement.

Alone, with our bags now firmly plonked on luggage racks in our rooms, we finally swung back the gilded portrait. It moved silently, like a book opening on top of a lacquered desk. There was a safe, alright, embedded in the wall, and a large dial showed the numbers at five-digit intervals. I entered the code, doubling the wheel back over itself for each successive number: 42-03-29.

A click. And a rather loud one at that. I pulled the handle down and the safe swung open. Inside were two curious items: a sealed plastic bag half full of white powder, and one bright-orange, plastic Gerbera daisy.

"What on earth?" I exclaimed, peering inside.

"Uh oh," Gertie said, looking over my shoulder. "I used to work with troubled youth, and this isn't good. In fact, don't touch that in case your fingerprints get on the bag."

"Come off it, Gerts. I can't see Aunt Edwina's Sherry Club ringleading a cocaine sales network." I stared at her, shocked. "Gerts?"

She harrumphed. "I know, they don't really go hand in hand. Perhaps they smuggled it in silver teapots and snuff boxes?"

"Honestly, Gertie. I don't think so. I doubt that it's drugs." I reached for the bag.

"WAIT!" Gertie yelped. "Don't get your fingerprints on the bag! I'll be right back!" She disappeared next door and was back in a moment with a pair of clear vinyl gloves. She handed them to me. "I use these when I dye my hair."

"Seriously." I tugged on the gloves then reached for the bag and the daisy. I held the bag up to the light. "It's too yellowy for cocaine."

"Says the world-renowned expert. The closest you ever got to drugs in boarding school was a bag of parsley on the annual ski trip."

I shot her a dirty look. "True. And I got far better marks than you, cousin. As I recall, you were more devil than angel back then."

"It was all a show. Just played loud music and wore a lot of black. I was in training for my future career," she said.

"Sure."

"Shhhh. Someone will hear us." She took the bag from me. Held it up to the light again. "The consistency is about right, but the color is off."

I smiled. "Oh, she got us good this time."

"What do you mean?"

"Look at the daisy, Gerts. What's another name for daisy?"

"I haven't the foggiest about the Latin name for a daisy," she said.

"Not Latin. The item itself," I said.

"What? It's a flower."

I crossed my arms and smirked. "Yes. It's a baggie of flour, and she just gave it away with the most visual clue she could think of. Dear Aunt Edwina. She's laughing up in heaven right now. I can hear her."

"Why would she leave us a baking ingredient for a treasure hunt?" Gertie asked.

"It's a clue to the next key or to explain the watercolor."

"I think we've exhausted the painting."

"So let's ask Lady Susan what flour has to do with Ludring." I took the baggie from Gertie and then tossed it from hand to hand.

There was a knock at the door. "Ladies?"

"Lady Susan!" Gertie whispered. I nodded and she went over to open the door. In glided Lady Susan, her gorgeous, flowing caftan encircling her like a cloud of perfume.

"Ladies, have you opened it yet? Oh good, I see you have. And?" She sat on a side chair, legs crossed, chin supported by an arm resting on her knee.

"We found these." I held up the plastic daisy and the baggie of flour. "Flour."

Lady Susan narrowed her eyes. "Whatever on earth was Edwina thinking?"

"Is there a miller family in town?" I asked. "Not the last name, but a family associated with flour milling in the past? It makes sense because Aunt Edwina was such a huge fan of family history and bygone industry research."

Gertie took the bag from me and investigated closer. She pressed her thumbs against the soft powder as if she was trying to spread it out within the bag. "Just trying to see if there is anything inside. It could be a bit of a trick, you see."

"I think it's pretty on the nose, Gertie," Lady Susan said. "Edwina wanted you to work for the clues but not be completely befuddled. I remember her telling me that."

"So do you know any millers in town?" I asked.

"I know a family that was extremely active in running the flour mill here in Ludring years ago before it closed due to lack of modern machinery. The flour mill moved to Ipswich; when it still operated here in town, it employed lots of people."

"Do we need to go to Ipswich?" I asked.

"Heavens, no," Lady Susan said. "The granddaughter, Harriet Tibbets, is an antiques appraiser and auctioneer in Medchester. I happen to know she's doing a large house clearance sale there this week, likely the best place to find her. She travels all over the United Kingdom, being so good at what she does."

"Well, that's brilliant," Gertie said with emphasis as she squeezed the bag a little too vigorously and popped it. All three of us were instantly covered in a dusting of white powder.

Gertie chortled as she looked at me. "You look like a badly made-up ghost."

"I look a fright," I said, going over to the mirror and wiping off the flour in long streaks.

But the funniest of all was Lady Susan. As she took off her fashionable glasses, her face was left with the clear impression of the glasses on her skin, making for a most odd look. I picked up a hand mirror and showed Lady Susan her reflection. We had a good laugh.

Gertie looked at me in dead seriousness. "Jules, at least you still had your gloves on."

***

I was excited to head to Medchester, partly because this was where King Charles the Second visited during his triumphant march to take back the throne in London in 1660. This monarch held a particular interest for me because I'd always felt he was a bit misunderstood. His love of women quite overshadowed his good deeds; one day it would be nice to see his achievements highlighted as well.

It was good to hear that Harriet Tibbets was an antiques appraiser, meaning that she probably knew Ewan Kilburn, a mutual, sane acquaintance to stand us in good stead during introductions. I made a mental note.

"You do know that a few other famous people visited Medchester, not just your favorite king," Gertie said as she guided our borrowed SUV down the A road.

I bristled. "King Charles the Second is largely underrated. He did much more than have a merry court. He led the nation through the Great Plague, the Great Fire–"

"Had umpteen spaniels, spent a lot of money on frippery ..."
Gertie grinned. "Sorry to burst your bubble."

"You're talking about the monarch who hid up an oak tree
to outwit Oliver Cromwell, had the courage to track down
and punish the regicides, reintroduced arts and holidays to
England, and founded the scientific Royal Society. By the way,
it was also during his reign that the first pineapple was grown
on English soil."

She raised her eyebrows. "You're just a fountain
of information."

"Better than a fountain of flour!"

"Oh, give me Henry the Eighth and his multiple wives any
day. At least he had the guts to marry all of those women."

"At least mine was smart enough not to!" I retorted.

"Touché, cousin, touché."

We drew up to Hinghurst Grange, a large house on the out-
skirts of town. This one was another odd design, likely created
by some eccentric aristocrat with more money than sense. The
home was of French Chateau style, a somber grey and quite
imposing. A large weathervane was on the apex of the tallest
roof peak, a thick bronze sculpture of an angel shooting a
bow, the initials 'W.H.' for William Hinghurst on the arrow's
shaft. Out front was a large sign boldly proclaiming *ESTATE
SALE TODAY!* and the front grounds were already parked up
with fifty-plus vehicles. One could tell the dealers from the

average joes: cube vans were parked in one area, many of them emblazoned with their owners' company names. The rest of the buyers, either looky-loos or serious folks, had parked transports ranging from tiny hatchbacks (miniatures and silver spoon collectors) to elegant SUVs (the wife was seeking a stylish side table she'd seen in the online auction catalog).

We were there in Lady Susan's loaner SUV and took up space with the rest of them in a long line. It was truly amazing how many people had the time and money to be here on a weekday at 10:00 a.m.

As we walked up the front path, I noticed that Gertie's eyes were a little red. "Are they sore?" I asked her.

"I think they're just irritated from the flour. After the auction we should stop and get some eyedrops. That'll fix it."

"You sure you don't want to go now?"

"No, thanks. I'll be alright," she said.

"Okay, just let me know if you change your mind."

Gertie linked her arm in mine and we walked up the path with renewed vigor. I recognized the back of the man we were following. I called out, "Ewan! We didn't expect to see you here." I had a smile on my face.

He turned to see us and gave us a warm greeting. "I'm here to buy a couple of key pieces for clients. It's also a good idea just to take a browse around to see if there is anything else that would suit the shop's inventory."

"We're looking for Harriet Tibbets, the auctioneer? She's apparently part of Aunt Edwina's mystery tour."

He grinned. "I was thinking about you two last night and wondered how your tour was going. Progress made?"

"Oh yes, the next painting and key have already brought us to a fancy car, a manor house, and an old sandwich," I explained. After I spoke, I realized how foolish it sounded. Then again, he'd already spent time with us, so perhaps it didn't sound so bizarre after all. I could only hope.

"And the flour. Don't forget flour," Gertie said.

"The flour?" Ewan looked quizzical.

"We had a bit of an issue with a baking ingredient," I explained.

"Aunt Edwina?" he asked.

Gertie and I both nodded.

"You two!" He held back a smile. "Come on, ladies, let's go inside and preview some lots."

***

The auction preview was set out amongst various rooms, and included everything from a George the Third tableware set to a fifteenth-century set of gleaming knight's armor. Even the intricately carved alabaster water fountains in the back were for sale.

A woman with sleek black hair and an elegant beige business suit came over to Ewan as soon as she spied him. She was a classic beauty, and obviously very well-versed in the business of today.

She extended a hand to him. "Ewan, so nice to see you. Welcome."

Her crisp coolness was impressive. Ewan turned to Gertie and I, and then we were duly introduced to Harriet Tibbets. She asked if we were looking for anything in particular.

"We are, actually. Lady Susan Marcelon said to seek you out and ask about your miller family background." I looked at the auctioneer for a hint of recognition.

Harriet's face yielded a kind smile, and she explained: "That goes back many generations in my family. The plant moved to Ipswich decades ago. Why are you interested in flour?"

"It's a bit of family history research we're doing for our Aunt Edwina. She recently passed away, and her last wishes sent us on this research journey."

"Did she think that your relatives were related to mine? That we have common ancestry?" Harriet asked. "It would be fun." Her eyes gleamed.

Gertie stepped in to help out. "Actually, we're not really sure. Do you have any unexplained family objects or traditions that perhaps link to Plumsden or to watercolor paintings?"

We received a blank look back from Harriet. "I'm sorry. Ewan?" She looked to him for inspiration and likely also confirmation that we were not completely bonkers.

"Oh, don't worry, Harriet, it's all legit. These ladies have got quite a mystery to figure out, and I've already tried to help them," he said.

"A mystery, how intriguing," Harriet said. "The only mysterious thing I can remember about our flour heritage is a large brass key that my grandfather used to hang over his mantlepiece. My brothers and I never knew what it was for, and our grandfather kept it pretty quiet. Just muttered about its importance to the town."

"And where is this key now?" I asked, very eager.

"I put it in my safety deposit box at the bank," she said. "I couldn't bear to part with it, not knowing what it opened. I'd be happy to show it to you, but not today. I have to run the auction."

"Of course," I said. "It sounds like your family was quite well-known in the flour trade."

She nodded. "My ancestors exhibited a steam-powered machine to grind grain at the Great Exhibition of 1851. It was the show Prince Albert set up inside his enormous glass house. Ludring's own silk works printed a shawl that caught the eye of Queen Victoria at that event. It brought home a gold medal for the town."

"The famous shawl. We've heard that story before," Gertie said.

Harriet stopped, waved at a few more locals, then refocused on our little group. "Look, here's my card. I'll meet you over at the bank first thing tomorrow morning and get the key out for you," she said.

"That would be wonderful, thank you," I said, watching as she went over to help a potential buyer who had a question. As Harriet traipsed off, she looked back over her shoulder. "Have Ewan show you the famous ruby ring. It's got wonderful provenance."

Chapter 25

Gertie and I both seized on that opportunity. "What famous ruby ring?" I asked Ewan.

He motioned us over with his index finger. We went to a clear acrylic case on a stand, fully guarded by a looming security officer. Inside the case was a solitary item, a man's intricately tooled silver ring, with one large, sturdy ruby in the center. The brass plaque said "Admiral Sir Leonard Byron Gyntonne."

"The naval man in the painting in front of the safe at Lady Susan's," I whispered.

"Yes, there is some sort of family connection there," Ewan said. "Sir Leonard was the Hampshire boy who rose from nothing to become a favorite admiral of Queen Anne in the early eighteenth-century. She actually paid for his funeral and interment at Westminster Abbey."

"He was a famous navy man, then?" Gertie asked.

"Famous navy man? One of the greatest who ever walked the earth, young lady!" boomed a confident male voice beside us. We all looked left to see a man in his late fifties or early sixties with porkchop sideburns, a waxed mustache, and heavy eyebrows. He had greying hair, stood over six feet tall, and had the sharpest creases in his dark-grey pinstriped suit that I'd ever seen.

My guess was retired military.

"Major Barry Whitcombe, retired," he said, extending a meaty hand. When he took my hand in his, I was sure he'd crush my fingers with his strong grip.

I rescued my hand as swiftly as I was able. "Julie Fincher, and this is my cousin, Gertie Porringer."

Gertie was subjected to the same death grip as I. Turns out, the Major was already a good friend of Ewan's.

The Major was just getting started. "The admiral rose through the ranks through his own hard work. He defeated the French fleet in the Mediterranean and then headed home to England. His ship was wrecked off the coast of Ireland, and when the injured great man crawled ashore, an old man stabbed him to death to steal his ruby ring. They found the admiral with broken ribs, head trauma, and multiple stab wounds. Queen Anne had his body moved back to the Abbey for a dignified burial."

I peered closer at the ring in the case. "And now they've found his ring?"

The Major nodded. "It's been hiding upstairs here at Hinghurst Grange in the dusty attic for hundreds of years. The letter they found alongside gave it perfect provenance, from the old tramp who stole it from the dying admiral on the beach right down through the next generations, to the final one who left it in the attic of the current owner."

"Amazing." It never ceased to astonish me what historical treasures could be found in old manor houses.

"It should fetch a princely sum at today's auction," the Major said.

"Shouldn't it be in a museum rather than squirreled away in some private collector's safe?" Gertie asked.

"And there you have the conundrum underscoring the basis of all antiques collecting," Ewan said. "Unfortunately, the museums of the world cannot afford to buy everything."

"Shame, really," Gertie said.

"The first order of business is to preserve the military history," the Major said. "The sacrifices made must be glorified."

"And where did you serve, Major?" Gertie asked.

"Commanded a crack unit in Iraq. Three tours of duty. Got out with mainly good health, just a bit of hearing loss from the mortar shelling. How I love the military. It's been like a family to me my whole life."

"Thank you for your service," I said.

"My pleasure. I am here, I must admit, on a bit of a rescue mission. I saw in the catalog that a uniform from the

Boer War is up for sale. I intend to buy it and donate it to a worthy museum."

"I hope no one bids against you. Your cause is greater than their pocketbooks," Ewan said.

"Are there a lot of dealers here?" I asked.

Ewan nodded. "Quite a few. Many have their own specialties. Gertie, you might want to whip over and take a look at the table with silver on it. I haven't had a chance to look at that yet."

Gertie was off like a shot.

I had an idea. I pulled out the photos housed in plastic sleeves that I'd bought at the antiques fair and showed them to the Major. "Do you happen to know anything about these uniforms? I've emailed them to a dealer in London but haven't heard back yet."

The Major whipped out a pair of small, folded reading glasses and peered at my photos. "I'd say these are from the First World War. Cavalry Regiment, likely. You can tell by the Lee-Enfield rifle, uniform, and bandolier."

"A bandolier?"

"The row of ammunition slung over his shoulder." As the Major leaned closer, I smelled his minty breath.

"See here? This badge? It's from the Dragoon Guards, a regiment used to counter Monmouth's attempt to capture the throne in the seventeenth-century after his father, King

Charles the Second, died. The Dragoons were raised, fought for England over centuries, and today are known as the impressive Prince of Wales's Dragoon Guards." He gave me a pensive look. "Where did you find these?"

"At an antiques fair in Waverly-on-Sea," I said.

"You should start with the museum in Cheshire. Send them scans of your photos and they'll be able to assist. Drop my name while you're at it."

"Oh, that's marvelous assistance, thank you. I'd love to reunite these photos with the right family." I beamed at him.

"My pleasure, young lady. We're on similar missions in life." He tapped my photo. "Every military person deserves a proper home."

"Thank you so much."

I watched the Major saunter away, eager to check out some rifles that were stacked up against a wall.

Gertie rushed back over to me, downtrodden. "They have a silver swans teapot but it's a fake. Bad hallmarks."

"Are you sure it's fake?" I asked.

She nodded. "No sense in bidding for it at all."

"You could try your luck with that fanciness," Ewan said with a quirky smile as he pointed to a gorgeous seventeenth-century English lime-wood carving with a detailed family crest and oak leaves. "Should go for well over £200,000."

My mouth dropped as quickly as Gertie's.

"My, my, the antiques business must be doing better than I expected," we heard. My art patron, the Duke of Conroy, approached. He was impeccably dressed in a navy blazer, crisp linen trousers, and a silk tartan cravat.

"Hi Bertie!" I exclaimed. "Are you here to look or buy?"

He beckoned the three of us close. "I'm after the ruby ring belonging to a certain admiral."

"It's a beauty, but it's attracting a lot of interest," Ewan whispered back.

"I almost bid by phone, but I wanted to see it up close, in case I'm unsuccessful, that is." Bertie made the admission, but it sounded halfhearted.

"Hardly likely," I said, knowing that when my ultra-wealthy sponsor truly wanted something, he simply bid higher and higher until he got it. The nicest thing about Bertie's antiques-buying hobby was that he was all for loaning his treasures to museums for public exhibition.

Harriet made an announcement requesting that people take their seats. The auction was very professionally run, and Harriet explained that the home's contents were being sold as part of the deceased's estate. After the contents were cleared, then the house itself would be sold. All the proceeds were going to charity, as the owner, William Hinghurst, had no heirs.

Three hundred and thirty-two lots later, we were sagging from auction fatigue in our uncomfortable fold-up chairs. The sunbeams in the long hall were fading, held back all day by tall curtains made from fabric printed with the Hinghurst family's coat of arms.

The ruby ring and the fancy woodcarving were the last two lots of the auction. Putting them last on the list was a smart move on Harriet's part; it kept people in their seats from start to finish.

"And now we arrive at one of the two cover lots of the auction," Harriet said, referring to the items shown on the front of the catalog. "Admiral Sir Leonard Byron Gyntonne's ruby ring. Stolen from him as he lay wounded on an Irish beach, yet passed down the thief's family members generation to generation. Provenance is superb, given the letter written by the priest who took the dying thief's confession. The ring and letter were only recently found here on site while we were assembling lots for this auction. Now, ladies and gentlemen, do I have £100,000 to start off the bids?"

Three hands went up. Bertie, a sly Duke of Conroy, waited to pounce.

The numbers rose to £289,000 and then started flagging. That's when my patron made his move.

Bertie raised his hand. "£310,000. And to a good home."

Harriet looked very pleased. "Thank you, sir. The bid is now £310,000. Anyone at £320,000? Anyone?" She cast her eyes around the room like a shark circling prey.

Nothing.

"I am going to sell Admiral Sir Leonard Byron Gyntonne's ruby ring for £310,000. Going once, going twice... I am selling..." The hammer came crashing down on its wooden base. "Sold for £310,000 to the Duke of Conroy. Congratulations, sir."

Bertie looked rather chuffed. I leaned over to congratulate him. "Well done, Bertie!"

"Jolly good show," added the Major, who'd taken a seat next to us and who was still reveling in his successful bid on the Boer War uniform.

Then I froze. I ducked down, ostensibly to get something out of my purse. "Gertie!" I whispered frantically.

She bent down with me, curious as to why I was scrabbling around on the parquet floor. "What?"

"It's Chris! Over by the entrance," I hissed.

"What?" She peered through the multiple pairs of legs and caught a tiny glance of my faux husband. "Oh dear."

"Where can we hide?"

The room was packed. Two empty chairs would be obvious if we kept bending down.

"How did he find us?" I asked.

"No idea. Breadcrumbs?"

I gave her a panicked look. "We need to hide. Over there, behind the curtains!"

And so we crawled on our hands and knees, disturbing a few other bidders, down the row, out the aisle, and four more painful feet across the hardwood to the curtains. Avoiding Chris was likely why wise Aunt Edwina had made us hide Athena. It was also why we were now considered to be the seriously strange ladies from Oakhurst.

We hid behind the curtains like vertical mummies. At that point, I didn't care how long we had to stay there, just so long as we could avoid meeting Chris. I tried to think calming thoughts, like warm cocoa, walking in a sunlit forest, and how special one felt after getting a new haircut. None of it worked to slow down my thumping heart, which was beating so loud it pulsed right through to the end of my fingers. I shut my eyes tight and focused on Harriet's professional auctioneer's voice. Hopefully we would get through this.

But it was a big ask.

Chapter 26

We heard the fancy woodcarving go for £249,000, quite a princely sum. We also heard Harriet announce that the auction was over. The scraping of chairs. The crowd noise. I peeked out from the break in the curtains and saw Chris aim for us like a dog after a bone.

"He's spotted us," I whispered. "How did he see us?"

"The hem of Gertie's floral dress. Quite distinctive," Chris said right in front of us, pulling the curtains open, pointing down, and talking in that little boy's whiny voice he used when I beat him at chess.

He separated the fabric even more and softened. "Julie, my love, where have you been?"

Chris put on his sad voice and face, the ones he used to wheedle and coax when he wanted me to cook his favorite meal or tend to his nasty cold.

"I-I needed some space," I stammered.

"Right after our wedding?" he said, dumbfounded. "And you had our priest help you to escape?"

Did I detect a note of hurt in his voice?

"I miss you. Please come home," he said. He looked ever so handsome at that moment. But Chris was a catch with a big catch.

"Chris ..."

People were starting to stare. I pulled Gertie and Chris off to a side room where auction house staff were already packing smaller lot items sold to telephone bidders. "Gertie was with me when I took the picture of you and Carlene," I said.

I'd just played my biggest card. Chris knew it too. The question was, how would he recover?

"So that's why you left without a goodbye," he said in a more clipped tone. He was buying time and thinking it over.

"Do you blame her?" Gertie shot back.

"My new husband was cheating on me. I think that's reason enough!" I said.

Chris turned on the nasty now that he saw I wasn't backing down. "Sorry sweetheart, we're wed. You've been holding out on me. I know all about Aunt Edwina's treasure hunt, and since the treasure hunt was acquired during our marriage, I can easily argue that the end result is communal marital property, dear wife."

I hate him.

"You cannot expect Julie to ever love you again," Gertie said to Chris.

"Chris, how very nice to see you," Bertie said, smoothly coming over to my rescue. He'd heard *You and Carlene* in my angry tone, obviously read the situation well, and knew I wanted out.

Or perhaps the Duke knew more than he was letting on?

Chris was distracted. Bertie's wealth always dazzled him. Bertie made a swishing movement with his fingers and gave us the signal to head out the door. From the corner of my eye I saw Bertie's SUV waiting outside, driver Finn Severs at the wheel.

Bertie saw that I saw. He swished with his fingers again, slung his arm around Chris and led him over to the payment stall. Chris loved the feeling of money on him.

Gertie and I had our exit.

Ewan came up beside me, looking for his friends. "Oh, hello, we're going for a cuppa in the tea rooms down the high street and wha–"

Gertie and I barreled past him like a herd of stampeding elephants. "Later perhaps!" Ewan looked confused and unsure all rolled up into one. He let us rush past him and then just stood, watching us go.

I wrenched open the back door of Bertie's SUV and dove in headfirst. Gertie followed me inside. As we both lay down on the seat, I let out a weak, "Hi, Severs. Can you please drive us somewhere away from here, and fast?"

"As you wish, miss," he said. Severs was a tall, angular man, extremely devoted to his employer. I'd heard Bertie say to him more than once, *if Julie ever needs anything, make sure you assist her*. At the time I thought it was really sweet of Bertie to say, but now I was gratefully redeeming my patron's generous offer.

We pulled out of the estate's parking lot only to be faced with a long line of cars trying to make their way out through the front gates. Severs looked behind the front seats. "Ladies, never fear. My security training taught me to know the back routes. Hold tight, please."

Twenty seconds later we were zipping along a small country road, crops, flowers, sheep, and cows all around us.

Gertie and I both sat up. "How did you know this way?" she asked.

"When one has employment as I do, it is important to share insider information with the other great houses' staff. I happened to get on splendidly with the chauffeur at this particular Medchester home."

"Severs, you are a gem." I settled back in the seat, not caring where he was taking us, as long as it was far away from Chris.

"I do try my best. Now please relax. There are cold water bottles in your armrests, and I shall take you somewhere private for refreshment."

It was good knowing a privileged person in times like this. Severs drove us to an out-of-the-way yet substantial country house in nearby Brambleford. It was hidden behind two sweeping curved brick walls and pillars that nearly obscured it from view. We were settled in a back room done in yellow damask, and plied with lemonade.

Forty-seven minutes later Bertie arrived. "That young man of yours, Julie, is quite devious," he said in an exasperated voice.

"Thank you so much for saving us," I said. "My marriage mistake is quite embarrassing for me."

Bertie took a lemonade and sat down across from us on a matching yellow sofa.

"I imagine you must have a good, factual reason for hiding from your newly acquired husband?" Bertie was old enough to be my father, yet played the vastly older brother role well.

My heart sunk into my shoes. "He's after Aunt Edwina's money, even though I don't have it. He's also romancing another woman, for how long I don't know." I brought up the picture of Chris and Carlene on my phone and showed it to Bertie.

Bertie shook his head. "If he's doing this, then it makes no sense to do that," he said, looking at my unexpectedly bare ring finger. "Oh, I see you have already taken care of that unfortunate advertisement."

"Pawnshop in Carlingheath," Gertie admitted. "Morning after the wedding. Plus, I've been defrocked, so the wedding wasn't for real."

Bertie grinned. "What a jolly good stroke of luck ... er, for the marriage, not for you, Gertie."

I was downcast. "Bertie, I'm sorry but there's something I need to tell you, a secret I've been hiding for far too long." And there it was. My moment of truth, the one I'd bottled up inside for many years. It had hung over me for years, only recently overshadowed by my problems with Chris. It was Gertie, my dear, boisterous, karaoke-singing cousin, who'd given me the confidence to fess up and start clean. With luck I'd earn a second chance. A do-over. Freedom.

"Go on." He sat up straighter in his chair and looked serious.

I forced myself to meet Bertie's eyes. "I was the one who took your beloved antique car out for a joyride when I was a teenager. I was the one who crashed it into the shop window and ran."

"Yes, I know," he said.

"You know?" I was incredulous. A gigantic weight was lifted from my shoulders.

He gave me a pert smile. "My dear, you left a violet paint smear on the headrest."

I sighed. "I completely understand if you no longer wish to be my art patron anymore."

Bertie shook his head. "On the contrary, my dear. But on two conditions."

"Two?"

"One. You consider us square. And two, you let me help take down that dastardly false husband of yours."

I couldn't help but grin. "I'd love your help defeating Chris. But square? I'm the one who wrecked your car, so I don't understand how–"

Gertie leaned forward to hear this one in all its minute detail.

Bertie started to explain. "Edwina knew that I crashed her yacht into a concrete dock after a charity polo match one summer. My crash versus your crash make us even. Right?" He extended his hand for me to shake.

"Good," he said. "And we shall say nothing more of it. Now this Chris of yours ..."

I nodded. "It's all so awful. But I didn't know about Carlene until the day after the wedding, honest."

"We nearly called to ask you to evict Chris from your converted barn, but Julie was worried about him slashing her paintings."

Bertie's face softened. "That's very noble of you, Julie. Some of the art in progress is due at my estate in the next few months. I'd hate to see it go to waste."

"So what do we do next?" Gertie asked.

"Take one of my cars from this house and go on to your next destination. Yes, Chris told me about your treasure hunt. He found out about it from the pub owner in Plumsden, who happens to be a chum of his. Chris just tracked down the closest person in Edwina's monthly Sherry Club and the jig was up."

I groaned. "I had no idea Chris knew Clint at The King's Arm."

Bertie took both my hands in his. "Buck up. We'll get you onto your next destination. Where are you at with the treasure hunt?"

"The key is with Harriet in her bank safety deposit box. She promised to meet us there first thing tomorrow morning."

"Very well, then. Have Severs bring your bags here so you can stay the night, and then we'll all go to the bank in the morning."

"Oh Bertie, thank you for being so kind. I really don't know what else to say." I literally felt like giving the kind man a gigantic hug, but I knew he didn't like that sort of thing.

"Speak no more of it. It is my duty as Lord of the Manor to protect friends in distress. The motto of my family is: 'Build Bridges and Fewer Fences'."

***

The five of us—Bertie, Ewan, Harriet, Gertie, and I—entered the bank at precisely 10:00 a.m. the next morning. We'd already congratulated Harriet on a successful auction yesterday. She replied that the auction house had done well, and the greyhound rescue society was most pleased with the estimated proceeds from a kind William Hinghurst who used to race greyhounds.

Harriet emerged from the small room at the bank, after making an important withdrawal from her safety deposit box. She looked triumphant, holding a large brass key in her hand. "Here we are," she said, handing me the key.

I noticed Gertie's eyes get awfully wide when she saw the key. "Yes, Gertie?" I asked.

"I've seen those before. They're for church parish chests, made in Henry the Eighth's time. He mandated that every one of his churches had a secure chest with locks on it." She looked at it much closer. "Yes. Somebody's actually scratched in an *H* and the number eight here into the loop of the key, see?" She passed the key around to us, and we all saw it.

"My goodness, this is a lot more exciting than my rotational grazing agricultural meeting this evening," Bertie said. He was really starting to get into this treasure hunt.

"Where's the closest church in town?" I asked.

Harriet answered that one. "Do you mean here in Medchester or back in Ludring?"

I thought on it for a minute and then responded. "It would have to be back in Ludring, where your grandfather was. Aunt Edwina assumed that you still live there because that's where the flour came from, at your family's multigenerational business."

Bertie checked his watch. "Right. Back to Ludring we go."

"We're not keeping you from anything else?" Gertie asked.

"Apart from my usual elevenses? No. Not until this evening," Bertie added.

Severs trundled the lot of us back to Ludring, Harriet following in her own car. We all agreed that it was doubtful Chris would tail us to a church, it being his least-likely place to frequent in any town.

St. Olave's Church had a fine history. It was famous for arches that were parallel to the pews, the ones that made for quite the slalom course whenever a bride walked down the aisle to greet her bridegroom. It also had a monument for the prominent Simpson family in the chapel with an unusual carving of a Chrysom Child, a stillborn child in swaddling clothes.

There was an old codger working in the churchyard as we walked in. I approached and asked if he was the churchwarden. The man in the flat cap and worn clothes stood, then cricked his back to get upright. "No, that's not me. Heck, I'm not even a local. I've only been here forty years."

We exchanged polite grins amongst ourselves and continued on to the church interior. Gertie knew exactly where to go. She strode with confidence up to the ancient vestry, the place where clergy would put on their official clothing for services. Unfortunately, the door was locked. She turned to look at us.

"We need the churchwarden. The porch should have signage as to where he or she lives."

"I say, this is very exciting," Bertie said.

Bertie, Ewan, Harriet, Gertie, and I trooped back down to the porch and read the sign. 'Fanny Gardiner, Churchwarden.' It listed her address in Ludring.

Harriet pulled up the address on her phone. "It's nearby, just over a couple of blocks," she said.

"How about I go with Gertie and the rest of you stay here, just so we don't look too obvious," Ewan offered.

It seemed to be the best plan, so we all went with it.

Fifteen minutes later, our search party was back with an intrigued-looking Fanny, who carried a large ring of keys. She was a solid, sensible woman in her fifties and duly impressed with our mission. I felt my anticipation grow as I heard the keys jangle against her hip.

"It's not too often that our old church is part of a mystery tour," Fanny said.

"Have you been working here long?" I asked.

"Not as long as the not-so-local man working in our churchyard," Fanny said with a smile. "I take it you've met Brian Flintmerle."

We nodded and shared a laugh.

"There was a bit of excitement here a few years ago when we had an escaped felon seeking sanctuary in St. Olave's," Fanny explained.

"What happened?" Gertie asked.

"The priest was away, so I sat with the felon for thirty-six hours, convincing him to turn himself in to the authorities. Can't say I liked having a gun in this house."

"How brave," Bertie said.

"I don't know how brave it was; it really was my only way out," Fanny said. She walked us over to the vestry door, unlocked it, and there stood the object of our quest: a dark-brown oak chest, six-feet long, three-feet wide, and four-feet tall. The chest was battered and weathered, undoubtedly from centuries of being moved over stone floors and from exposure to damp interiors. Two heavy clasps were fixed onto the front of the rugged lid as well as down its front. Fanny motioned me close and pulled out one key to open the left lock. Harriet's key then fit in the right lock. Both padlocks now opened, and we took them out of their metal loops on the chest and opened the lid.

Inside was some old, used silver plate, an envelope marked *Julie,* and a wrapped package in the definite shape of a water-color painting, also marked with my name. Fanny gently lifted both the envelope and the painting out and handed them to me.

Harriet refused to take her own key back, telling Fanny that it was now back where it belonged. Fanny wished us well on our way out.

Gertie stopped halfway down the cool stone floor, panic stricken. She patted herself down. "I need two pounds. Does anyone have two pounds?"

I rolled my eyes. "The penance."

"I'm sorry?" Fanny said.

I gave Fanny the brief summary. She laughed. "I'm sorry, but being defrocked for too-lively karaoke seems a little overzealous, considering what else is going on in our world today."

"I blame it on the stealth punch," Gertie moaned. She looked at our group, getting frantic. "I still need two pounds. Does anyone have two pounds?"

Bertie looked blank, because obviously he always paid on his good name's credit or got things gratis. I was clear out of change, as were Harriet and Ewan.

Then Gertie smiled. She slowed down her frantic movements and pulled a two-pound coin out of a hidden pocket. "First rule of travel. Always carry emergency funds."

The coin made a satisfying clank onto the pile already at the bottom of the donation box. The world was made right again. And today, I felt that this would, eventually, all work out for the best.

I looked outside at the churchyard and felt my stomach rumble.

Chapter 27

After profuse thanks to Fanny, we all went back to Bertie's country home outside Medchester for tea. Bertie called ahead, and so we sat down to a wonderful spread literally twenty minutes after we arrived. Staff of great houses had a peculiar intuition that anticipated their host's every need. For example, serving roast chicken within a twenty-minute window was impossible. However, the cook noted that the Lord of the Manor was touring in the area with friends and that they would be staying the evening. So she put three birds in the oven to roast, knowing that they would be used either at tea, as a late dinner, or as a staff meal the next day.

We were spoiled with roast potatoes, carrots, broccoli, brussel sprouts, leeks, and a wonderful strawberry rhubarb pie for dessert. Bertie would hear nothing of opening the painting or the envelope until we were at least finished the first course. It was a seven-year-old's Christmas-present-opening-delay agony all over again.

Now that we'd all finished our pie and lingered over dessert wine, Bertie motioned for me to retrieve the artwork and envelope. Once the larger dishes were off the table, he had an entire clear end on the tablecloth. He had his staff put down extra folded tablecloths just to protect the artwork. No food or drink allowed within ten feet. He left the package wrapped while I opened the envelope. It contained another piece of Greymore Hall stationery with a small brass key taped to it. I read Aunt Edwina's beautiful handwritten note:

> *Dear Julie:*
>
> *Your treasure seeking quest continues!*
>
> *This royalist town has a flute and silver salt tower,*
> *And a princess born while an older king clung*
> *to power.*
> *An explorer gave coffee that surely did entertain,*
> *Sea captains in town trading goods for gain.*
> *A shipwreck's victims rest here, sunk against their will,*
> *While other scared bodies rest on their exotic hill.*
> *A city famous for trading wool from sheep,*
> *Heed the wild ponies as they wander the heath.*
>
> *Love always,*
> *Aunt Edwina*

I went over and opened the package. Inside was a watercolor painting signed by 'E.E.', depicting a boy and a girl sitting on a medieval stone bridge.

Gertie was the first to pick up on it. "Is this the sixteenth painting that Algy over at Holgarth's Hall was looking for?"

"Possibly," I said. "What do you think, Ewan? Algy's a client of yours, right?"

"Yes, but he's looking for another artist, a G.Z. Norton. Does that frame come apart?"

I looked it over closely and saw no join in the wood. "No, not this time."

"So we have the watercolor and the riddle."

Bertie leaned back in his chair. "If we put our heads together, I think we can solve this tonight."

There was silence in the room. But only for a moment. When one put good minds together, including Bertie, Ewan, the Major, Gertie, and I, ideas were bound to percolate to the surface.

The men gave it a shot first, with Bertie sharing his insight. "I say, there is a coffeehouse where Sir Walter Raleigh did entertain foreign diplomats, about two-hundred miles south-west of here. King Charles the First's daughter Henrietta was born there, and it's famous for being a royalist town."

"Sea captains trading goods for gain," the Major said. "Could be any one of the port cities."

"Scared bodies on an exotic hill." Gertie shook her head. "This riddle is harder than the prior ones."

"I think I've got it," Ewan said. "There's only one town I know that has a flute you drink from, and the salt tower is now part of the Crown Jewels."

"A flute you can drink from? Surely all the liquid would fall out of the holes on the way up?" I said.

Ewan shook his head. He looked at Bertie, who was nodding in agreement. Those two knew what was going on.

"It's not a musical instrument flute, Julie. It's a champagne flute," Ewan said. "Tall and thin, made of glass, etched with King Charles the Second's likeness for a local celebratory banquet."

"And when Charles the Second was restored to the throne, the city's residents gave him an intricately made salt tower that is definitely one of the prized possessions of the Crown Jewels," Bertie added. "I've held it, and it's marvelous. Reputedly used in 1660 at a celebratory banquet when the king arrived en route home to London from his landing at Dover."

"Okay. And it's got to be near Dartmoor because that's where wild ponies roam the heath," I added.

"They also have wild ponies in Exmoor and other national forests," Gertie said.

"Not with champagne flutes," I retorted. I looked at both Bertie and Ewan. "Okay, gentlemen, fess up, please."

"And would you like to do the honors, kind sir?" Bertie asked Ewan.

"Certainly, my esteemed colleague," Ewan replied, really drawing out the suspense. "The referenced town in question, I believe, is Pixleton."

Gertie was busy scrolling through her phone. "I agree. A few 'Glory Boymead' shipliner victims are there, and the 'exotic hill' means the hillside Egyptian-like catacombs that were built but never used to their full extent. They were built in order to prevent grave robbers." She shivered. "Imagine that. Going toes up and someone stealing your corpse."

We all shivered.

"Right then, we have our marching orders," Gertie said. "Julie and I will leave in the morning."

The men all harrumphed.

Bertie was brave enough to go first. "Ladies, I would rather you take one of us with you. With Chris now roaming around after you, I just don't think it's wise for you ladies to go by yourselves. Also, you're still distraught over Aunt Edwina."

Wrong thing to say.

Gertie and I both bristled. "We're not damsels in distress for you to rescue, Bertie," I said.

"Of course not, however–" he started.

"Of course, it would just be preferable if we took a man with us, right?" Gertie finished for him.

He took offense. "Good grief. It's not like we're asking you to run naked across the village green. We're just offering our help," Bertie said.

"It really makes sense, ladies," the Major said. "As with any great battle plan, you need strategists with every different type of expertise to best outflank and outwit the enemy."

Ewan looked a bit bashful, yet eager. "My aunt owns a self-catering cottage near Dartmoor National Park. I also got my undergrad art history degree from the University of Pixleton and offer that, as well as my antiques expertise, which has come in handy quite a few times on this journey so far, I might add, and–"

I held up a hand. "Fine. Ewan can come. But not all of you. A larger group would just slow us down."

"Slow you down? When I was in the military, I'll have you know my lightning raids were legendary," the Major said.

"I believe Bertie and the Major can work at home base and play an important supporting logistical role," I said. "Besides, the idea of Bertie surviving a self-catering cottage just does not ring true to me at all." I raised my glass, and we toasted to that concept.

"You're likely correct," Bertie said. "I do like my ironed newspaper and three-minute boiled eggs with their one-and-a-quarter inch strips of toast at precisely 7:45 a.m."

"Then it's settled," Gertie said.

"And I have another toast to make, if you'll indulge me," I said. I raised my half-full glass of dessert wine and stood. "I wish to offer a simple, yet kind thank you to all of my friends here tonight. Your warm smiles, kindred spirits, willingness to protect the past as well as cherish the future, all in Aunt Edwina's good name, are greatly appreciated. To Aunt Edwina!"

Everyone responded with raised glasses. "To Aunt Edwina!"

It was warm, cozy, and quite frankly, exactly the morale booster we needed. Because there was one thing—no, one person—on my mind, and I didn't want him to be.

I sighed. "You all know how my marriage to Chris was a mistake and not really official, correct?"

Everyone nodded.

"Well, Gertie and I caught him with another woman the day after the wedding. And I also know that he's only after money, what little I currently have. He's aware of the treasure hunt, however, and that's what's egging him on."

"In other words, we need to lose the dude," Gertie said.

Ewan gave me a sympathetic look. I could tell he was upset, learning all I'd been through.

Bertie cleared his throat. "I cottoned onto that a while ago. Actually, Edwina gave me an inkling before she passed. So at the Hinghurst auction, I set Chris up." Bertie looked rather chuffed with himself.

I frowned. "What do you mean?"

"I told him you two ladies keep everything in Athena and that she's in for repairs right now. I told him about the storage shed at the retail park in Ludring and that Athena would be back in the shed tomorrow night, packed and loaded to go with everything for the next destination. I made it up as I went. I just played dumb, you know, the jolly old aristocrat."

I grinned. "Bertie, you are a peach."

"I hope you're not upset with my taking such liberties with your other half?"

"Never. Besides, Chris is a half I want to lose, and the sooner the better," I said, giving a shy glance to Ewan.

The Major banged his spoon against his wine glass. "Friends, allow me to interject a moment. The lure is out in the water, however, what bait do we use to get the fish to bite?"

Bertie sat up straight. "How about a riddle, composed just for Chris?" The look on his face was genuinely scheming.

Gertie spoke next. "I love it. Send Chris on a wild goose chase, somewhere up north in Scotland where he can get stranded at high tide. Just him and the seagulls."

I had to add to that one. "Plus Carlene. She'll probably come along with Chris for the ride."

"Every operation needs a name," the Major said. "Let me brainstorm. Operation Suede Shoe, Operation Hall Table, Operation Stormy Seas, Operation Guinea Pig, Operation Salt Cellar." He stopped when he realized everyone was staring at him, mouths agape. "Completely standard military operating procedure," he advised.

"Operation Suede Shoe sounds too obvious, like a smarmy sales guy," Gertie said.

"And Operation Guinea Pig sounds like it is a trial, and we need something that's definitely going to work," Ewan said.

"How about Operation Salt Cellar?" I asked. "It has a nice ring to it, and plus it's one of the pieces Gertie is still trying to find for her silver collection."

Ewan was busy scribbling something down on a piece of notepaper he'd pulled from his pocket. He was just that kind of person, organized and always with the right tools at hand.

No one argued with 'Operation Salt Cellar', so that's what our takedown stealth operation was coined. The Major was tickled pink at having named it.

"There are no dead bodies involved, are there?" I asked half joking, half serious.

Both the Major and Bertie frowned at the thought. "Of course not," the Major said. "That's just not done amongst men of honor."

Bertie was confident. "Remember, you're looking at two men who were masters of the payback game in their youth." He stretched his arms. "A brilliant military strategist plus a toffee-nosed aristocrat. What more could you possibly want?"

"How about a place and a riddle?" Gertie said in a sarcastic tone.

Ewan looked up from the note he was working on. "And while you lot are bandying about fancy names and strategies, I figured out where to send Chris as well as a rough riddle for us to leave inside Athena."

We all leaned forward as Ewan started to read:

> *This tartan isle is green and pure,*
> *Inside the clutches of Cromwell for sure.*
> *This castle was wrecked by a garrison sincere,*
> *To protect deer from poachers every night, every year.*
> *Look for the trap that captures something with claws,*
> *Enjoy your treasure, you're set for life, cue applause!*

"Pray tell, where is this fabled destination?" the Major asked.

"Tuttle Island in Scotland," Ewan replied. "It's a tiny little island off the Firth of Clyde. All that's left is the castle keep. Cromwell knocked down the rest. The island's connected to the mainland at low tide, but at high tide you're in for a swim."

"And the claws?" Gertie asked.

"Yes, do tell us about the claws," I added.

Ewan smiled. "Lobsters, of course. They still trap them on the coast. It will be interesting to see what Chris does with all this information."

Gertie grinned. "If he's smart enough to figure out the riddle."

"We'll leave him a few maps, with the proper island circled. Leave him no doubts at all," I added. "But we need to leave the riddle in the right format. I can forge a note from Aunt Edwina, along with her stationery. But I'm going to need the right paper stock and a gold paint pen."

The Major looked at his watch. "I think the stationers is still open. How about I nip down to the shops and get what you need?"

"Perfect."

I looked at Gertie. "While the Major gets the stationery supplies, I'll whip off a watercolor with a ruined castle on a tiny island."

She frowned. "But how will we age it to the 1940s?"

"In the oven, carefully, and on very low heat. It's been a classic forgers' trick for centuries."

"And you can use a key from this house," Bertie offered.

"I don't think that's wise," I said.

"Oh, not my front door. No, from my odds and sods collection." He gestured for us to follow him to the front hall. Bertie pulled open the drawer to a heavy side cabinet and there rested a jumble of fifty keys of all types, sizes, and finishes. Our host started to rummage.

"What are all these for?" I asked.

"No idea," Bertie said with a nonchalant shrug. "Most have been in the family for centuries. I have no use for them."

Ewan picked up a handful of loose keys, focusing on those that looked a few centuries old. "You could sell these to a collector for a tidy profit."

"Really?" Bertie gave him a smug smile. "Oh, let's not give Chris anything of real value. Try this one ..." He handed me a mid-sized brass key that was nicked in a few places but a bit shinier than the rest.

"What's this one?" I asked.

Bertie explained. "This one I do know. It's from a broken bicycle lock our cook used a couple of years ago. We can recycle it to a higher purpose."

"Perfect."

Overall, it was amazing how incredibly well we'd set the trap. With the right people and tools, we could get Chris to leap onto the nearest motorway destined for the land of tartan, scotch whiskey, and bagpipes.

***

The next morning, Gertie and I returned to Lady Susan's house. She was out back, set up with an easel, painting a watercolor of her grandchildren's swing set and the rose garden off in the distance behind it. Today she was wearing a beautiful royal-purple caftan interspersed with peacock feathers of green and turquoise. She was definitely a free spirit, a privileged one, but not afraid to speak her mind and help out friends in need.

"About 'E.E.'," I began.

"Edwina warned you'd be asking me about him," she said. "All I know about the mysterious man is that his first name was Elliot, and he was from Pixleton."

"Elliot from Pixleton," Gertie breathed. "Did you ever see a picture?"

Lady Susan shook her head. "I knew he was in the RAF during World War Two, and that she loved him dearly before she married her husband. It's almost like Edwina's left something undone with him that she wants you to finish for her."

"That's what we're thinking," I said. "I'm also wondering if Meadows could drive us to the old silk-printing works site so we can put some things in Athena. For the ruse, you know," I said.

"Of course, just let Meadows know when you'd like to leave," she said. "And you're staying with me one more night, correct?" She winked at us. "Have to give the thief some time to forage into the shed and find the planted riddle and watercolor, don't we?"

"It's all about making it look on the up and up," Gertie said.

Thirty minutes later we filled our suitcases, all except one, and put them in the back of Lady Susan's SUV. I had forged the riddle on Greymore Hall stationery the night before and also circled Tuttle Island on a map of Scotland with a thick, pink highlighter. To make things even more authentic, I'd even included a train timetable that showed how to get from Ludring into London and then zip, via fast train, all the way up north to Scotland. It made it look like we'd really researched all possibilities. We deposited these items inside Athena, securely locked the shed with the same padlock, and then left with Meadows once more.

My mobile phone rang just after 8:00 p.m. that evening.

It was the Major. "I am pleased to report that Operation Salt Cellar is now officially underway. The subject didn't just take your watercolor, riddle, map, and timetable, he also took Athena. Left here about twenty minutes ago."

"Oh dear. Gertie's not going to like that," I said, watching her towel off her hair as she entered my room at Lady Susan's.

"Gertie's not going to like what?" she whispered.

I put a hand over the phone and shushed her. I spoke back into the phone: "Thank you very much for the field report, Major. Well done."

He had one further question. "Did you want me to follow him?"

"To make sure he gets to Scotland?"

"To ensure we know where he dumps Athena before he gets on the fast train."

"Very wise idea," I said. "Glad I thought of that."

I'd just hung up from the Major when my phone rang again. "What did you forget?"

An officious man's voice that I didn't recognize came across the line. "I'm sorry? My name is Constable Bud Snowdrop, and I'm with the Ludring police. We've had a report of a break-in from the site manager at the old silk works and armaments factory retail park. I understand you store a vehicle there?"

This was an interesting development. "Who reported this?" I asked.

There was some shuffling of papers in the background that I heard. "Appears to be a Mr. Stan Trentworth of Ludring. Would you like to come down and identify the missing items?"

"Well, Constable Snowdrop, I can tell you that my cousin is likely missing a mint-green-and-cream-colored 1963 van, fondly known as Athena."

He emitted a high-pitched giggle, most unbecoming for a serious policeman. "Your vintage van is named Athena?"

"Do you find that amusing?" I asked in my sternest voice.

"Well, it's different. At any rate, it is customary for the owner of the property to come down and describe what property is missing."

So, for the second time that day, Meadows was commandeered to take Gertie and I in Lady Susan's SUV to the retail park shed complex.

We saw a very chagrined Stan standing there, cap in hand, looking quite apologetic. "I'm very sorry to have disturbed your evening, but I thought I'd better ring the police as soon as I saw the padlock had been broken and your vehicle was missing." The padlock was indeed hanging askew at a very ill-looking angle on the heavy clasps that kept the door shut. Someone had used effective bolt cutters. Yellow police tape prevented anyone from walking inside the shed at present.

Gertie stood up straighter. "Of course, there's not many like her in England. Athena's quite rare."

Constable Snowdrop was about five-foot-ten-inches tall, had a shock of black hair falling over his forehead, and was rather pudgy in his tight uniform. He looked like a man who took no nonsense from anyone unless he was bribed with a juicy Sunday roast dinner. His black service boots had thick soles, meant for walking his beat. Constable Snowdrop watched us with extreme interest, his pen and notepad out at the ready.

Gertie peered inside the shed and then looked back at us. "The thief took Athena, my suitcase full of two-pound coins, most of my clothes, most of Julie's clothes, and our trip planning itinerary."

She had Constable Snowdrop at 'suitcase full of two-pound coins'. He looked up from his notepad. "I'm sorry, you said a suitcase full of two-pound coins? Any idea of approximate value?"

She only had to think on it for a moment. "Just under £10,000."

"How on earth did you lift that into the van?" Constable Snowdrop asked.

"I'm joking. It was about £3,000," she replied.

Constable Snowdrop scratched out his recent notes. He looked rather perturbed that Gertie was toying with his investigation. She obviously didn't know of the unspoken rule not to joke with border guards or the police. Constable Snowdrop made a big show of once again crossing off the first number she gave him and then correcting it with the £3,000 figure.

She shook her head. "I think the only thing you'll find left in the shed is car wax, some old rags, and a fossilized lunch kit. Everything else was stolen."

"Well, fingerprinting will be here soon. We had a rather bad incident at the other end of town earlier today, and they're just finishing up at that crime scene."

"Oh dear," Gertie said. "I hope no one was hurt."

"Only people's minds," Constable Snowdrop said. "These petty vandals are quite intrusive these days." He loved being in the know. It was obvious. So obvious that he couldn't help but let slip more details. "I was interviewed for the local news."

"Really. That must've been some crime," I said.

"It was reported as vandalism by a couple of office workers. Then they discovered it was street art, although rather forward in nature, shall we say. They're pressure washing it off as we speak."

My antenna was up. "Anonymous street art can be worth a small fortune, you know."

Constable Snowdrop looked confused. "It was graffiti."

"Or a small fortune never quite making it into the local council's coffers," I countered in a heartbeat.

Constable Snowdrop looked like he was about to lose his lunch.

"They did a big documentary on it about a month ago. Didn't you see it on the news?" Gertie asked.

"I, er, well ..." Constable Snowdrop took off, then came dashing back again to close the conversation, slight panic now brimming in his eyes. "We'll keep you informed."

"Thank you very much, Constable," I said.

And then there was Meadows, standing quietly off to the side, pretending to polish the SUV. It was his job to shuttle us around, not to ask questions. I'm sure he thought we were all barmy by now. Thank goodness for his discretion.

Constable Snowdrop wasn't sure what to do next, but falling back onto police procedure was his obvious fail safe. "Right then. I've made a report and also taken pictures of the scene. Do you have additional contact information I can take for now?" he asked. He peered at me, then at Gertie, as if he was sizing us up. Then he refocused on Gertie. "Your face looks very familiar to me."

Gertie got agitated. "I don't think we've ever met, Constable. I'm pretty sure about that."

He peered at her some more and then cracked a grin. "I know. You're that singing priest, right? That's it! I never forget a face!" He looked awfully pleased with himself, as if watching a viral karaoke video was the penultimate in his policing career.

"Well, you're probably never going to believe this, Constable ..." Gertie started.

Chapter 28

—

Gertie and I borrowed a deep-burgundy-colored SUV from Lady Susan's fleet. It wasn't an ostentatious, fully decked-out exotic one, and that was perfect. It was good with us because it meant we were far less obvious on the road. En route we stopped off at a roadside station for refueling, lunch, and the toilets. It bears repeating because of the totally modern rest stop that this place really was. I was amazed to walk into the restrooms that were totally automated, each stall being a complete floor-to-ceiling individual room for each customer. One paid to get in by inserting coins into a turnstile, and each stall was even self-cleaning. After finishing, one could actually use the facility receipt for a discount at the restaurant.

The food offerings included a full selection of the standard soda, juice, and water array, and the business distinguished itself from other roadside stops by making sandwiches and salads to order, plus having an amazing dessert selection. We sat at a table off to the side and enjoyed ourselves, quite liking this respite from the frenetic activity of the last few days.

"All this skullduggery takes it out of you, doesn't it?" Gertie said.

"Agreed. I never thought art and letter-writing could be so complicated or carry such high stakes," I said.

"All I know is that when this is over, I'm going to sit out in my backyard with a deck chair and a good book. I may not even open the book. If it's sunny enough, I may just snooze for the afternoon."

I smiled back at her. "Do you remember the time we were traveling on the autobahn to Germany?"

"From Denmark?"

I nodded. "I came out of the restroom so impressed with this new modernized toilet, but forgot to do the coin exchange in my head. I ended up telling you it cost me €75 to use the toilet. You should've seen your face."

She laughed. "I remember asking you three times if that actually was what the toilet visit cost. You kept saying yes, so I eventually told you to stop drinking anything until we got to our hotel."

"I then realized I was trying to say 75¢ instead of €75!"

After a good chuckle, we clambered back inside the SUV and got underway.

***

City of Pixleton.

Pixleton was a lovely city, well-known for its cathedral and museums. University students loved this city because it was within close proximity of major train destinations. There were one-off specialty boutiques as well as high street shops plus a variety of restaurants. What got me the most, however, was the scenery leading up to the city and beyond. This part of the County of Devon had rolling hills, green fields separated by tall hedges and deep lanes, plus quite a sheep population. Dartmoor was behind the city, its groundcover a bit more purplish than the farmers' fields of spring green below.

We made our way to Pixleton Cathedral for obvious reasons: Gertie's two-pound donation. As we walked the high street, I noticed a bookshop selling new and secondhand tomes and pointed it out to Gertie.

"Let's just pop inside. I'd like to get a detailed guidebook for the area. One of those good ones that has history, pictures, and maps," I suggested.

It was a quaint little shop, tucked in between a cobbler's shoe repair and a solicitor's office. The building itself was at least Georgian, perhaps earlier. The door was painted bright red and the sign outside said 'Todling Books: Astonish the World with Superlative Reading'. We had to duck as we went inside because of the lower-than-expected doorframe. A tiny bell announced our arrival.

The shop was a delight for the senses as the slightly musty scent of ancient tomes reached our nostrils. It was literally jammed floor-to-ceiling with bookshelves, some with only two feet in between opposing pieces of furniture. There was order in this treasure trove of reading material, displayed with clearly printed topic placards at the end of each row. Behind a couple of stacks of genealogy magazines sat one unique man sucking on a piece of striped ribbon candy. He wore a rumpled tweed suit, a polka-dot bowtie, and scuffed shoes. His meaty hands held the candy in one and a sweet romance novel in the other.

"Good afternoon!" he exclaimed, springing to attention and knocking over one of the magazine stacks in the process. His candy emerged from the fray mashed into the front pocket of his lemon-yellow dress shirt, and his face turned beet red at the effort of returning all things to good order. His bowtie went askew, and he didn't seem at all embarrassed by what he was reading. He held out a hand. "Frederick Aloysius St. John Todling at your service, still better known as Fred Todling. How can I help?"

"Thank you," I said, still trying to take all of this in without being overly obvious. "We're looking for a comprehensive Pixleton-area guidebook. Something that also shows the surrounding villages."

Fred nodded and gave us a kind smile, showcasing a gleaming-white, perfect-toothed grin. "And are we heading for the shops, a quaint country drive, or a walking tour on the moors?"

Gertie and I looked at each other, undecided.

"We're really not sure. Do you happen to have a very thorough book that covers everything?" she asked.

"I do, I do." With a laser-like efficiency, he guided us to the exact spot on the exact shelf in the exact location in his shop that offered a brand-new Pixleton guidebook. He pulled it off the shelf, showing remarkable agility in his thick fingers. Quick on his feet, he spun around and handed it to us, resting it in both his open palms. "I believe this should do the exact, perfect, and precise trick."

The guidebook was, indeed, perfect. Lots of color pictures, a great index, and many of the local surroundings. We'd correctly guessed that Aunt Edwina's painter had decided to stray a little outside the formal confines of Pixleton city. There was a hint of open country, perhaps, behind the boy and girl sitting on the bridge watercolor. I sensed that perhaps he used a smaller village near Pixleton as his muse.

Fred loomed closer, wringing his hands. "How did I do, ladies?" He looked genuinely worried, and was checking we'd found what we needed.

"This is spot on, Fred," I said. "Thank you for the recommendation. We'll take this one."

He rubbed his hands together. "And is there anything else you are looking for? Perhaps a fancy bookmark or a gift for a loved one's upcoming birthday?" It seemed as though his entire life depended on up-selling us at this particular moment.

"No, thanks. This is all we need," I said. "Although, you don't happen to know a painter who goes by the initials of 'E.E.', do you?"

Fred looked devastated that he didn't know the answer. "Alas, I could tell you about every sun, star, and moon in the sky with my vast collection here in this bookshop. Every composition of Homer, every sonnet of Shakespeare ... yet it gives me great, unyielding sorrow to inform both shop visitors who stand before me at this precise moment in time that I do not know of the aforementioned phantom painter 'E.E.'"

This man really got into his books. And words.

"All right, just thought we should ask," Gertie said briskly, guiding me by the elbow to the register. She obviously wanted to beat a hasty retreat.

Fred fascinated me. And I had to pose the question. "Have you owned this bookshop long?"

Fred was busy ringing up our guidebook, and as he did, he shook his head. "This glorious commercial enterprise actually belongs to my illustrious and well-beloved uncle. I've just passed the arduous, rigorous and altogether mind-bogglingly intense bar exam, and pending my establishment as a new solicitor with clients, I'm minding the shop for him while he takes his annual holiday in sun-drenched Spain."

"You certainly seem very well-versed in English language books. Well done!" I said.

Perhaps my comments sounded a little lame, but Fred was just such an unusual person that I didn't really want to leave him hanging.

"Thank you, dear lady, your words warm the cockles of my heart." He made a big show of wrapping up our guidebook in fancy patterned paper, and then tying it with a textured, spooled ribbon that he curled using the end of a big pair of shiny scissors. He leaned forward. "Now there's just the tiniest matter of your invoice settlement, please." He spoke in a whisper, as if he was sharing some deep, dark, national secret. He said it like he was politely asking us to hand over the nuclear codes.

I rummaged in my purse and pulled out my credit card, doing a contactless payment for his wonderful local guide-book. I decided right then and there the recently qualified and overly verbose barrister was the most unlikely bookseller one could ever imagine.

Invoice now paid, he handed us the wrapped package, resting it again on the two open palms of his hands. We were given another courtesy brilliant-white smile.

"What type of law was it you intend to practice?" Gertie asked.

"Intellectual property," he replied.

"Why does that not surprise me? Best wishes with your new career," she said.

"Take a card, spread the word if you feel the urge," he said. "I would be most obliged."

"What exactly is intellectual property?" I asked as I turned his card over in my hand. His slogan was 'Todling Law: Minding IP for Pixleton and Beyond.'

Minding IP.

Rather unfortunate when one spoke it aloud.

Gertie couldn't resist. "Minding IP? Er ..."

Fred's face went red again. "The full intellectual property wording wouldn't fit within the design parameters of the card. And then the teenager doing graphic design at the copy shop forgot to put the periods after 'I' and 'P', so it became 'IP'."

Gertie nudged me.

"You could ask for a reprint, you know," I said. "Your business card is your first impression to a client. Don't settle for something you have to explain away every time. But I shouldn't have to explain breach of contract law to a solicitor."

"Ah, but it is a memorable slogan, is it not? I find it a rather unexpected bonus promotional gimmick, this ever-so-teensy typo of mine."

The best marketing gimmick in the world surely was his flowery manner of speaking.

He continued. "Now, intellectual property law involves trademarks, copyrights, and even things such as literary work ownership. I've always found it fascinating to consider that a body of work is copyrighted the moment an artist creates it. Now, that's not discounting someone's ability to formally register the copyright, but I like to think of that particular nuance of the law as meaning that the jolly good fellow—or gentlewoman—does usually win in the end."

"Were that only true for everything in life," I added.

**

Pixleton Cathedral was a truly amazing place of worship. We stood in awe of the intricately carved classical arches plus formal figures and gargoyles that covered the front façade of the building. The building dated back over 900 years and had been lovingly cared for ever since by devoted parishioners. Its largest bell was over a ton in weight. Fancy oak choir stalls and the bishop's throne were inside, as were rows and rows of dedicated parishioner pews. It had bravely survived the worst of the enemy bombing in World War Two. We looked for the donation box. It, too, was sturdy and well-crafted, four-sided with plexiglass, and already had a good pile of coins and bills inside.

Gertie strode up, pulled out a two-pound coin, and heard the satisfying clank down on top of the pile of prior donations. I could see in her mind she was counting out how many more boxes she'd have to find before she considered herself squared with the institution. It was a lot more to go, because really she'd only just begun. I didn't know how she would start over, or what her next career vocation would be, but knowing Gertie, she'd take it on full tilt and with gusto. She was never one to shy away from a challenge. I envied my cousin for her innate ability to pick herself up and move forward. Even if it did involve a smeared smoky eye and bright-red hair.

It was hard not to be overwhelmed by the beauty of the cathedral. One walked around with reverence, enjoying the multitude of artwork and even the smallest comical item on display. A raft of animals and wise people were carved in lifelike detail, placed around the perimeter of the stone walls, obviously created by artisans of great talent. Perhaps it was places like this that had attracted Gertie to the priestly robes in the first place.

Gertie came back over to me, a gentle smile in her face. "Well, that's that. Are you ready to leave?" she asked.

"It makes you wonder, doesn't it?" I asked her.

She was just as captivated by the soaring stone arches in the roof as I. "What does?"

"Why there's so much wrong in the world when it contains so much beauty like this."

She took my hand in hers and squeezed tight. "That's why God put people like you and I here on his earth. We're supposed to remind others of that fact."

***

Dartmoor National Park. Later.

Ewan wasn't joking when he said it was a true getaway holiday place. The self-catering cottage was right on Dartmoor National Park's heath. Set into a tiny alcove of meadow, Ewan's aunt had bought herself a jewel. With no neighbors in sight, this was a wonderful little hideaway. Clad in grey stone, and at least a couple of hundred years old, the cottage had a variety of mature trees around it. The inner border ringing the driveway was a stone wall absolutely jam-packed with wildflowers. There were a lot of flowers that crawled over the rock-wall face and cascaded down below: yellows, purples, and pinks, all in a wonderful display of green thumbs. The hills behind us were just starting to turn purple as the heather put on its annual display. The gravel drive wound around the side, where there was ample parking for up to three cars. The cottage itself was two stories and approximately fifteen-hundred-square-feet.

Ewan wasn't there yet. Earlier, he'd texted me the electronic door-code entry and told us to make ourselves at home. We walked in on a thoroughly modern holiday cottage that was a wonderful surprise. The front entrance hall boasted a large hanging wall embroidery that read 'Welcome Guests!' in the center and was surrounded by residents from the ancient city of Pixleton through the centuries. There was also an embroidery of an old blacksmith's forge, a man bent over in half, working hard as he held up the hoof of a black-and-white Shire horse. Someone had spent a lot of time embroidering smoke from the forge as well as the breath the horse exhaled onto the frosty morning scene.

The cottage opened up into a warm living room with a fifty-inch flat-screen television and an L-shaped sectional sofa done in tan fabric with lively purple and cream throw pillows. A low coffee table sat on a modern rug, which covered part of the hardwood floor. An interesting lamp, Art Deco vintage, hung over the middle of the room, and there were a couple of lamps on the side tables at either end of the sofa. To the left was a modern kitchen, smaller appliances than for a full-size house but definitely more than adequate for a holiday. The kitchen table sat underneath a couple more embroidery pieces: the first showing a full English fried breakfast including eggs, bacon, mushrooms, black pudding, and tomato plus toast, as well as another depicting the beautiful moorlands of Dartmoor. I marveled at the patience of the hands that created such beautiful embroidery. I, for one, did not have the patience nor skill for that type of handiwork.

We rightly assumed that all the bedrooms were upstairs. Separated by a long hallway that spanned the length of the cottage, there were two small, twin-bed rooms at one end of the cottage. The other end of the cottage had another bedroom, this one with a queen-sized bed. There was one bathroom upstairs for everyone to share. The skylights on the top floor were amazing and let in a lot of natural, warm light. Each bedroom had a window that opened out onto a view of the glorious carpet of green lawn out back, surrounded by wildflowers and mature trees.

After we came back downstairs, I turned to look at Gertie. "It's perfect."

"It is lovely. When is Ewan arriving?" she asked.

"In about an hour," I said, checking my watch. "He had some kind of a roll-top desk he was selling to a client at 10:00 a.m. today."

"Did you want to get supper started? We didn't even stop for tea this afternoon, what with the drive, the bookshop, and cathedral."

"No need. Ewan said he was bringing groceries and dinner with him. He ordered a grocery delivery straight to his antiques shop so he could take off directly to Pixleton."

"Well, isn't he a dear," Gertie said. "And I think we have visitors." She pointed outside the window.

There, on the wide expanse of lawn, were three wild Dartmoor ponies. One was a dark brown, the traditional coat color, and the other two were skewbald, white and brown. They were foraging out amongst the mature trees.

"Do you think they're welcome?" she asked. "This place does have a nice garden."

"I think out here on Dartmoor, the wild ponies rule the roost. Not much we can do about it."

We put our bags in our rooms, and noted the ponies were still there the next time we looked outside the downstairs window.

"To be that wild and free. What an interesting life," I observed.

"But you have no warm stable to sleep in at night. And these moors can get pretty rough in the wintertime. Windswept, cold, snowy ..."

"I suppose it's a romantic idea," I said.

"Speaking of romance, I noticed you're enjoying our time with Ewan," Gertie said.

I felt my cheeks go a little red. "Yes, unexpectedly so. He's a nice man, very kind."

"Is he married?"

"Honestly, I've never asked. I don't know what his situation is."

"Would you like me to find out?" And there was Gertie, standing straight in front of me, a knowing look on her face. She looked so sincere, her eyes focused directly on me, not a hint of a joke or put down inside them. All she offered was help and understanding.

"Well, considering I'm not really married ..."

"Then we must find out if he is," she said with a nod.

"I wouldn't be averse to moving in that direction. But be subtle, don't make it overt; that would just ruin what we're all doing right now for Aunt Edwina."

"Roger that."

We looked outside at the ponies again. "Somehow, Gertie, I think they've got the best life. Wild, free, and they just roam about making friends without any major drama involved." It did seem to be quite an idyllic life.

"Until they have the annual round-up; that can't be fun for them."

"I suppose not." My mobile phone rang, and I answered. "Hi Ewan."

He had questions for us about what individually packaged desserts he should be buying. He was in Pixleton, just finishing his grocery shopping because he'd forgotten to order dessert for his earlier shop delivery.

I put a hand over the receiver and asked Gertie if she wanted chocolate sponge cake or sticky toffee pudding. I then went back to Ewan on the line. "We'll both have sticky toffee pudding, please. And it's very sweet of you to call and ask. See you soon. Bye!"

I hung up and Gertie just looked at me with a syrupy smile on her face. "And once his situation is revealed, I think you'll do just fine on your own," she said.

I wagged a finger at her. "Just please don't make it awkward. I've had enough awkwardness with Chris to last me a lifetime."

Chapter 29

___

It indeed turned into an awkward moment when Ewan arrived. He was fully laden down with grocery bags. After he put them on the counter, we didn't know whether to just say a casual hello, shake hands, or give each other a hug. It was like that with burgeoning friendships. So we settled on a stiff hand wave all around.

"How was your drive in?" he asked.

"Fine. We took one of Lady Susan's lower-end SUVs to travel under the radar," Gertie explained.

Ewan grinned. "With hair that color, I don't think you're under the radar regardless of what vehicle you're driving."

"Ha." She shot him a dirty look. "In that case, I shall wear a hat."

Ewan turned his attention to me. "I thought I'd make us a stir-fry tonight. Brought all the ingredients, easy to toss the vegetables and meat into a skillet, boom, done."

"Sounds great," I said, returning his smile. It felt good to have him back with us. "We're just about to take another look at the watercolor. Did you want to see it too?"

"Er, I'd better get dinner going. Maybe later," he said, our eyes meeting.

I read the attraction between us in his eyes. I felt it too. Yes, there it was. *Awkward.* Exactly what I didn't want.

Gertie wisely made herself scarce.

I decided to tackle this head on so we weren't stuck in a vapor lock of discomfort for all eternity. "Look, Ewan, I think you're great, but we have to do Aunt Edwina's work first. We can't get distracted," I said.

He nodded, military-efficient like. "Of course. I understand. Just save me a place when this is all over. I'm very single, er, just so you know." He grinned.

And there it was: an easy way out of a difficult situation, figured out in an instant by a very caring man. I felt totally comfortable and relieved.

Gertie and I now had a definitive answer to the question about Ewan's situation.

"Do you need any help with dinner?" I asked.

He shook his head. "I'm pretty good in the kitchen. Go look at your painting with Gertie. I'll call you when our meal's ready."

"Great, thanks." I left him in the kitchen, the half door open to the outside air, and went to find Gertie.

She had the watercolor out on the coffee table in the living room right beside our guidebook, which was open to the history section. She was bent over, peering at the bridge. "This looks awfully similar to the medieval bridge in Pixleton." It was true, the girl and boy sitting on the bridge, their legs dangling over the side, did make it look as if the unused medieval bridge was where the painter had situated his models.

"But it's got the countryside in the background instead of the low-rise shops and taller buildings behind it. I think the painter has mashed two different scenes together," I said.

"That makes the most sense to me. Like I said back in Medchester when we were all having dinner together, I think this riddle and painting are more difficult than the last ones," Gertie said.

Twenty minutes later, Ewan came into the room. "Supper is served, ladies."

We made all the right sorts of rumblings and appreciative noises as we headed to the kitchen. The cottage was far too small for a formal dining room. Besides, it would've been way too ostentatious for us anyways. All we needed was good food and a warm, quiet place to sleep, and then we'd be ready to tackle Aunt Edwina's mystery tomorrow.

Ewan was quite an unexpected talent in the kitchen. His stir-fry was packed full of crisp, tender zucchini, orange peppers, bean sprouts, and onions. Nothing too soggy or overcooked. It was seasoned just enough to be tasty yet not so peppery it gave one heartburn or stomachache. The meat was also cooked perfectly, and he'd added a small side bowl of rice for each of us. Dessert was perfect, and we had sparkling water as our beverage. Simple, last-minute, but everything tasted really good.

He toasted us with his glass. "So we've got antiques, churches, and art all covered with our knowledge here. What a team!"

Gertie and I knew that he deserved strong thanks.

"Ewan, you've been more than generous with your time in our family's quest. Thank you so much for all your help. We enjoy spending time with you and really appreciate your expertise," I said.

"It's the least I can do for the person who saved me from losing more than three hat pins at the antiques fair in Waverly-on-Sea. You probably saved our industry six figures or more by breaking up that ring of thieves." He toasted us again and then drank some more water.

"Imagine a thief dressing up like an elderly woman to take advantage of good people. That's just not cricket," Gertie said.

We all shook our heads and focused on dessert. This was just three good friends enjoying an evening together after quite a series of adventures to date.

***

Gertie and I were already set up in our bedrooms at one end of the top floor. Ewan took the bedroom at the other end of the hall. We worked out a bathroom schedule for the morning, where each person got half an hour. He let us go first as long as we were out by 7:00 a.m. We were all soon sound asleep.

Later on, I awoke to a horrible shriek from downstairs.

I met Ewan at the top of the landing, both of us rapidly tying on bathrobes, hair askew and wild-eyed.

"It's coming from downstairs!" I urgently whispered.

"Where's Gertie?" he asked.

"I think she's the one shrieking. Come on!"

We pounded down the stairs two at a time and headed into the kitchen, where the shrieking continued. Ewan gently ran into me from behind as I stopped in shock upon seeing Gertie facing an enormous two-hundred-pound potbellied pig beside the kitchen table. The pig was black, with bristly hair all over it. His feet made tick-tack contact sounds on the floor, and he grunted every once in a while as Gertie prevented the pig from leaving the kitchen.

The only thing louder than the pig's grunts were Ewan's guffaws.

Gertie shot him a look of doom. "I'm glad you find this funny, mister 'my aunt has a holiday cottage in Dartmoor that will be perfect'."

Tears ran down Ewan's face. He held his stomach with both hands. "It's just ... it's just, that's the neighbor's pig. He wouldn't hurt a flea; he's just looking for food. I forgot to padlock the door after leaving it open to air out the kitchen a bit after dinner. He's a smart one and knows how to work door handles."

Gertie had her hands on her hips, a skillet still clutched in one of them. "I'm so glad to hear that. It could have been a wild boar, you know."

That was my cue. "Charles the First actually did reintroduce them to England–"

"Not now, Julie!" Gertie said, wielding her skillet as the pig grunted and moved closer.

We heard heavy boots tromp up the path, and then the last person on the planet we expected poked his head around the door: Fred Todling, verbose solicitor and bookseller. He was also in his bathrobe, his hair not perfectly combed, and sans bowtie. We all looked quite embarrassed at ourselves, standing there staring in shock at each other in our bedclothes.

The pig flopped down on the floor and started napping.

It was Fred who first broke the silence. He got a very cross look on his face and glared down at the potbellied pig. "BAR-NA-BY, how frightfully rude of you! How on earth do you expect Ewan's guests to feel welcome when you come rooting around in their kitchen during the small hours of the morning.

Very rude." Fred looked up at us with an apologetic smile on his face. "Ladies, please permit me to extend you the most fervent and complete set of apologies I am able to offer. This is a personal affront to both our dignities as well as to your quiet, peaceable enjoyment of this property. Barnaby and I take full responsibility for the intrusion."

There was really nothing one could say after that incredibly complete apology.

"Well, at least we can see your legal training is being put to good use, Fred," Gertie said. "Now can we please have a removal of the pig from our kitchen?"

Fred clipped a leash onto the pig's collar and then tapped his index finger against his thigh. The pig obediently heeled, and Fred had him squirreled away faster than one could say 'grunt'. As a parting gift, Fred looked back over his shoulder. "And to all good night."

The three of us left in the kitchen first checked if there was anywhere we shouldn't step. Seeing that the pig was house-trained, we all sank into kitchen chairs, wondering what to say next. There really was no protocol for this experience, because waking up in the middle of the night to encounter the neighbor's potbellied pig inside the house didn't have a guidebook.

"I'm so sorry, ladies," Ewan said. He was still wiping tears from his eyes.

"Do you think, perhaps, a warning might've been issued?" Gertie asked. She wrapped her bathrobe around her sturdy frame a bit tighter, as if she wanted to protect herself against any other animal intruders disturbing her slumber.

Ewan shrugged. "Barnaby's a pretty smart boy. He keeps figuring out how to unlatch his pen and does these night wanderings, much to the chagrin and embarrassment of his owner."

"Fred just didn't strike me as the type," I said. "What on earth is he doing with a domesticated pig?"

"What is anybody doing with a domesticated pig?" Ewan replied. "And a two-hundred-pound one at that."

There was a knock on the door. Fred popped his head in through the top half. "Sorry to disturb, however, in light of the vast apology that I owe you, please accept a free one-hour legal consultation from my law firm, courtesy of the founder himself." Ewan got up to take Fred's business card, on the back of which he'd written: *One Hour Gratis. Signed Fred Todling.*

Fred wasn't done yet. "I only live a half mile up the road, and you know where the bookshop is, so any time you feel the need for some confidential legal advice, I would be more than happy to oblige. As you know, I'm an expert in intellectual property law and can help you register any type of copyright or trademark that you need processed forthwith, including all the necessary follow-up notifications and notarizations."

Ewan was up at the door again, hand on the upper half, trying to shut the conversation down. "I'm absolutely certain Julie and Gertie will let you know if that's of any use to them. Right now, I'm not aware of any copyright or trademark issue that they have, but you will certainly be the first to know, Fred."

"Well, thank you, kind sir. I must say, you are the most cordial and courteous neighbor I've ever had the pleasure of interacting with. You're so understanding, and of course so good with Barnaby that we consider you a dear friend and trusted confidant." Fred looked like he was just getting started on another diatribe.

Ewan started swinging the upper half of the door closed this time. "Goodnight, Fred."

Chapter 30

———

The next morning we headed back into Pixleton in pursuit of other local knowledge that matched Aunt Edwina's riddle for this place. The fact that she mentioned both 'sea captains' and 'trading goods' led us to the Brown's Customs and Trades Building, a 1681 building that stood the test of time as well as contributed a massive amount to the city's history. It was at this very location, resplendent with its gold-leaf plasterwork ceiling, that trade was done over several centuries. All this was courtesy of the founder Gill Brown. Pixleton cloth was stamped with a tillet block before it was ready to board a ship. Cloth was traded for items such as rice, wine, sugar, coffee, and much more. Smugglers were also rampant in the area, and this added another layer to the complicated network of ships, captains, and commercial merchants keeping the economy going.

Today the Brown's Customs and Trades Building was a museum open to the public. We walked in just as a woman who looked very much in charge was explaining to a visitor how customs officers used to burn smuggled goods in a stove on site. The three of us admired the intricate ceiling. The woman with the visitor acknowledged our presence and held up an index finger, indicating she'd be with us in a moment. It looked like she was giving directions to the visitor, and once heads started nodding yes, we knew she was nearly free to help us.

The petite woman had her hair done up in a messy bun. She rushed over to us, full of apologies. "I'm terribly sorry. Two of our guides called in ill today, so we're quite short staffed. How can I help you?"

Ewan started. "We're wondering if you are an acquaintance of Lady Edwina Greymore?"

She smiled. "Ah, I've been expecting you. I have a replacement guide coming in half an hour. Can you wait that long, look around the museum, perhaps, until that time? I'd like to give Edwina's travelers my full, undivided attention."

***

Thirty minutes later we met in her office. Her name was Lisette Gilbert-Durand, and she was obviously incredibly organized, judging from the various file folders and pencil cups she used to corral everything on her wide expanse of clear desk. It looked like this was a typical not-for-profit organization where funding was tight, yet ideas were big.

We sat in the guest chairs and the door was closed. Lisette leaned forward, clasping her hands together. "You must be Julie," she said, looking directly at me.

"That's correct," I said. "Do you happen to be the lady from France that Lady Susan Marcelon was telling us about?"

"The lady from France." Lisette chuckled. "Do you know I emigrated from France over thirty years ago, and they still call me the lady from France? I'll never escape it. Some days I wonder if I should tattoo the Union Jack on my forehead and carry a fish-and-chips-stained newspaper in my purse."

We all had a good laugh over that one.

Gertie and Ewan introduced themselves.

"We have this riddle from Aunt Edwina, and it's led us to Pixleton. Because it mentions ship captains and trading, we assume this is the best place to start. How are we doing so far?" I looked to Lisette for any hints that we were on the right track. Quite frankly, after this harder riddle and the painting that was not making total sense, it would be a devastating blow if we were wrong. Worse yet, none of the guidebook's surrounding villages and their histories had struck a chord.

Lisette took a deep breath. "You have deduced correctly. I am the lady from France in the Sherry Club with Susan and Edwina. And yes, Edwina roped me in to be part of her riddle quest. She was quite a good sport."

"She left us a key." I started to feel inside my pocket for the key from St. Olave's Church. I looked aghast and then realized Gertie had it for safekeeping.

Gertie hauled it out of the pocket of her floral dress and handed it over. "Key."

Lisette held the key in her hands and turned it over a few times. "Yes, I believe you have brought me to my 'Open Sesame' moment. And trust me, I'm just as excited to see what Edwina locked inside my historical desk as you are." She got up and led us to a small back room. Behind a narrow, floor-length curtain stood an antique writing desk. It had a lid that opened up to showcase an upright wooden letter-sorting box. Underneath were various cubbyholes for things like stamps and spare jars of ink. The writing surface actually folded down from the front of the desk, and there were two smaller cabinet doors that opened underneath. The entire unit was covered in inlaid wood and was lacquered to produce a high sheen.

"Somehow it almost looks too fancy for the high seas, but apparently it went out a few times before the ship was retired and ended up here as part of payment for duties owing," Lisette explained.

The desk certainly captured Ewan's attention immediately. "It's a very lovely piece. Late nineteenth-century?"

"So I understand," Lisette said. "A former ship captain's desk, and it's been here at Brown's for much longer than I."

Ewan took a closer look and noted the quality brass lock as well as the marquetry on every gleaming wood surface. "May I?" he asked. "I deal in antiques."

Lisette stepped aside. "Of course, be my guest."

Ewan inserted the small brass key, the one we'd brought from the envelope that I'd opened at Bertie's house after our visit to St. Olave's. He turned it in the lock and rotated a handle of one of the small cubbyhole doors in the top part of the desk. There was a slight click. Suddenly, a secret compartment sprang open towards the top of the desk, revealing Aunt Edwina's next letter inside.

Lisette looked shocked. "And here I was expecting a letter to be front and center in one of the cubbyholes. I had no idea that secret compartment even existed. Edwina obviously knew her antiques."

"It was very popular in Victorian and Edwardian times. Secrets and tricks amongst friends were well-known amusements," Ewan advised.

Lisette took the letter out of its secret compartment and handed it to me. The envelope felt a bit heavy, and I knew that meant there was another key inside.

Ewan handed Lisette his card. "It's a lovely desk. If you ever want to sell it, please contact me first."

"Well, that would have to go through the board of trustees, but I will let them know you're interested," she said.

"I have several clients who would be thrilled to have this piece in their collection." Ewan couldn't take his eyes off the desk. It truly was a lovely specimen and had been preserved in the utmost best condition.

"Edwina always said that Julie would come looking for this desk. All of us in the Sherry Club vowed to keep her secrets safe until you came to collect what she wanted you to have. I'm almost sad that the excitement's over so soon," Lisette said.

"Well, team, I think we've done very well this morning. Now it's on to the next site," Gertie said. "Unless you know anything about two children sitting on a medieval bridge?" she asked Lisette.

All we got back from our new friend was a puzzled look followed by her emphatic and polite 'no'. We then issued our thanks and went back to our vehicle. As we walked, Gertie looked at both of us. "It almost seems too easy, doesn't it?"

"Well, the riddle and watercolor were harder, maybe that's why when we finally figured it out, it all came together fast," I said. "What do you think, Ewan?"

"All I can think of is how wonderful that antique was. I've never seen a ship's captain desk in such fine condition, nor one with such intricate marquetry. She must know she has a one-of-a-kind object there. I was practically drooling over it."

"And that's an image I'd like to immediately scrub from my mind," Gertie shot back. She screwed up her face in disgust, and we laughed together.

I spotted a cozy café on our walk. Our little team decided to sit down and review what Aunt Edwina had left in her latest envelope for us.

Chapter 31

——

Dirk's Bean Easy Café, Pixleton.

We all ordered cappuccinos in order to get some serious caffeine flowing through our veins. This had been a long trek already, and there was still more to go. It's not like we wanted to give up, not by any means; we were just trying to pace ourselves and not make any mistakes with the clues.

In the middle of our quiet contemplation, my mobile phone rang, and caller ID said it was a London number. My heart sank to my stomach. "I hope this isn't Chris who's figured out the ruse before he even left the capital."

"Well, if it is, you can't avoid him forever. You might as well answer and get it over with," Gertie said.

And so I did. Quietly, so as not to disturb the others in the café.

And thankfully it wasn't my false husband.

"Hello, I am trying to reach a 'Julie Fincher'." A rather posh accent accompanied the male voice speaking.

"This is she," I said.

"This is Michael Eppelton from Eppelton Military Memorabilia. I'm a friend of Lance Holgarth's. I believe he had you send me some photos by email?"

"Oh, I'm so excited you called!" I whispered who it was to Gertie and Ewan.

"I would like to thank you for taking the trouble with these photos. I'm sorry for the delay in my response; our internet's been down, something about an unfortunate fault with an underground cable. I don't think you realize exactly what you have, hence your email to me, correct?" Michael asked.

"They just looked so forlorn sitting there in a box of post-cards at the antiques fair. I wanted to rescue them and reunite them with the right family if I could."

"Well, Julie, you've done much more than that. You've actually found some rare photos of Horace Griffins, a famous British Special Operations Executive, or SOE agent. He was an expert saboteur and the one who decimated a secret ammunition store the enemy kept on the coast of France during World War Two. Horace saved fifty-one lives that night and was awarded the George Cross for his bravery."

"Wow. I had no idea. Were the woman and baby his family?"

"Yes, indeed. Mary and daughter Rose. Mary and Horace are actually the grandparents of a current Member of Parliament representing a London district. I'm reaching out to see if it would be alright to pass your contact information along to them so they can issue a proper thank you."

"Oh, it's wonderful we've brought the photos back home. Thank you so much for your help. How could you tell from the photos?" I asked.

"I recognized the uniform and the scar on his hand from his famous work in France. Just so you are aware, the Member of Parliament happens to be a good friend of mine, and a long time ago he asked me to keep on the lookout for a photo of his grandfather. Apparently, the family home was bombed out in 1942, and all the other photos were burned. They read in the family bible that these photos existed, but no one had ever found them."

I smiled. "I'm absolutely amazed. Yes, please have the family contact me. You can give them my mobile number, and I'd be happy to speak with them."

Michael rang off with promises to do just that. I turned to look at Gertie and Ewan, my eyes shining with happiness. "Now this, friends, this is what family history research is all about."

***

Pixleton Family History Society.

The office near the high street was the flagship location of the city's family history research action. Inside was a treasure trove of parish register transcripts, microfiche, maps, books by local authors, plus various unique and donated items the organization had acquired over the years. Public computers were available to both members and nonmembers. The knowledgeable staff were simply excellent at helping everyone from the novice to the advanced researcher find out more about their ancestry. Most staff were eager seniors, researchers who finally had the time to dedicate themselves to this intriguing pastime. It was certainly not uncommon to walk in and be greeted by a sea of grins and eager faces, wondering what puzzle on a family tree a visitor had brought them today.

Family history research wasn't for the faint of heart, at least not for those who wanted to get it done right. This hobby was all-consuming, very addictive, and usually produced unexpected results. One considered the ethics of, for example, shocking an elderly man with the news that he had an illegitimate son, now fifty years old, living a mere twenty-eight minutes away by car. One had to balance the calamity of heartbreak with the gut-wrenching heartache of not knowing.

Aunt Edwina had schooled me in such worries before she passed away. Gertie and I had both been subjected to her many 'teaching talks', as we called them in our youth, as she patiently explained the ins and outs, the ups and downs, and the rights and wrongs, of properly conducting family history research. Family History Societies were absolute goldmines of information and had research facilities staffed mainly by dedicated volunteers. One respected the volunteer men and women who were willing to share their knowledge for free, all in the name of helping others untangle their silent past.

The three of us approached a lady at the front counter who wore a name badge that said 'Sue'. When we explained why we were there, she asked us to wait a moment while she scurried away to get the director of the facility, Amelia Georges. Amelia was a fountain of information, and led us to a quiet table with chairs. She brought out a custom leather-bound book from a cabinet, and on the book's long side was a heavy clasp and lock keeping it firmly shut. Gold tooling was on the spine; this obviously was someone's pride and joy.

Amelia started to explain. "Edwina was a frequent patron of this establishment. She also donated quite a princely sum to help with our operations fund. So, when she asked us to keep this book for you, I was very happy to oblige. It's been inside the locked cabinet in my office for a few months now. She was so certain that you would arrive, Julie, and I'm glad that she was right."

"So is that what our key unlocks?" Gertie asked.

"Only one way to find out, isn't there?" Ewan said.

I held up the key that we'd found in the desk at the Brown's Customs and Trades Building here in Pixleton. It looked like it would be a good fit, but one could only tell for sure by trying it in the actual lock. Lo and behold, it fit perfectly, and when I turned it, the clasp sprang open, allowing us to leaf through the book. It was a Greymore Hall visitor book, 1890-1942, Volume Eleven. As I leafed through the handwritten pages and signatures of who's who in England and the world, I saw another one of Aunt Edwina's telltale envelopes slid up against the spine, in between pages 290 and 291. I opened it, seeing a letter and a folded family tree inside. I read Aunt Edwina's letter aloud:

Dear Julie:

I'm so glad you found this letter. I'd like you to review E.E.'s family tree, but don't worry, all the hard work's been done. This exercise is just to show you what families can overcome.

Julie, you took on a self-confidence issue when you chose art and a lower-paying job as your vocation. Things will improve as you gain experience and new opportunities come your way; look at how E.E.'s family went from the workhouse to posh boys school then RAF pilot in one generation. Hard work does pay off; just embrace change like you always do.

The initials 'E.E.' simply stand for Elliot Edwards of Pixleton. Just like a Frank Farmer from Plumsden or a Henry Hillman from Ludring. Elliot was an RAF pilot who was stationed at the airfield near Greymore during the war, and that's where he got his flight training. I met Elliot when I was running the canteen as part of the homefront volunteer work during the war.

Elliot was my first true love. He was also the grand-nephew of the famous painter Gerald Zachary Norton. Algy's missing sixteenth watercolor is now in your hands: the boy and girl sitting on the stone bridge. Elliot painted it using childhood photos of he and I as his muses.

I had a friend in the war office who confirmed Elliot's death (tragically shot down in a dogfight) and then my letters got returned. They were very careful about that at the Returned Letters Office. My subsequent marriage was pleasant but not a great love, not like what I had with Elliot. My husband Bruce, your grandfather, is long passed on now, so I can share my secrets from the grave.

Please go back to Greymore and find a lasting memory Elliot left for me all these decades ago. The enclosed family tree will give you an appreciation of what the wartime generation went through. Please handle it with care and ensure it's preserved in the family records.

I trust you to do the right things.
Love from Aunt Edwina.

We examined the ornate, hand-drawn family tree, amazed at the various branches and reproduced photos appearing beside names.

"What does she mean by 'do the right things', plural?" Gertie asked.

"I think it means preserve the family tree in an archival safe facility and get the sixteenth painting back to Holgarth's to complete Algy's collection."

"Does she say anything about mixing up the open country background with the real background of the medieval bridge?" Ewan asked.

I shook my head.

Amelia leaned forward. "It's not uncommon for painters to compose an image made up of several pictures from reality. It's their choice what they're trying to get across to the audience."

"We thought it was there to mislead us, but perhaps it was just what Elliot thought would be best in the painting to finish up the series." Gertie was giving this some serious thought.

"It could just mean she wanted you to appreciate Elliot's work and ensure Algy was put out of his misery about the missing painting." Amelia was indeed a wise person. We stared some more at the family tree on the circular table we all surrounded.

An envelope fell out of the family tree when we unfolded it, and it revealed a photo of Elliot in his plane. The RAF pilots obviously had a good time painting the machine because the plane's nose was all done up in a yellow-and-white toothy snarl, with a bold, frowning eye over top of it to make it look really fierce. The plane was named *Edwina's Everlasting*, and one could just see the moniker below the fierce face of the plane.

"So we have a letter telling us to do the right things, a family tree for Elliot, a picture of his plane, and the missing painting that belongs back with Algy," I said.

"Plus the directive to go back to Greymore," Ewan said.

"Edwina was usually pretty upfront with things, and we all know she loved riddles and puzzles. It sounds to me like you've gathered all the evidence and Edwina now wants you to go back to where you started." Amelia's words made a great deal of sense.

"But why send us all around England if only to send us back home again?" Gertie asked.

Amelia and I exchanged a knowing glance. I gestured for her to add her thoughts first. "Because that's what family history research is all about. You do go on a journey to learn, grow, and appreciate those who came before you and all they've accomplished. It makes you a better, whole person, more able to take on this complicated world of today by understanding the struggles of the past."

What else could we say? Amelia had succinctly summarized the entirety of Aunt Edwina's treasure hunt. Now it all made sense. The quest wasn't there to cause us consternation or frustration. Rather, it was there to help us bond and feel a greater love for those who trod the earth before us. It was Aunt Edwina's absolutely marvelous gift from beyond the grave.

Chapter 32

The Chortling Willow Pub, Pixleton. Later.

"I've spent many a fun evening inside this pub," Ewan announced as we slid into a window booth with tall wooden sides and worn seat cushions. "It's a great student hang-out as well."

We all ran tentative fingers over the tabletop that bore an inlaid piece of glass covering reproductions of ancient maps.

"I'm glad they're not papering their tables with the real thing. Those should all be in proper, professionally managed archives," I said.

"Agreed. I once went into a doctor's office and saw an original map from 1790 hung on the wall like artwork. I was shocked," Gertie said.

"Did you know that back in medieval days, they were so unsure of what lay beyond their country's borders that they simply wrote 'Here Be Dragons' on the edge of their maps?" Ewan asked.

"Today it's more like 'Here be Peace and Quiet'," Gertie said. "The frenetic pace of today's lifestyle really leaves a lot to be desired."

"Rumor is this pub is haunted," I said. "Have you ever seen ghosts here, Ewan?"

He nodded. "Once, on a dark, late night, I was here with a few mates from university. One of us thought he saw a man staring at us from outside the window. So, we all piled over to take a look. There was no one about, and we even went outside to check. Still saw no one around. But what we did find on the windowpane was a nose print from the ghost who'd been watching us."

"That's pretty spooky," Gertie said. "Do they know who it was?"

"They think it was a local cooper named William Murlow," Ewan said.

"Why?" Gertie asked.

"Legend has it that he got lost walking outside in snowy weather and knocked himself out on a hitching post. Didn't kill him, mind you," Ewan said.

I groaned. "And the punchline is?"

"He was so drunk that he stayed knocked out until the milkman came along with his horse and cart the next morning. Didn't see him in the snow and ran right over him. They say

Murlow's ghost now roams Pixleton, curious if today's world is better than his back in the late nineteenth-century."

"Interesting," Gertie said. She cast a glance over at the window. "No nose print tonight."

"I don't think you can request a haunting. It's just something that happens," I said. "Just like you can't predict falling in love."

"And I'll be heading for the loo," Gertie said in a bright voice, leaving Ewan and I to ourselves.

"She's not so subtle, is she?" Ewan said.

I rolled my eyes. "Subtlety is definitely not one of Gertie's stronger suits," I said.

"Ahem. Look, I thought we agreed any idea of 'us' was on hold until this quest was completed?"

"Agreed. It's not that I'm not interested, it's just … "

Ewan handed me his mobile phone. He brought up a minute-old text from Bertie: *Journey to Scotland underway as planned. B.*

"Well, that's great news," I said. Trying to avoid another awkward moment, I came up with a question. "What do you suppose Aunt Edwina meant when she said go back to Greymore and find a lasting memory that Elliot left for her?"

Ewan thought on it for a moment, taking a sip of his dark ale. "It's referring to something in the past that you should know about."

"But none of us ever knew of Elliot. Greymore is a huge estate. How on earth would we know where to look?"

We both thought on it for a moment or two.

"Could it be something in her estate's legal paperwork?" he asked.

"I don't think so. She wanted it to be something specific, something obviously hidden for decades because she married another man after Elliot was killed."

"Was there anything in her earlier letters that we found?" Ewan was really trying to help.

"A 'lasting memory' Elliot left for her. What lasts over the decades yet wouldn't be discovered by anyone unless they knew what they were looking for?" I asked.

"A piece of furniture with a secret compartment in it? We just saw how that worked. Or maybe an old piece of crockery kept way high up on a shelf that only gets dusted when royalty's coming to visit?"

"Okay, that's a bit far-fetched. Something secret, sturdy, that we'd know when we recognized it. A 'lasting memory'. Something customized, something printed, something carved ..."

Gertie came back to the table and heard my last sentence of musings. "How about the tree where Elliot carved their initials in the bark? That was in one of Aunt Edwina's letters to Elliot."

Ewan and I both looked at Gertie, shocked.

I smiled. "And not just another pretty face."

I'd taken photos of all the letters we found inside the water-color painting frames along with me just in case they had some relevance during our traveling quest. I thanked my lucky stars for having this foresight. I rapidly scanned through the images and found the one sentence that proved Gertie's hunch was correct:

I sat under our oak tree at Greymore today and saw where you carved our initials in the bark, a lasting testament to our love and commitment to each other.

"Gertie, you're brilliant. We need to get back to Greymore first thing tomorrow morning."

Her face crumpled up in a bit of a frown. "So that means another night at the Dartmoor holiday cottage?"

Ewan stifled a laugh. "Don't worry. I promise to firmly latch the door tonight."

Chapter 33

—

Greymore Hall, Near Oakhurst. Next Day.

It felt good to be back in Oakhurst. It was a village I knew and loved well. Nearby Greymore Hall was like a second home to me when I was growing up. Aunt Edwina was so kind to both Gertie and I, seeing us through the awkward stages of adolescence when we were back in England on holidays from our boarding school in America.

As we drove, I looked over at Ewan and Gertie. "Greymore is 350 acres. How on earth are we going to find a single oak tree in the midst of all of that land?"

"Well, we know it was somewhere she used to sit. So that means probably not more than a mile or two away from the house because it would've been too long a walk," Gertie said.

"Remember, they used to keep horses at Greymore," I said. "It could be a few miles away."

"Good point," Gertie said.

We were stumped again.

"Did she ever mention a favorite hike or picnic place?" Ewan asked.

"No, but I remember her saying there's nothing as beautiful as your favorite sunset," I said.

"Meaning it was likely on a hill."

"With a bench and flat spot for picnicking?"

They nodded.

A smile came naturally to me. "Then I know exactly where it is. I just never realized there was an oak tree there because the lilac trees always dominated with their petals and scent."

"I know the spot too," Gertie added. "Does everyone have decent walking shoes on?"

***

We walked across rolling green pastures, avoided cow patties, and saw sheep scurry away when they saw us coming. I knew it was a couple of miles' walk. When Gertie and I were younger, Aunt Edwina took us out on an electric cart to her special place amongst the lilac trees. But now, I also knew that she didn't show us absolutely everything about it. She saved some of that for her and Elliot alone.

"Kind of funny, isn't it? Edwina and Elliot?" Gertie said.

"Perhaps they saw it as a sign," Ewan said.

"Okay, Mr. Romance." Gertie stepped up the pace and raced him up the next small hill in the meadow.

And then we reached it. A flat plateau overlooking a small stream, with an estate cottage far off in the distance. A disused riding trail. A fox den. A robin's favorite nesting nook. Aunt Edwina had taught us well.

We were surrounded by dozens of lilac trees. Their scent was glorious in May. Right now the blooms weren't at their best, and only few stragglers remained here in June. That made our hunt for the oak a bit easier. And when we found it, we certainly owed it reverence. The oak stood four stories tall, dwarfing us. It had a hollow trunk, about eight feet up from the ground, clearly because the tree was aging out over the decades. It looked at least 375 to 400 years old, perhaps even planted by the founder of Greymore Hall himself in 1629.

In the autumn, this would be a place of glory, the oak's green, moss-covered branches reaching out like octopus arms, large burls like feet at its base. It did indeed look a bit like a muscular person frozen in time, with limbs and a strong torso that had all grown thick over the centuries. An aura of golden yellows and oranges would surround it as the younger trees did their best to impress their eldest arboreal cousin.

"Think of what this oak tree lived through," I said. "The Restoration, Waterloo, both World Wars, wow. And look at this!" I peered around the oak, around the saplings that were ten feet tall and still spindly. We walked a bit further into the wooded area and suddenly were treated to a magnificent view of a valley below us that stretched out for miles.

"Quite impressive," Ewan said, admiring all the tidy green fields, corralled by hedges framing the land.

"Aunt Edwina never took us back here," Gertie breathed. "I remember her always talking about the lilac forest. Nothing about a hollow oak." She pointed to a tiny heart carved into the bark, an 'E.E.' marked inside, yet largely obscured by time.

"And while we were busy here making lilac bouquets for the house, she was reminiscing about her days with Elliot," I said.

"It's tragic that his plane was shot down," Ewan said. "What a tragic end to a love story."

"Indeed."

Gertie motioned us over. "I think we found her hiding place."

"What, did you play hide and seek as children?" Ewan asked, not quite following.

"No, where Elliot hid something for her." I signaled to Gertie. She reached down inside the hollow of the tree and pulled out a one-foot-long plastic tube. It rattled. We sat on the bench beside the lilac trees, all three of us like bumps on a log. We undid the strong latch on the tube and retrieved two pieces of paper and a key. The letter from Aunt Edwina read:

Dear Julie:

This poem was written by Elliot for me before he died. It's always meant so much to me, and I lost track of the times I came up here to read it all by myself. Now that I am gone, I want you to understand what we shared and hold it dear to your heart, in hopes that you, too, can find the same love for yourself one day.

The key opens a secret room behind a bookshelf in my office at Greymore Hall. That is where the treasure hunt will end, and your final instructions will be given.

Love from Aunt Edwina

We read Elliot's poem next:

She waits underneath an oak so strong and true,
All I can fathom is being here with you.
The fires light up London, and the sirens wail,
Crushing most dreams like evil hammer and nails.
Behold she stirs.
I am not worthy
To delight in her loveliness for all I feel is fury ...
At the fires blazing across the land.
A spring flower, petals so delicate and pink,

Are likened to the pretty blush feathering her cheeks.

Oh I wish I were worthy of all we could have now,

But, my love, I leave you, with a final bow.

Be bold, be brave, pine forever for me not–

Find another one, build a life that can be got.

You deserve the world, and although I fly up high,

If you read this Edwina, I am forever in your sky.

Love E.E.

Gertie had a steady hand on her chest as she wiped back tears. "It's lovely."

I was a similar blubbery mess.

"Can I borrow your phone?" Gertie asked me.

"I doubt you'll get service out here," I said.

"I don't want to make a call. I need your pictures." She scrolled and brought up the picture of the watercolor girl and boy sitting on a stone bridge. "There," she said, showing it to both of us. "Doesn't that look familiar?"

She turned our line of vision out to the vast scenery behind the grand oak. Sure enough, Elliot had used the medieval stone bridge from his city, the boy and girl from his and Edwina's childhood, along with their favorite backdrop at the Greymore Hall estate. Finally the watercolor painting made perfect sense.

"The watercolor was a tribute to their love. How devastatingly sweet," I said.

Chapter 34

——

Aunt Edwina's office was a noble lady's hideaway, a place where she took care of estate matters surrounded by gleaming cherrywood furniture, a well-stocked library, a high-backed executive chair, plus her standard vase of fresh roses. When I say library, I mean one that could keep a small village adequately entertained for months, what with her vast history and topography titles, royal biographies, full range of classics, as well as London city collectibles. She even had three special shelves for the younger set when they came to visit. I remembered many times when I sat beside her on the chintz loveseat in her office while she read to me as a child.

With over a thousand books before us, choosing the right one was a bit of a large ask. We all started scanning books' spines to see if any titles jumped out at us.

No luck. It was just too overwhelming.

Then my eyes roamed to Aunt Edwina's collection of visitor books, the one with a single volume missing and now about to be put back in its rightful place. That was, until I spied a lock set back into the wall immediately behind the gap on the bookshelf.

"Guys! Come and see this!" I cried out.

"You found it?" Gertie asked after she came over from looking at some delightfully illustrated children's books, the ones both of us remembered reading in our early years.

Ewan was hot on her heels and held out the key we'd brought. I put the key into the lock and turned. With an electric hum, the carpet started to vibrate. A fingerprint sensor below the lock lit up and glowed green, the words 'press index finger here' now apparent. I put my finger to the small screen, and we heard a satisfying click, as if a lock were disengaging.

"What's happening?" Gertie yelped. "The floor's moving!"

"I think it's supposed to," Ewan advised us while Gertie clung to his shirt with all the power of an old washerwoman's mangle.

We all looked down and saw a circular piece of carpet disengage from its surrounds. We jumped onto the inside of the circle that started to rotate clockwise, grabbing the bookshelf and each other for support. We spun around 180 degrees and then the turnstile stopped. A concealed door swung open. We were now in Aunt Edwina's secret room, a room neither Gertie nor I knew existed. It was a vault with heavy steel walls. Inside were shelves bearing financial papers, stock market certificates, three gold bars, parchment estate deeds, the family silver, plus, most importantly, two letters propped up between stacks of silver coins in plastic tubes.

I picked up the first letter and broke the seal:

Dear Julie:

Congratulations on successfully completing my little treasure hunt. Yes, Plumsden, Ludring, and Pixleton were the three places where Elliot painted. I took you to see what he saw and loved ... because I loved him so very much.

The background for the girl and boy sitting on a stone bridge was here at Greymore. Look behind the hollow oak and you'll see it, exactly like he did all these years ago. Please put flowers on Elliot's memorial stone for me (on the hill near the hollow oak). You may let the world know about us because secrets don't matter anymore now.

Love from Aunt Edwina.

PS: I hope you've made some new friends on your journey.

There was still one more letter from Aunt Edwina that we needed to read.

Chapter 35

"Hello? Hello?" We all heard Bertie's plaintive voice calling out. It got closer and closer, till he was poking his head around the sideways bookcase that led into the vault. "I say, this is rather fabulous! A secret vault, good on Edwina."

Bertie had a thick newspaper in his hand. "Before you make off with the family silver, I suggest you let me entertain you with this." He waggled the newspaper up high.

"What have you got there?" Ewan asked.

Bertie came into the vault and handed it to me. "Proof that the home support team came through with flying colors."

Gertie read over my shoulder and was amazed. "You must be joking."

"I suppose that's what one calls hook, line, and sinker," Ewan said, also reading it.

The newspaper was the cherry on top of our day ... no, our year.

LOBSTER TRAP VANDALS ARRESTED IN SCOTLAND

Police have arrested two people for an odd crime: vandalizing lobster traps off the mainland near the Firth of Clyde. Chris Undermead and Carlene Munsonthwaite were both found stranded on Tuttle Island at high tide without emergency supplies or mobile phone service. Their SUV was swept away with the rising tide. They were rescued by helicopter and taken to local hospital for treatment of hypothermia.

Both suspects rode out the storm in the ruined castle's keep. After surviving for thirty-six hours without food or water, a light plane noticed an SOS sign written in the sand, which led to their rescue. After passing a health check, both suspects were arrested without incident. They paid for their bail using an astonishing amount of two-pound coins kept in their mainland hotel room. Neither suspect explained why the lobster traps were of such great interest.

Local fisherman Angus Garfield McTaggart, sixty-two, plans to bring a civil action against the suspects to recoup the cost of ten lobster traps and his missed catch. McTaggart stated, "Never in my forty-five years of trapping lobsters have I seen such blatant disregard for a man's way of living. City folk ought not to be on such a wee island with such wee minds."

We all had a belly wrenching laugh.

"Imagine Chris and Carlene stuck in the ruined castle's keep, no phones, no luxuries, just picking apart salty, rusty lobster traps ..." I said. "It's all too good to believe."

"Hunting for treasure that was never there in the first place!" Gertie said with glee.

"Perfect." Ewan was also a fan of Chris's predicament. I was beginning to think that Ewan was a keeper.

Bertie looked awfully pleased with himself. And he did look quite dapper in his pinstriped suit. But there was one thing trifling him: "On a sadder note, I have to report that the police found Athena."

Gertie brightened considerably. "Really? Where?"

Bertie shook his head. "She's not drivable. Dumped at the side of the road in Mossmarleigh. I believe it's a town known for its cheesemaking."

Gertie looked aghast. "Mossmarleigh?"

Bertie nodded. "That is correct."

"How badly is she 'not drivable'?" Gertie asked. She looked about ready to cry.

Bertie looked from each one of us to the next as he tried to compose words in his head, probably pondering how to reveal such horrific news.

I gestured for him to go ahead and spit it out.

Bertie looked awfully apologetic. "Well, Athena has a dented roof–"

Gertie winced and clutched her chest as she heard his first description. It only got worse.

Bertie continued. "She's missing her left front door, has red spray paint on all the bench seats, and all the upholstery was slashed, including the, er, rather unique padded ceiling. They also jimmied the glovebox open and removed that door as well."

"Is that all?" Gertie asked.

"My friend, I think that is enough tragedy in your life for this month," Bertie said.

"I'm so sorry, Gertie. I know how much Athena means to you," I said, putting an arm around her. I hoped she wasn't too distraught.

Gertie looked at Bertie, her eyes ever hopeful. "Is there any-thing at all remaining of Athena's soul?"

Bertie straightened his silk tie and contemplated her question. He shook his head. "I'm afraid there was too much mayhem."

Silence in the vault.

"Perhaps it would be wisest for all of us to let Athena rest in peace," Bertie suggested.

Gertie spoke in a cracked voice. "You mean, rest in pieces ..." Her upper lip trembled, and she fought back tears.

We gave her a group hug, then headed for the kitchen for much-needed tea and cakes.

Gertie dropped her bombshell just as I was about to sink my teeth into a lovely scone with farm-fresh strawberry jam over top of a slight smearing of butter.

"Just so you know, I don't have a problem with Mossmarleigh, per se," she said.

"I'm sorry?" I said.

"It's just that Mossmarleigh, well, that's where my viral karaoke video was filmed. Rather a vivid blur of a memory, you see."

I chewed rapidly and swallowed even faster, in hopes of getting a bit more out of her. However, my mobile phone rang, and I had to give that my primary attention because caller ID said it was Chris.

"Julie speaking," I answered, heavy apprehension in my voice.

"Julie. It's Chris. Can we talk?"

"There's really not much left to talk about, Chris."

"Obviously, you'll be wanting an annulment–"

"Already taking care of. We were actually never really married in the first place."

His silence was overwhelming. He managed to scratch one lousy word out of his parched throat. "What?"

"You heard me. We were never really married. Gertie didn't have a valid ministering license when she married us, ergo we are not wed. Quite convenient, considering the bind you put yourself in." I couldn't remove absolutely all of the acid dripping through my voice.

"Oh."

"That's all you have to say? Oh?" I asked. "Do you have any idea what you've put me through?"

"I've been a real disgrace," he admitted.

"You think?"

More silence. Then Chris tried again. "Julie, I just phoned to wish you well. I'm not going to bother you anymore."

"So Mr. Stockbroker actually has a bit of heart. Good. Because I now have a question for you."

"Yes?"

"The small question about your mistress. Shall I have your things sent to her office?"

Chris groaned. "Carlene and I broke up in jail. Just send everything to my parents. I'll sort it out with them later."

"As you wish," I replied in a singsongy voice, because now I knew I would be rid of the man who'd been haunting me. "Have a nice life, Chris."

Everyone at the kitchen table was staring at me. They'd all watched, wondering how I would handle this. By the looks on their faces, I'd done an awesome job.

I could tell Ewan was relieved that I was rid of that dastardly man forever.

I basked in their applause.

Chapter 36

The reading of Aunt Edwina's will was a rather dour affair conducted by her long-serving solicitor. He summarized the key points for us after going through the legal preambles including the formal responsibilities Gertie and I would share as executrices.

Re: Greymore Hall and all of my estate

- Greymore Hall's grounds and first-floor fancies, historical furniture, and artwork that tourists like to ogle are bequeathed to the Greymore Hall Charitable Trust with input on display and maintenance quality standards overseen by my Executrices.
- £1,000,000 is bequeathed to each of my children, Donald, Catherine, and Robin.
- £1,750,000 is bequeathed to my granddaughter Gertrude Porringer. I have no issue with her donating to a religious organization of her choice as she sees fit.

- Everything else, including £5,000,000 in liquid assets (cash, stocks etc.), is bequeathed to my granddaughter, Julie Fincher. My rightful heir, Julie's father and my son, has no desire to assume the responsibility of running and maintaining Greymore Hall. I trust Julie to do what's right.

All of this was fine with me, mainly because my father was a modest man and had no interest in living as Lord Greymore. Neither did I, to be quite honest, however, Aunt Edwina's treasure quest gave me a wonderful idea as I sat there listening to the solicitor drone on. Over the last little while, I'd learned valuable lessons: the biggest teachings were to do right by others, disassociate with negative people, and help move the world forward in one's own little way.

After the will was read, I spent hours thinking about how to best honor Aunt Edwina's legacy. For such a distinguished estate, it made perfect sense that the charitable trust would raise money for Greymore Hall's building and grounds upkeep by partially opening them to the public. Tourists would be awestruck by the wonderful sculptures, ornate plaster work, and gilded treasures on the first floor. The grandfather clock in its three-centuries-old case would continue to tick tock along, sounding out the beats as people walked through, amazed at how yesteryear was lived. The grounds, with their lush gardens and the outbuildings, would no doubt be turned into an interpretive walk where tourists could ramble solo for the day, enjoy a hike out with the family, or simply take a couple's romantic stroll. The charitable trust would likely build a gift shop and a tea room. Plus they'd have nice toilet facilities, exceptionally clean and well organized. I could hear Aunt Edwina now: *Greymore Hall will have none of those ridiculous charges to use the toilet. I'll never forget being granted four sheets of toilet paper, maximum, at that so-called fancy castle we visited on the continent.*

I'd make sure that the gift shop stocked tons of interesting books, ranging from cookery to local guides to craftsmanship. There'd be books on hiking, on British fauna, on family history research. The tea room would have twelve different kinds of tea and an assortment of fancy cakes and healthier fare, depending on how exotic one wanted to be that particular day.

Aunt Edwina was clever. She'd created a charitable trust that signed off on a perpetual maintenance clause, meaning the estate was not responsible for anything else except for the second through fourth floors of the main house and not including the roof. Perhaps I could renovate the fourth floor into suites, even offering one of them to my father out of courtesy and respect.

It absolutely broke Aunt Edwina's heart when her letters were returned. She'd had a great love and lost it. She'd quietly protected me from Chris, and somehow life granted me a coveted do over. I firmly believed a great love was out there for me too: I just had to find it. Or perhaps it had already found me in the guise of a local antiques shop owner.

Aunt Edwina left me a private note scribbled at the bottom of the will in her elegant handwriting—straight and true, right up until the day she died: *Julie, you must fill your life with positives and let me enjoy watching you succeed.*

Once the will reading was over, I looked skyward, a copy of her note clutched in my hand. "Oh yes, that will be taken care of, Auntie. I promise." It was a glorious day, slightly windy but with fierce sunshine. It was the perfect day for new beginnings, and I intended to ensure Aunt Edwina's kindness and wisdom were never forgotten.

***

Aunt Edwina's funeral was held two months to the very day after her death, exactly as she requested. She requested a celebration of life instead of a somber march to dreary church music. All the flowers were pink, cream, and lavender roses, her favorites. I used the same florist she'd chosen for my wedding and just told her we were doing a different type of display this time.

Absolutely everyone showed up. And by 'everyone,' I mean all the members of her Sherry Club, Algy and Lance, all of the major and minor aristocrats of the area, every villager who was in town that day, as well as big city London merchants. Family filled the first four pews of the ancient parish church in Oakhurst. Then came the friends, acquaintances, and business colleagues who filled the rest of Aunt Edwina's world.

The church was packed.

I wondered how Gilligan the Afghan was doing and made a mental note to ask the Holgarth Hall brothers after the service. But now was a time to celebrate the life of a grand old dame, one who had lived over nine decades and witnessed the transition of her country through fierce industrialization to make more munition supplies and homefront defense in the 1940s, all the way through the casual 1960s, ending with today's mobile phones, internet connections, and email accounts. So much had changed since the day she was born, yet Aunt Edwina had ensured that the important things stayed consistent: family, friendship, and community.

It was beautiful to see how Aunt Edwina forged such strong, honest relationships with the community and the circles in which she traveled. Great people didn't advertise their good deeds. Rather, their good deeds were eventually discovered belonging to them, with the responsible party shunning public credit. Some people were eager to promote where they had spent their charitable dollars or donated volunteer time. It was exactly the opposite with Aunt Edwina. She knew she could often do more good by staying as a supportive figure in the background on many of her causes. She wanted others to learn for themselves, including me. There was no sense in simply tossing money at a problem; problems had to be managed properly in order to be conquered. But given a little guidance, and then some quiet charitable assistance in the right areas, a community could flourish. Today was when people found out that Aunt Edwina had been silently supporting so many causes without their knowledge. Bertie summed it all up in his eulogy:

"Lady Edwina Greymore was one of those rare beauties who graced this earth for ninety-two years. Everyone who knew her was privileged to be in the company of such a lovely, caring person. But mark my words, if you ever did cross her or were dishonest with her, her quiet fury would unleash itself, and the wrong would be corrected. Trust me, I would know after crashing her yacht into a concrete post when I was twenty-two! I spent twelve full Sundays at the shipyard helping repair the damage while her yacht was in dry dock. I suppose if I ever need a second career, I could take up boat building."

The crowd laughed at that one. Then Bertie continued:

"As you know, Edwina and I travelled in many of the same circles, ate much of the same rubber chicken at various gala dinners, and smashed champagne bottles against various ships being launched. Many of you saw her do those things. But many of you did not know all of the silent things she did behind the scenes to improve our way of living and this community. In doing so, she always understood that people are inextricably linked to each other. They are linked by the water, the land, and the air. Many of you do not know that Edwina was the one who made sure that the appeal for less-fortunate children's Christmas gifts always reached its goal by digging into her own pocketbook. Many of you would be surprised to learn that Edwina alone was responsible for the new roll-in shower stall at the seniors' care home. And finally, the new football turf and nets out at the Plumsden Grammar School were paid for by none other than the lovely and irreplaceable Lady Edwina Greymore."

At this point, Bertie looked out at the crowd and spotted Roger the Mustache, postmaster for Plumsden. "Don't worry,

Roger, you'd already shaved your mustache off for the Plumsden historic village-green fundraiser, so the school's football turf committee had to look farther afield for funding."

Everybody chortled. Bertie wrapped up:

> "I choose to remember Edwina as she wanted to be remembered. Vivacious, lovely, elegant, well-mannered, eloquent, caring, a wonderful mother, wife, grandmother, and aunt. She was also one heck of a tough negotiator, a keen investor, and fiercely devoted to maintaining her beloved Greymore Hall and all its precious memories. Edwina, we love you dearly and we will miss you. Today, as you wish, we celebrate your life. Thank you."

After such a rousing presentation, one always felt the urge to clap, but it just wasn't the done thing at funerals. The other thing racing through my mind was how Aunt Edwina had another first love that nobody else really knew about—well, other than me, Gertie, Ewan, the Major, Bertie, and my father. Aunt Edwina said we could share more details of Elliot, but it just didn't seem appropriate anymore. Why dig up the past like this when she'd made peace with it and we had a private memorial stone that we could visit on her behalf? I decided right then and there to leave it be. It was one of those ethical family history questions that was just better off left alone.

Bertie went back to his front row pew. I caught my father's eye, then he reached for my hand and squeezed it tight. I knew Bertie had done an excellent job and saved my family the heartache of having to give a eulogy for their beloved mother and grandmother.

After the priest led us through a couple of hymns, all personally chosen by Aunt Edwina, it was my turn at the lectern. Luckily I didn't have much to say, and it was all written down in case I experienced a last-minute freeze in my throat and vocal chords.

I stood and hoped I could get through this. *Be Brave. Be Strong.* I could hear Aunt Edwina in my mind. I took a deep breath.

> "On behalf of Aunt Edwina, I would like to thank all of you for coming today. I realize you have busy lives, and she would be so touched to know that you took the time to celebrate her life. The family would like to invite you all up to Greymore Hall, where we have an extensive food and beverage service prepared for you. I also have a surprise for the community that I'm unveiling today on behalf of Aunt Edwina. We hope you will join us. Thank you."

As everyone filed out of the church, the front rows going first, I saw many people holding back tears, trying desperately to celebrate Aunt Edwina's life because that's what she asked everybody to do. Yet, losing such a valued person from the community was something that brought tears to the surface. As Bertie hit the second row of pews, I looked to the priest and nodded. He cued the soundman to start playing an up-tempo gospel song from Aunt Edwina's youth.

I looked up to the heavens. *This is for you, Aunt Edwina. I love you.*

Chapter 37

I met Bertie in Aunt Edwina's office. He was one of the first guests to arrive following her funeral. I quickly ushered him inside and shut the door. "I just wanted to say a heartfelt, private thank you for your eulogy. It was very, very kind, and you've made her so proud."

It was hard for me to hold back the tears. In looking at Bertie, I could see he was struggling with his emotions as well. "You're very welcome. I spoke from the heart, and it was all true. She was a very special lady."

"Indeed she was."

"How are things for the wake? Everything ready for the guests?" he asked.

It's not like Bertie was offering to be a waiter. That was a little out of his comfort zone. No, I knew he was checking I had enough money to pay the caterer and wondering if anyone messed up and needed a stern talking to. Big brother in the room again.

"All actually appears to be going fine, thank goodness for that. I can just see Aunt Edwina up there looking down on us, clucking her tongue at a missed tray of hors d'oeuvres or somebody's drink not getting refilled on time."

Bertie smiled. "We will do her proud today. I promise."

"Thanks also for your help with the treasure hunt. I don't know what we would've done without the escape to your country house, plus the brilliant Scottish ruse."

"I rather enjoyed the excitement," Bertie said.

"Maybe you should have traveled up to Scotland and helped the police take down Chris and Carlene," I suggested.

He scoffed. "I hope he pinched his fingers really hard on those lobster traps. After what he put you through ..."

"It's all in the past now. Chris is out of my life, so things are back to normal. I can start working on your watercolor again, that new one for your study."

"Marvelous. Simply marvelous. We must have a grand unveiling of your entire year's work at my Winter Solstice party. And do bring along that Ewan friend of yours. He seems like a rather good sort."

Bertie held a Winter Solstice party instead of a Christmas one, simply to ensure he wasn't infringing on anyone's family time. It was celebrated a few days before Christmas and was a bonafide local hit. His Summer Solstice party was also something to look forward to each year, and the invitations had already gone out.

"You know, the watercolor might even be ready by Halloween."

He tapped a finger to his chin. "Halloween. That means costumes. What if I could convince Severs to dress up like a goblin and–"

I held up a hand. "Bertie, roping your gallant, ex-security-service chauffeur into acting as a ghoulish Halloween character is far beyond his job description."

"I suppose you're right. Perhaps he could dress up my antique convertible like a pumpkin, and then we at least have something as a centerpiece while people walked in. Let me think on that." He gave me one more focused stare. "So everything is fine? You don't need any help?"

"Everything is running smoothly."

He took a deep breath. "Right, then. I shall go back to entertaining the guests."

"Excellent. Thanks again, Bertie."

He saluted and then left. The door was open. I'd no sooner sat down behind Aunt Edwina's desk when I looked up to see Major Whitcombe and two strangers standing behind him.

"Hello, Major," I said. "Thanks very much for coming to the service and wake."

"Wouldn't have missed it for the world. Edwina was a rare jewel. Do you remember how you were so pleased to learn that we'd found the descendants of the military family in your photos?" he asked.

"Yes, of course."

The Major got a big grin on his face. "Please allow me to introduce the descendants of Horace Griffins, his two grandchildren."

My mouth must've dropped open a mile and a half wide. I had no idea the Major was working on this meeting. The two strangers he had along stepped forward to introduce themselves. The first was a woman in her forties, slender and very businesslike, in a tailored suit. The man with her, who I would quickly find out to be her brother, was the spitting image of the military man in the photo I'd found. It was uncanny.

"I'm Vera, and this is my brother, Dudley Smythe, MP. Thank you for rescuing our ancestor from the pile of oblivion. You have no idea what this means to our family. We've been looking for those photos for over a decade." Her eyes were kind, and she was quite emotional as she gripped my hand, shaking it several times.

"You're quite welcome. I just saw them sitting there all forlorn and couldn't let that be. I was so hoping that I could reunite him with his family."

Dudley stepped forward and said a few niceties to me.

I fanned myself with my free hand. "You'll have to excuse me, we're in the middle of a wake for my dearly beloved aunt, and I'm finding all of this a little bit overwhelming," I said. "But I'm absolutely thrilled that you're both here."

Vera gave me a kind smile. "We are ever so grateful," she said. "Had it not been for my godmother knowing the Major, who knew the dealer in London, my goodness, we never would've met here today."

"That's the power of family history. You have to keep pushing down brick walls, keep rattling door handles, until something appears in front of you that you've been searching for what seems like forever," I said.

The Smythes nodded, very eager.

Vera spoke next. "We've actually become very interested in genealogy, and we're planning to work on a couple more lines in our family tree. My brother has everything entered onto an online genealogy program, and we're keeping it all very organized."

"You should talk to my cousin Gertie. At our recent family event, she had a twenty-foot-long family tree, all computerized, tacked to the wall for people to make additions. I nearly fell over when I saw a cousin had written in his dachshund's name."

"Oh, what fun!" Vera said, emitting a laugh. "I'd love to meet Gertie."

"Look for the bright-red hair. And please, stay for some refreshments. Do you live nearby?"

"We have a family cottage about twenty miles away but spend most of our time in London for work. The Major tells us you found the photos in Waverly-on-Sea?"

"That's correct."

Dudley got a pensive look on his face. "Well, if our ancestor can travel so many miles to fight in a war, then who's to question his photo ending up in Waverly-on-Sea?"

It was good food for thought. Speaking of food, I heard the hum of the crowd now here at Greymore Hall. I was due to go and officially welcome our guests, then also reveal my fabulous surprise.

***

When I walked into the great ballroom, I saw many familiar faces. Of course, they'd all been at the church, but one could never be sure who would make it back to the house for the wake. Many people I knew were just too distraught at funerals and didn't want to be seen in public with red eyes after the service was over. They just signed the guestbook at the church and left. To each his own. I certainly made no judgements; I just wanted to ensure everybody got what they needed in order to properly mourn—and celebrate—Aunt Edwina.

I waved hello to Algy and Lance, and then felt a tap on my shoulder. I turned to see Ewan standing there, looking somber yet supportive, and likely wearing his best suit. It wasn't tweed; rather, it was a proper tailored suit likely hailing from London. After seeing him in action for the last little while, I knew that the formal suit was certainly not his preferred attire, but it was so sweet of him to dress up for the occasion and support his new friends.

"How are you and Gertie holding up?" he asked.

I sighed. "Tough day, but we're surviving."

"I'm sorry. This has got to be just terrible for you to go through. From what I knew of your Aunt Edwina, she was quite a lady."

"Yes, they definitely broke the mold after they made her," I said. "Did you get some food? There's loads of it in the other room." I knew this as fact because I'd arranged the catering myself.

The Fizzleywick Hotel had kindly stepped in and done a wonderful job of catering a multitude of finger foods, both hot and cold, plus an assortment of desserts and nonalcoholic beverages for the wake. They'd even sent over some waiters to help us at no charge. It was kind, but of course also good business because the hotel's logo was prominently displayed on the tent card announcing each dish.

Ewan gave me a focused look. "Are you getting enough sleep?"

I shrugged. "I get by."

"Make sure you take care of yourself. You don't want to be getting sick. The world needs people like Julie Fincher."

I smiled. "What a kind thing to say."

Our eyes held for a moment. There was a brief spark that could be ignited after all of this, today, tomorrow, and perhaps a little bit down the road, when the rest of this mêlée was finished.

"Question. What would you have done if you'd missed a clue or gone to the wrong place during your treasure hunt?" Ewan asked with a small grin.

"Never fear. That's when the Sherry Club would be called into action," we heard behind us. We turned to see Maude Livingstone and Lady Susan Marcelon standing there.

Maude spoke first. "We had a secret envelope kept in the Plumsden Family History Society safe. It had the master clue list from Edwina. All of us in her Sherry Club were to be on the lookout and call in a report if we saw Julie going astray."

"At first we thought Edwina was a bit off her rocker, but it turned out to be all in good fun," Lady Susan said. She patted my arm. "And you did an excellent job, dear. Just excellent."

"Truly, thank you," I said. "And now if you'll excuse me, I must make my rounds."

I circulated around the room, making sure I said hello to everyone who had been kind enough to attend. I had a quiet word with the waiters to ensure that everyone's glasses and plates were promptly refilled. It was a mixture of people who attended because Aunt Edwina had touched the lives of so many, from every class of society. I was glad to see everyone getting along.

Lance came over and shook my hand. "Condolences from the Holgarth family to yours," he said.

"Oh, Lance, I wish we were meeting again under better circumstances," I said.

"At least there are no odd vegetables or animals involved at this event," he said with a teasing smile.

"That's right, thank goodness for that." I scanned the crowd, looking for Algy. "Did you hear we found the sixteenth watercolor?"

"Yes, we heard. We just didn't think it would be appropriate to bring it up today."

"Nonsense. Now that we've finished our treasure hunt, Aunt Edwina would want it to go to Holgarth Hall. It's got fifteen brothers and sisters waiting for it on your family home's wall."

He looked shocked. "Gosh, that's awfully nice of you. Algy will be thrilled."

"I hear my name, and I trust it's spoken with a great deal of affection and reverence?" Algy said, striding over with a glass of punch in one hand and a plate full of fine cheese and grapes in the other.

"Hi Algy. I was just telling your brother that we have the six-teenth watercolor, and I'd like you to hang it at Holgarth Hall."

Algy looked stunned. "But those models were Edwina and her first love, Elliot. Surely your family would want them here at Greymore?"

I shook my head. "I have many, many family photos of Aunt Edwina with us over the years. Plus the Major's helping us dig up some photos of Elliot from the recently released RAF archives at The National Archives in London. I think we can stand to be without one watercolor. It just means so much to your collection, and it would be a shame to see the sixteenth sit here all by its lonesome when you have the other fifteen waiting beside an empty gap on the wall."

Algy's eyes were shining with excitement. "To finally fill that gap in our wall. You have no idea how happy that makes me. It's been a gap ever since I was a little boy at Holgarth Hall."

"It's wonderful to fulfill a lifelong dream," I said.

Algy put his glass and plate down on a nearby high-top table and then took both my hands in his. "Edwina would be so proud of you."

We shared a smile.

The clock gonged a strong 3:00 p.m.

"And now it's time for our grand reveal," I said. "You'll want to stick around for this one." I left amidst a sea of wonder and curiosity, as many guests heard me make that statement before I disappeared out the doors to retrieve what I needed for my presentation. I was back inside the ballroom hosting our guests in under two minutes. Under my arm, I carried a remote control as well as a stack of recently printed brochures. I walked up onto the small stage to the lectern and microphone that the audio-visual contractor had installed at the side of the room. It was right next to the screen where we'd been showing pictures from Aunt Edwina's life.

It was time for a new set of slides for the audience. And this was the focus of my presentation now. I leaned into the microphone. "Ladies and gentlemen, may I please have your attention?"

The audience fell silent. Everyone focused on me.

"I have a surprise, and it's presented to you in Aunt Edwina's memory."

There were murmurs in the crowd. They knew something good was in the offing.

I continued. "As you know, Aunt Edwina was very involved in family history, always encouraging everyone she met to research their ancestry, taking care to make sure that the research was correct, using multiple sources, and recorded so future generations would enjoy the work. It was in that train of thought that I looked at my inheritance of Greymore Hall and decided that there was more to its legacy than simply a show-case of old furniture and fancy flower gardens for the tourist world. Tourism is welcome, however, I feel that Greymore has a higher purpose, a true calling, all based on the wonderful woman who guided it for so many years."

The big screen beside me flipped to a picture of the ballroom we all stood inside.

"What you see today is a place to hold large society gatherings and fashionable dances for aristocrats. However, this isn't the 1930s anymore. I also feel a great duty to preserve the past and ensure that the people of our community and beyond have the resources to do that. We are responsible for what we leave to the next generation. Part of Greymore Hall is to be a museum for the charitable trust, many of Greymore's lovely furnishings and collections on display. And, with great excitement, I'm announcing the creation of the new, additional charity, the Greymore Genealogy Research Site, a research library open to the public. It's a collaborative project with the Plumsden Family History Society, giving the society much-needed additional space plus more modern computer and digital equipment."

I beamed with excitement. I felt Aunt Edwina's presence in the room, approving of what I was doing with her legacy. The room erupted into applause. There were even some hoots and hollers from those not accustomed to clapping. I looked around the room and saw only the faces of those whom I loved the most: family and friends. My father was there, a proud parent. Gertie and her parents stood off to the side, as did Aunt Edwina's youngest son who'd flown in from New York. Everybody was there and everybody was in support. I continued:

"I'm going to run you through some of the construction diagrams now, and remember, these are just concepts. I welcome any input and suggestions you may have as we embark on this new journey together. It is by working together that we will make this a true community resource, just like Aunt Edwina would have wanted."

The architect had prepared some rough sketches for me, and I showed the audience the twelve new computer stations and equipment, a list of well-trained staff positions to be filled, desks that moved up and down to accommodate various disabilities, a breakroom that offered complimentary tea and snacks, as well as plans for an annual volunteers' award determined by number of hours donated. One needed peace and quiet, a good local reference library, up-to-date computers, new model printer and photocopy machines, and a place to store the oversized maps. Everything was as digitized as possible, but there was still something special about opening up an old book that someone in the eighteenth-century had once touched.

Algy banged on the side of his punch glass with his fork. I wasn't sure if it was proper aristocratic behavior, but at least he got the crowd's attention. "A few words, if I may?" He had an expectant look in his eyes.

"Come up and use the microphone, Algy," I said.

He was up on the stage beside me with alacrity, and then gave me a kiss on the cheek. "Don't worry, this is a family-friendly comment." He leaned into the microphone. "I just wish to announce that Holgarth Enterprises Limited will make the first donation to the new Greymore Genealogy Research Site, in the amount of £25,000."

I came back to the lectern after he headed back into the cheering crowd. "Well, that is incredibly generous, Algy. Thank you so much. Quite unexpected but also quite welcomed. Those electric sit/stand desks are more expensive than one would think!"

More laughter throughout the crowd.

I flipped through more architect renderings on screen.

"I should also add that the new research site will include a large classroom for training, and also a boardroom with video-conferencing abilities. All the latest technology is being used: no more cobbled-together machine parts or cannibalizing one to keep another one going. This will be a modern and efficient resource site in every meaning of the word. Having professional staff is key, and they will ensure that research is done in the most accurate and best recorded manner possible."

The slide deck on the big screen came to a rest at the end of the presentation. The grand finale was a lovely photo of Aunt Edwina, Gertie, and I standing under an archway of purple wisteria in the garden at Greymore Hall. We each had a family photo album in our hands. I remembered that day when Aunt Edwina took us children out for a weekend at her private cottage in Devon for a good chat about our ancestors. It was my first introduction to family history, and I was hooked from that very day.

It was how I chose to remember Aunt Edwina: regal, beautiful, wise, and caring. It was how she would wish to be remembered.

**

I threw a 'Happy Annulment' party, albeit a much smaller event than the wake, a week later. The only guests in attendance were me, Gertie, and Ewan. I left my father out of it because I didn't want him to remember anything more about my failed marriage than need be. He said he totally understood, and I knew he was being honest with me. Father had resolved that he simply wanted me to be happy in life, and if that was without Chris, well, then that's how it would have to be.

It had been quite a whirlwind of activity over the past week as Gertie and I returned all of the wedding gifts. I'd actually turned it into a bit of a sales tour for the new Greymore Genealogy Research Site, giving everyone a brochure about the new facility as we handed back their gift with my apologies. For those who'd gone to the trouble of getting engraved glassware or anything else customized, I offered them a gift certificate of the same estimated value to their local grocery store. All the guests were surprised to see me at their door. And everyone was exceedingly gracious about the entire fiasco. Many of them had seen the article about Chris and Carlene in the paper and said it had been a constant source of amusement in their household. I was now at the point where I could laugh about it too; by now I'd heard every joke on the planet about lobster trapping.

So that's how it was. The three of us ended up again at Elliot and Edwina's favorite hollow oak tree, overlooking the beautiful meadows and trees below. Together, we had laid a beautiful bouquet of cream, lavender, and pink roses on Elliot's memorial stone.

I wondered how often Aunt Edwina came up here during World War Two in hopes of seeing Elliot again. It must have been so hard for her to lose him. As I ran my hand over the etched marker she'd installed up high on the hill, I knew my hand traced hers against the cool, smooth stone.

Touching the stone made me feel closer to her and also closer to an era gone by, one that seemed a bit lost in more modern times. Aunt Edwina was a young woman during the era of fighting a World War that nobody really wanted, dealing with rationing and nightly bombing raids. I spent a great deal of time thinking about sacrifices prior generations had made for someone like me. I wanted to be part of the growing hordes of dedicated volunteers intent on sharing this history with new audiences.

The Greymore Genealogy Research Site would change with the times. It would have online offerings including social media posts, short videos, and podcasts to keep audiences' attention. I was fascinated with family history by the age of nine and knew that once captivated, many others would be too.

The sun began to set over the hills in the distance. We thought fondly of Aunt Edwina and Elliot as we enjoyed the apricot and rosy streaks covering the sky. The light would quickly fade from the day now, but we'd been here to celebrate all that was good and all that was happily coming in the future.

EPILOGUE

——

Julie's Barn Residence, Scotford Castle Estate.
That Evening.

"Gertie, you know this karaoke video went viral for all the right reasons, don't you?" I was sitting on the sofa while she made us hot cocoa on the stove. She refused to use the microwave because she wanted to catch the milk the second before it boiled; that's apparently what made the ultimate evening drink.

She looked back over her shoulder at me, still stirring, as she replied. "Why's that?"

I pressed *play* on my phone again and was rewarded with my being the 16,103,497th viewer of her karaoke video.

Long black tunic? Check.

Disco ball above her head? Check.

Purple lipstick and loose, bright-red frizzy hair? Without question.

Gertie cradled the microphone close to her chest and then started to belt out her song. Her dress was modest, and there was nothing provocative about her stage moves.

She was off key, out of tune, and stumbled over half the lyrics. I saw the offending stealth punch bowl in the background, multiple empty cups beside it, as well as a reusable coffee mug Gertie was swigging from during the song's bridge melody.

Her performance was so bad it was good, in a hilarious way. But it wasn't so bad that Gertie deserved to be banished from one of the things she truly loved doing: ministering. I watched it three times and failed to see what was causing all the church hullaballoo.

There was a knock at the door. I roused myself from deep cushion oblivion and padded over in my slippers, leggings, and hip-length top. I pulled open the door expecting to see either Ewan, Bertie, or the Major. Instead I saw Fred Todling, our favorite solicitor and bookseller from Pixleton.

He looked like a drowned rat standing outside in the pouring rain.

"This is a surprise, Fred. Do come in. Please excuse the mess, we weren't expecting guests," I said.

"It is most incredibly thoughtful and kind of you to invite me into your humble abode," he said. "I am like a stranger coming in from the dark, pelting sheets of battering rain, a careless, wanton stranger who disturbs your evening, and for that I am most apologetic."

"You didn't bring Barnaby, did you?" Gertie shot over her shoulder as she stirred frantically.

Fred shook his head. "Master Barnaby is not in my good books at the moment."

"No?" Gertie and I both said.

"I took him out rooting for truffles, he slipped his collar, took off down the hill and across the meadow to Farmer Jones's landholding."

It was almost too funny to imagine, Fred barreling down the hill after a two-hundred-pound potbellied pig in search of his next meal. I tried to hold in my laughter. Gertie just bent her head over the stovetop, but I could see her entire face was getting red restraining herself.

"Well, at least the farmer wouldn't be scared of a pig, right?" I said, helping Fred off with his jacket.

"Ahem, there was one slight problem. Indeed a rather large, extreme problem. You see, Master Barnaby has taken a liking to Farmer Jones's donkey Daisy, and once those two get together, there are some rather violent disagreements if we try and pry them apart. Their friendship is purely platonic, let me assure you, but they do miss each other so when separated."

"That's in Dartmoor, Fred. How can we help you here tonight?" Gertie asked.

"I bring a most effusive and enthusiastic update with me tonight. I have looked into the intricacies of ecclesiastical law. As you know, my expertise lies in copyright and trademark protection, intellectual property law. However, considering the scant evidence that was used to defrock the said Gertrude Porringer here in this abode with us tonight, I would humbly suggest that a solicitor better versed in the specific specialty of the law be engaged to see if a compromise could be reached and the frock returned to its rightful owner."

This had Gertie's attention. "You think they had no reason to strip me of my priesthood?"

"Ah, yes, here we have a lady able to succinctly understand the law and summarize its meaning for us here in this room. What a delight it is to listen to those melodic legal tones tumbling from your lips," he said.

Now Gertie had her hands on her hips, the steaming cocoa in three smaller mugs instead of two large ones. "And how do you think I should proceed?"

"Well, I would show them the staggering increase in church youth membership that has occurred since said viral video gained over sixteen million views. According to my online research, which included multiple websites and statistical expert postings, churches all over England are now reporting an uptick in youth engagement. The main reason cited is your, well, viral singing work." He took a sip of the cocoa that Gertie offered him and rocked back on his heels, wiping his shoes frantically on the stiff mat to ensure he wasn't bringing in any mud or rain from outside.

"And you think that's enough to get me my job back?" Gertie asked.

"My dear friend, I know it is," Fred said. "My uncle happens to be a bishop."

"You mean the one who was away in Spain?" I asked.

"Yes indeed, the very man himself. I happened to share with him the experience of having two delightful customers in his shop, looking for a Pixleton guidebook, not too long ago. When I described your rather, er, effervescent appearance, it became clear that he'd also seen the video while he was on holiday in Spain. Down in his holiday country, the video was seen as a positive way to entice young people back into a delightfully fun and healthy status of worship, one where all sorts are welcomed and rejoicing is not limited to the stoic, overly conservative bunch."

"Even if that was true, and I do thank you for at least floating the idea past your uncle, I'm sure there would be guidelines for the future," Gertie said.

Fred and I both nodded.

"There would definitely be guidelines," I said.

"Most assuredly, there would be a new list of guidelines to follow," Fred said.

"So have we used up our free hour of legal consultation with you?" Gertie asked.

Fred spied the plate of warm oatmeal cookies on the kitchen table. "I suggest we broker a rather unwittingly simple arrangement. Were I to partake in cocoa and cookie consumption with these two lovely ladies here before me now, I could be convinced, and somewhat easily at that, to share the name of my uncle and his email address, as well as draft correspondence he would be willing to sign as a letter of support, on a non-fee-paying basis, of course, completely avoiding the ticking and tocking of said costly time clock."

"So in exchange for hot cocoa and cookies, you're willing to get Gertie's job back?" I asked. "Sounds like a great deal to me."

"I was hoping you would say that," Fred said. "Because I sense there will be many more adventures between us in the future."

"Especially with the new Greymore Genealogy Research Site opening in a couple of months as well as the next antiques fair I'm going to in London next week with Ewan," I said.

Fred's eyes roamed the room. He could see some of my watercolors hanging on the walls. The one I was working on for Bertie was still unfinished, but it was nearly done. It was a lovely scene of a Scottish crofter's cottage surrounded by stone walls and a wide expanse of open heath. This was the Shetland Islands, a place close to Bertie's heart ever since he discovered that one of his fifth great-grandparents grew up in those remote Scottish Isles.

I realized now that in the midst of all this chaos and things going on, I wanted to be nowhere else in the world. In fact, I wanted to dive so deeply into this world that it would become an all-consuming passion for the rest of my life. That's just how close I felt with bringing the past to the present. I looked at Gertie and Fred, now engaged in animated conversation about their strategy to get her job back. It was absolutely amazing to think that a Pixleton guidebook and a potbellied pig had brought us to this particular moment in time. Yet, that's what family history research, friends, and family brought into one's world: a chance to learn from the past, live a full life in the present, and create a wonderful future.

THE END

Acknowledgements

——

It takes a lot of talented people to produce a finished book.

To my beta readers and fact checkers: you are my favorite people, and I am so grateful for all your kind efforts.

Extra-special thanks to Wolf Wenzel for his cover artwork: Wolf, you are a maestro in the graphic design world.

Thanks to Kaitlyn Johnson for initial story review and guidance on next steps.

Kudos to Bret Newton and the team at FriesenPress for helping bring this book into the big, wide world. Special thanks to Kellie Rendina and the team at Smith Publicity. Thanks also to Bekah Sine and Nikki Pierce at Method Agency.

And my sincere appreciation to the dedicated archivists, historians, genealogists, and family history society volunteers who ensure our valuable records are preserved, transcribed, and available for future generations. You are unsung heroes and make the world a better place. Thank you for all that you do.

About the Author

Lynne Christensen is a world traveler who enjoys visiting museums and archives. She grew up roaming around grave-yards in Europe with her genealogy-loving parents in search of elusive ancestors. A lifelong learner, she earned both Master of Business Administration and Bachelor of Commerce degrees plus has over twenty-five years of experience in marketing and corporate communications. Her writing is published in numerous magazine articles, case studies, advertisements, and technical manuals. She lives on the West Coast of Canada in a house full of fascinating books.

Northleo
WRITING INC.

www.auntedwina.com

Printed in Canada